MARKED EXCHANGE

OTHER BOOKS BY ANJULA EVANS

Novels:

COVID ICU

Antares Trap

Illustrated Children's Titles:

Kids & COVID Questions

I Kicked the Ball in Gym Class: Self-esteem & Being Different

School Day Worries: The Link Between Thoughts & Anxiety

The Anti-Bullying Project

Why Is Skin Color Different?

Where is My Gigi? Losing Someone You Love

What Is Foster Care: Emma's Journey

The Super-Hero Survival Guide

MARKED EXCHANGE

Paradigm Shifters

ANJULA EVANS

First paperback edition 2021
First hardcover edition 2021

Cover Art by Gareth Brown
garethnbrown.co.uk

Paperback **ISBN** 978-1-989803-19-6
Hardcover **ISBN** 978-1-989803-20-2

Thank you Alanna, Gareth, and Karen, for your hours of dedication, and thank you to Mind Forward and the Writers' Collective of Canada for the inspiration and support.

CHAPTER ONE

Th-thump, th-thump, th-thump. As I run down the old, decrepit alleyway, my heart pounds in my ears, blocking out sounds of my pursuers. I leap over an upturned garbage can, tripping at the last moment, scrambling back to my feet, taking a split second to glance behind me.

Th-thump, th-thump, th-thump. My heart races, this time faster and stronger. In the darkness it is deafening, diminishing my other senses. I need to get out of this side of the city, the area where people disappear without a trace. I force myself to push through the air surrounding me which is clear gelatin, matching the consistency of my legs beneath me.

Th-thump, th-thump, th-thump. I turn briskly around the next corner, and meet with a rattling smash. A fence. I groan. I hear them gaining behind me. I. Must. Get. Out! My muscles contract as I climb the chain links, and I hear the raspy tear of denim while jumping over the top.

Th-thump, th-thump, th-thump. My senses are suddenly heightened from another shot of adrenaline, as I hear my pursuers quickly leap over the fence and close in behind me.

I'm running out of steam and I can't keep going at this pace much longer. The lactic acid buildup is too much, I'm cramping, and my lungs can't handle inhaling the frosty air. I make a quick decision, and race toward the only light that glows in the black of the night—a street lamp. I'll have to take a stand where I can see. I'm at a disadvantage as my pursuers seem to be able to see in the dark.

I brace my back against the chilly lamp post, waiting for my pursuers to surround me, not knowing if I'll survive this encounter. Moving toward

me, coming out of the darkness but disguised by the pre-dawn mist, is a creature—I can only imagine the teeth and claws—the grotesqueness of my demise.

It moves closer to me and my body stiffens as I ready myself to fight. I see two more shadowy figures emerging behind the first one, hidden in the fog. My pounding heart swells with regret, both over my life which is now flashing before my eyes, and over my actions during the last hour which set me on this fateful path.

TWO HOURS EARLIER

Although I've only ever heard rumors of the mythical beasts that supposedly inhabit the east end of town, I do believe in the validity of their existence. Whether they are responsible, or there's another origin of the evil that is depleting the female population, I am unsure.

Urgency overtakes me as I leave the police station after filing a Missing Person's report. In my hurry to get to my car, my strides are longer than usual. My shadow is stretched and oblong, as the lights from the precinct parking lot pierce the darkness around me. The light is then sucked in by the shadows of the night, the black holes that deplete the world of its glow, leaving only coldness and emptiness behind.

It's ironic how that metaphor represents my life right now. Although my sister has only been missing for twenty-four hours, the fear grips me and my life feels cold and empty. "Only" twenty-four hours is how they referred to her case when I filed the report. But she's never been reckless or irresponsible before, and she's never disappeared like this.

After driving my car down the streets where she often walked, finding no sign of her earlier, I stopped by the precinct in her area. All other avenues have come up blank, and the many phone calls I made earlier in

the evening were futile. None of our family or friends have seen her, including her roommate, Julia, who was the one to initially call me. Natalie hadn't come home after work last night.

"Psst. Hey, you!" I whip around, quickly analyzing my surroundings. I'm not afraid, due to the bright lights and the fact that the parking lot is next to the police station. However, I am startled as I am jolted out of my thoughts. "Over here!"

I look around until I am able to locate the owner of the voice. Tucked behind the large sign announcing that this indeed is police headquarters, is a scrawny man in a beige trench coat. *Oh God, please no.* I hadn't thought an exhibitionist would have the guts to expose himself right beside the police station.

But when he keeps his trench coat closed, I re-evaluate him and see he's wearing a brown tweed fedora. The way he's dressed and acting so secretively, he seems like he's just stepped out of a detective comic book. The corner of my mouth quirks up a bit and I shake my head as I continue to walk to my car.

"I heard you asking about your sister." In the quiet darkness of the wee hours, his voice carries so I can hear the words he's speaking, even at low volume. He apparently wants to stay hidden and doesn't move from the place he seems to feel most secure.

I pause mid-step and turn around to face his direction. "What about my sister?" My level of patience is low, considering my exhaustion and the emotional toll of the day, but I try not to snap at him.

"I think I might have a lead for you."

I roll my eyes. *Everybody wants to play detective.*

Nevertheless, although I'm not about to stake my hope on his "lead", I feel I should at least listen to what he has to say. "What kind of lead?"

"An address and a name."

Riiiight. Ambush. At least that's my first thought. But I second guess myself, and that's what will eventually become my downfall.

Mr. Detective-wannabe scribbles something down in a notebook, then I hear the ripping of a page. I walk closer to where he's standing behind the sign, but not out of sight of the police station. He stretches his arm over in my direction and gingerly hands me the scrap of paper he's torn from his notebook.

I look at the address and name scrawled on the paper. I don't recognize the area of town. "What is this place?"

"It's on the east side of town. Old industrial area. Knock on the door three times, then three times again, then twice slowly."

This just keeps getting better and better.

"When they answer, ask for the name on the paper."

"Speaking of names...what's yours?" I feel like prying a bit. Get a better feel about this guy.

"Dick. Just call me Dick. Short for Detective." I roll my eyes again.

Okay, Mr. Dick-wannabe. "Alright...Dick. Where did you get this info and how is it connected to my sister?"

Even with the shadows masking his face, I can make out a small smile on his lips. "The place is linked to the missing girls. Your sister is missing and is a girl." *Well, duh.* "The guy's name. He's a trusted informant." I can barely hear him mutter under his breath, but pick up the words, "...at least he used to be..."

"Why didn't you give this info to the police?" I'm still skeptical. It all feels fishy to me.

"I respect my contacts' anonymity when it comes to staying away from the boys in blue, and the guys at the club can smell a cop a mile away. Plus the officers think I'm a crackpot, anyway." I resist cracking a smile.

I need to stay focused—even though this whole scenario in the parking lot is almost comical. Under any other circumstances I'd find it amusing.

I carefully fold up the scrap of paper and put it in my jean pocket. "Well, thanks...Dick." I back up toward my car. "See ya' around."

I watch as he nods and tips his hat to me in the shadows. "Glad to be of service, Ma'am."

I walk the rest of the way to my car, unlocking it on the way, then slide into the cold seat behind the steering wheel. *Thank goodness for faux leather gloves.* My fingers would be falling off without them. I turn the ignition and put the heat on. *And thank goodness for heated seats.*

And I might just be thankful for weirdo Dick-wannabes before dawn today. That's if what he says helps me find my sister. I drive past the sign where he was standing, and through my partially defrosted windshield I notice he's mysteriously disappeared. *Gone with the wind.*

I make my way to the other side of the city, depending on GPS to help me find the location scrawled across the paper given to me by Dick. I park on the street next to an older brick warehouse. *I'm not sure I like this scenario.* I pull out my taser from my glove box to take with me. *That's better.* Now I feel more secure.

I sit in my car, debating if I should use the absurd secret knock and ask for the person listed on the paper. But then I remember time isn't standing still. It's the only lead I have to find my sister.

I decide to do whatever I need to—I really don't have a choice if I want to find her. Although I have to admit, I'm following a standard trope from a movie script that seems a bit ridiculous. However, I get out of my car, and walk to the warehouse.

Not all lights shine clearly in the parking lot. Instead, one is burnt out, another has been smashed, and a third one flickers violently. Overall,

there's not much light. Just enough to cause the shadows to reign fear and havoc on my emotions, in the eerie silence of the night.

A low fog gives the area an otherworldly feel. I feel dampness settle in with the morning humidity. Today it feels like that same dampness is seeping into my bones. I reach the door in the red brick building, wondering the whole time whether anyone is inside.

I press a lit-up doorbell, but hear no ring or indication it's done anything. Well, apart from sating that internal urge I have to press buttons. *It all starts at age two, trying to press every button in sight. Then it becomes a growing urge to press other people's "buttons".* Let's hope I can keep that under control tonight and not anger anyone.

Then I remember the secret knock. I'm embarrassed to use it, like I'm part of some secret society or treehouse kids' club. *Three quick...three quick...two slow.* I rap my knuckles on the door following that pattern. And of course, as if I'm in a spy or gangster movie, a barely visible panel slides open and two emerald eyes stare out. They narrow suspiciously as they see me standing below.

"What d'ya want?" The voice speaks gruffly to me.

"I'm here for Justin." I try to keep the quiver out of my voice.

"Ya'are, are ya?" Then I hear a mutter, barely audible. "That lucky bastard." I hear numerous locks on the door being opened, and finally the door swings outward violently, with no regard that I'm standing in front of it. I stumble backward to avoid being clipped by it, and land on my butt on the hard pavement.

I am about to stand up when I notice the dark shadow of a man towering over me. He steps backward, and I can see his face in the light. He rolls his bright green eyes, and with an exasperated "Well? Come on then!" he turns around, expecting me to follow him. I jump up and dart through the door just before it bangs shut.

We walk through a lit corridor, then Mr. Emerald-eyes yanks back a black curtain, revealing an adjoining room. I try to take in my surroundings as we weave our way between round tables, but my eyes are still adjusting to the dim light.

I start to make out colors, noting booths with plush velvet burgundy upholstery. Deep purple tablecloths caress the bottoms of the many drink glasses scattered across the room. And the owners of those glasses—well, let's just say everything screams "Godfather". Suddenly, I'm wondering what in heaven's name possessed me to come here.

We arrive at a large booth, close to the back of the room. "Yo, Justin!" An incredibly handsome man lifts his head and looks up at us. "Another one for ya." Justin eyes me, starting from my toes up to my nose, then his deep blue eyes raise slightly and look into mine.

When we make eye contact, he seems to startle and his eyes widen. He doesn't stand in greeting, just whispers something to the girls on either side who are seductively trying to capture his attention. The two scantily clad goddesses leave the table with a grumble and a huff. I can feel their glares boring into the back of my head.

"Have a seat, my dear." Justin points to the seat beside him. I slide between the table and bench, watching Mr. Emerald-eyes saunter off back to his post. As he goes, he drinks in some of the dancers, offerings of the night.

I glance at the stage, complete with poles, cages, and posters of dancers. I notice a screen with a photo of a girl projected on it. It seems out of place, as it doesn't fit in with the rest of the dancers' photos.

As I watch the screen, it changes to another girl's photo, who again doesn't fit in. She's absolutely gorgeous, but her face doesn't hold the expression of a typical model's. It holds confusion and an element of

desperation. As her photo appears, I hear feet scuffle, and watch as several silhouettes exit a stairway down to who-knows-where.

The sweet scents of cinnamon and cedar linger around him, becoming stronger as Justin moves closer to me. "So what is it you want to talk about?" I sense a hunger in him that stirs me uncomfortably, because it's so alluring.

There is an undeniable attraction between us—I feel like a magnet that's just found its match, the connection is so intense. The longing I sense in him just serves to increase that attraction, as it taps into my own craving. His desire for me augments my burning need for him, and increases the obvious draw between us.

What is wrong with me? Why do I feel this way toward him?

I am at a loss, not knowing where to begin; I am overwhelmed by the pull toward him. As I make eye contact, trying to speak but finding no words, I am mesmerized by the blue oceans found in his eyes. Rough, wild oceans, not tranquil seas, that speak of untold horrors that have shipwrecked many a soul. Alarm bells go off. *This man is dangerous.*

"Well? Tiger got your tongue?" He looks amused as he speaks softly.

I sigh, breaking my eyes away from his and willing my dry mouth to speak. I take a deep breath. The words come out in a rush.

"My sister's gone missing and I'm trying to discover her whereabouts."

Justin tuts his mouth at me, shaking his head. "Would you like something to drink?"

Normally, I don't make a habit of drinking, and in a place like this I'd rather avoid it. Never know what someone could slip into my drink. So I decline.

"I was given this address and your name as a contact person who could help me in my quest to find my sister."

He doesn't say anything, and I begin to feel nervous as the seconds stretch on. He glances between me and his whiskey, almost as if he's comparing me to his drink on a set of scales. *I knew this was a bad idea.*

Suddenly, I blurt out, "You know what? I'm so sorry I bothered you. I'll find my own way out." I attempt to rise, but his powerful hands press on my shoulders, keeping me in place.

"Sit." His voice is quiet, yet commanding. I sit back down, feeling uneasy. "This sister of yours—she looks like you? If so, I may have seen her.

I draw in a quick breath. *Yes! I knew this was a great idea! No, you didn't,* I answer myself back. Internally I facepalm. *Oh great, so now I'm not just talking to myself but arguing with myself? That's got to be a whole new level of strange.*

I quickly answer Justin. "Yes, people used to think we were twins. She has the same dark hair and eyes I have—"

Justin interrupts me. "Rosebud lips, heart face, amazing body." His eyes sweep over me hungrily. "Yes, I've seen your sister before."

"Before? You mean in the last twenty-four hours or before that?"

"I saw her several hours ago, and to be honest, it didn't look like she was doing too well."

My heart plummets to the ground. "Oh my God." I put my hand to my chest. "Was she hurt? Do you know where she is now?" My nervousness has morphed into full-fledged anxiety.

"One question at a time, Love. Firstly, I need you to answer a question of my own." I nod. "How the hell did you find this place, and who in God's name told you to contact me?" Regardless of his words he doesn't sound angry, just exasperated. He seems more focused on our surroundings than on me.

I feel embarrassed to disclose my strange source. My words squeak out like a question. "I met a strange man in a fedora and trench coat?" I hear him groan as he rubs his face with his hands.

"You're talking about Dick?" I nod again. His eyes close and he follows up with another groan. He mutters under his breath, thinking I can't hear him. "He's trying to set me up. What a dick."

"Please tell me about her!"

Justin takes a deep breath and rubs his face with his hands. "Look." He glances over my shoulder. "She was here, but she no longer is. She was taken elsewhere. But the important thing right now is that you leave immediately."

He stands, straightening his tie, offers his hand, and assists me when I reciprocate. I'm startled by the electrical sensation I feel as we touch. Then he pulls me to his side, too close for comfort. I start to move away, but his grip is too tight.

He whispers in my ear. "Stop it. Don't draw attention and look forward or at me. Play along." I stop pulling away and melt into his side as we walk. I hear footsteps behind us. He waves at someone, and the footsteps stop.

We walk farther into the establishment, until we get to a set of rooms. A man in a suit and a woman in a short red dress, black heels and hose, with golden hair piled on her head, are making out. I have no idea where Justin is taking me. Then the lovebirds open one of the doors and fall inside—onto a bed. The man kicks the door closed.

Suddenly, I'm concerned he's got the wrong impression. "Oh no. I'm not...I'm not here for that. Please, let me go!"

"Shush! Play along!"

Justin stops before one of the rooms, loosens his tie, and takes me in his arms. His voice is commanding. "Pretend to make out with me."

I lean into him, and we kiss, arms wrapped around each other. He puts his mouth to my ear. "Make it more convincing."

We kiss again, and this time I let my mouth open as he runs his tongue along the inside of my lower lip. His tongue darts into my mouth and our tongues touch. I'm so startled by the physical sensations brought on from the kiss, that I allow myself to start free falling.

Our kiss becomes more passionate, and as we sway back and forth, a yearning stirs deep inside me. I can tell we're moving closer to another set of doors, but I keep playing along. *I am just playing along, right?* I blush. Before Justin backs me around a corner, I open my eyes for a second, and see several sets of eyes looking at us.

Justin swings me around the corner, grabs a handle, opens a door and forces it to slam loudly, although we're still in the corridor. Once we're completely out of sight, he drops the charade and pulls me hard, by the wrist. After our kiss, I don't know which end is up, and because of my dizziness I trip. I fall...right into his arms.

"I've got you." Justin smiles at me as he stands me upright. "But we have to move. Fast. Follow me." He pulls me along and I try to keep up with his long strides.

"Where are we going?" He doesn't answer and keeps walking swiftly in silence.

A minute later he rubs his lips. I hear him muttering to himself. "She didn't have to be *that* convincing." Then he speaks at a more audible volume. "C'mon, I'm getting you out of here, before things go sideways."

I yank on his arm and stop. "What about my sister? Where is she?"

I hear a growling sound emerge from Justin's throat. "She's not here. Long gone. But unless you want to face the same fate, you need to come with me. Now!" He tries to pull me along but I resist.

"Look." He runs his hand through his dark chestnut hair and looks exasperated. "You're not going to find her here, and if you don't get out of here fast, you won't be able to look for her." That prompts me to continue walking with him, matching his pace.

After another few minutes of walking through what appears to be an enormous compound, Justin opens a door to a men's washroom, and walks me in. He pulls me up to a wall with a window that looks out on the blackness outside, with faint orbs shining but somewhat blocked by a partial obstruction.

"So the building is surrounded by hedges, but there's a small opening you should be able to squeeze through about twenty steps to the right. Once you get out, you run as far and as fast as you can, okay? Get out in the open and out of this area of town."

"But what about my car?" I'm confused. "Wouldn't it be better to double back and use my car to leave?"

"Oh, that's even better. Just watch out for *them*."

"Who? What are you talking about?"

Justin grips me by the shoulders. "Look, just get out of here. They hunt in groups. Your life and future are the important things. Okay?" He waits until I nod. "Good girl." That phrase sends a wave of pleasurable shivers up my spine, and makes me want to comply even more.

"You ready?"

"For what?"

"For this." Justin spins me and faces me against the wall, gripping my ass with both hands.

Oh. My. God. Spikes of pleasure rocket through me as I'm in his grasp.

But that pleasure only lasts for a moment. "Umm. Your arms? Grab the window sill?" He starts pushing me upward.

Oh. My face flushes deep red and I feel mortified. Thank God I'm facing away from him and he can't see my face.

I grasp the window sill with one hand, and use the lever with the other hand to open the window. Once it's open, Justin gives a final thrust and I'm leaning outside. I pull myself over the sill, so one leg is on either side. I look down at Justin's deep blue eyes, and see something there that I can't ignore. An unstoppable yearning. The odd thing is—I feel it, too.

"Okay, pretty girl. Time for you to get out of here. We've bought some time from that earlier charade, but not a lot. Unfortunately, you're going to be a target, now that you've attracted attention. They'll be able to track you wherever you go. Stay in crowds and don't walk alone, especially at night. Hopefully, after a while they'll lose interest and stalk someone else."

Oh great. Stalkers. Just what I need. I'm somewhat confused, but nod.

"Thank you, Justin." I speak in earnest, thankful that someone was looking out for me tonight.

He cracks a small smile. "Goodbye, Princess. Stay safe."

I swing my other leg over the sill, grip it to lower myself partway to the ground, then drop the rest of the way. I land on my feet on a skinny line of grass, sandwiched between the hedges and the building. I work my way in the direction Justin instructed me to go, but see no space twenty steps down. I move another ten steps, then see a tiny opening. *Right, twenty steps for him equals thirty steps for me.*

I squeeze through the opening and the orbs are slightly brighter, now they are no longer obscured by the hedges. I take off running, trying to get the hell out of there.

CHAPTER TWO

Damnit!!! From my vantage point behind shrubs across the street, I see that my car is gone. I try not to freak out. I can't afford to attract attention, so I force myself to keep it together.

I try to order an Uber with no luck, then call for a cab. No one is willing to drive to this part of the city. I hang up my phone, trying not to panic. So I guess I'm on foot for now. I follow Justin's instructions, and start running like my life depends on it.

I've been weaving in and out of side streets to avoid notice. Whenever I hear raucous laughter or signs of a scuffle, I scoot in another direction. I'm gradually making my way west to get closer to the downtown area and its bright lights. However, this early in the morning, there won't be as much of a crowd as I would like. I'd prefer to hide myself in a throng of people.

I'm no longer running—I'm keeping to a swift jog to avoid tiring myself out. The important thing is that I keep going. After a while, I start to get a creepy feeling that I'm not just being followed, but being hunted.

My anxiety increases and I start glancing over my shoulder. I need to either get to the city center, or make it through the next two hours safely. Then I'll have the added bonus of bright street lights or sunlight, and morning crowds that would discourage anything shady.

After glancing backward again, I notice a few men walking briskly, about a block behind me. Their bodies have become silhouettes as they scatter lamp light around themselves. After a few minutes I glance back again, and see only one man. The other men are no longer anywhere to be seen. I have an uneasy feeling.

I decide to cut through an alley to test if the guy is following me. I know it's a risk, but it should also throw anyone else off my track. So I move back to weaving in and out of streets, using alleyways as the conduits through which my dance flows.

I cut through an alley and see a man walking swiftly on a parallel street, keeping pace with me. I feel like I'm being corralled. Because the first man is definitely following me, it's likely the other men are involved in his game.

I pick up the pace to lose them in the maze of alleyways. However, before I make a turn and run out of sight, I see the most extraordinary and frightening thing I've ever witnessed. *It can't be. It's impossible!* I'm certain I saw one of the men morph into a biped cat-like being. It's times like these when I wish I had a giant cat toy, a few cans of sardines, or at least some catnip.

I know my mind must be playing tricks on me, but I continue to run through the maze of alleyways, tripping over a garbage can, and later scaling a rattling fence. I know someone *or something* is still after me. Images of that human-cat creature fly through my mind, striking fear into my heart and urging me to keep running.

It must have been my imagination. It's running wild because of the rumors about this place.

I run toward a lamppost, fueled by adrenaline, and decide to make my stand there where I can at least see who or what I'm fighting. My hands clench, but I have no weapon. It's at that moment when I feel entirely and utterly alone.

Wait! My taser! I pull it out of my cross-body bag and check the cartridges. At least my odds are a bit better now.

I watch as a man walks out of the morning fog, wearing jeans and no shirt. He's very tall and exceptionally good-looking. Behind him, two

more men materialize. They could be twins with their high cheekbones, and similar musculature. They're also wearing jeans but no shirts.

I take in these details as I back up. Then my back hits the lamppost. I get my multi-shot taser ready, and point it downward.

The first man speaks. "Time's up." His last consonant makes a "popping" sound. I shake my head, not really believing the situation I'm in. I feel like I'm having an out-of-body experience, and everything is in slow motion. My ears are ringing and my eyes have razor sharp focus. "You're coming with us, Girly."

I hear one of them snicker as I move into a defensive posture. I try to discourage them from approaching me. "Don't come any closer!" I wave my taser toward them, and my warning evokes a snort of laughter in another.

Suddenly, a giant roar shakes the stillness of the night. *What the hell?* To my right, I can see a shape stalking us through the silver fog. As the shape nears, the fog shimmers, and lets through the most beautiful yet terrifying creature I've ever set eyes on. A Siberian tiger in all its splendor.

I was sure I'd refused anything to drink at the club, but now I'm not so sure. Someone must have slipped me something, especially considering how impossibly huge the animal is—and the fact that I haven't been torn limb from limb...yet.

I glance back in the direction of the three men, and see they've scattered. There's no sign of them. The only prey left to be stalked is me. The tiger has stopped within pouncing distance. Although it's still partially obscured by the mist, I can see how majestic the creature is.

Looking into its slit eyes, I see a glint of recognition. Although every second tightens the coil of anxiety ready to spring from my stomach, it's one second more I'm alive. But the anticipation is unbearable. Part of me wishes the ordeal, my painful death, was over.

Will tasing it just make it angry? Do I roll over and play dead to make it lose interest? Or do I try to look as though I'm a greater threat to scare it away?

My mind is unraveling faster than I can follow, and all my survival skills I used to know, from my one summer in Girl Scouts, seem to fly right out of my head. But before I can take action, the majestic creature tilts its head and nods, then disappears into the night. The welcome interruption from a stranger, a literally "strange" tiger may have just saved my life. However, it may just be a temporary divergence from what is fated to come.

I continue walking in the direction of the city center, and although I still feel shaky from the two encounters, I force myself to endure travel at a brisk walk. I jump at every sound as my startle reflex has been heightened. By the time I reach the city center I'm a taut bundle of nerves, ready to explode. I order an Uber to take me home.

Back in my apartment, I sip on a hot chai tea latte and watch the sun rise. The hues of pink and orange are gorgeous, but there is no comfort for me. I stare at the crumpled piece of paper Dick gave me.

What use is this lead if it's too dangerous to follow up on?

Now that I've talked with Justin, I know the key to my sister's disappearance lies in that building. *Maybe the police will follow up once I give them the info.* Although Natalie may no longer be there, it may be the last place anyone's seen her alive.

Oh no. I need to stop thinking like that. She's got to be okay.

The other option is to talk to Justin or Dick-wannabe. I don't know how to find Justin, but maybe Dick can give me more answers now that I know he's legitimate. *He's dick-legit.*

I shower and set my alarm for four hours. My body desperately needs rest. I know I'm becoming more and more non-functional the longer I go

without any shut-eye. I resign myself to talking with the police, dealing with my car, and hunting down Dick once my body is somewhat functional again.

After I drag myself from my bed a few hours later, I Uber to the police station, and search around the grounds for Dick. He is nowhere to be found. I walk into the station and report my car as stolen.

"So where did you last park your car?"

"At 530 East York Drive."

The officer loses his composure. "What the hell were you doing in that part of the city?"

"I had a lead on Natalie's whereabouts, so I followed up on it."

"Look, little lady, that part of town isn't safe. Hell, we cops don't even patrol that area, it's so dangerous!"

"But I need to find my sister, and it's the only lead I had! Besides, someone at the club said they saw her just hours before."

"You went *inside?*" The officer shakily rakes his hand through his hair. He sits back and sighs. "For your own good, stay away from that place. Unless you want to end up a statistic like your sister."

A feeling of horror grips me. "A statistic? I don't believe she's dead." Realization dawns on me and my eyes open wide. I give him a questioning look. "You know what that place is, don't you?"

The officer is reluctant to talk. "All I can say is the investigation is ongoing, and I can't go into detail or it would compromise the operation."

A flicker of hope starts to brighten. "So you might find her while investigating then!"

"To be honest, Darla, with the way that place works, if we don't get in there within the first 48 hours of a kidnapping, the chances are that you won't see her again." The police officer sounds apologetic. "Our investigation is ongoing, but I don't want to give you false hope. The

chances are remote that there will be a raid before she's moved—if she's even still there."

The stress and lack of sleep are catching up to me. I feel tears building in my eyes. "You mean the police aren't going to do anything?" My voice starts to rise.

"Shhh, shhh." The officer hands me a tissue to mop up the tears that have escaped from their carefully guarded mask. "I'll make a note on her file about the possible connection with the club so they know to keep their eyes peeled during the investigation. That's about all I can do right now.

"In the meantime, check to see if your car was merely impounded. I'll hold off on filing the paperwork for a stolen vehicle until you give me a call." I nod, thank the officer, shake his hand, and leave the precinct.

I pass by City Hall and enter the public library to grab a strong coffee from the small cafe inside. I look up the address on Google Maps, then locate the impound lot closest to it. I give them a call, and find out my car wasn't in fact stolen, it was just impounded. I call the precinct and let the officer know not to file the paperwork.

"Make sure someone drives you out there to pick up your car, okay? No walking, and go this afternoon. No going when it's dark." The officer sounds concerned.

"Okay."

I call work to let them know I won't be in for a couple of days, and they arrange for another mental health professional to take over my caseload. All my clients are high-risk youth, and I've never taken time off before, but these are exceptional circumstances. I'm frantic to find my sister and ensure she's safe.

I arrange for my friend, Susan, to drive me to the impound lot to pick up my car. Once we get there, she makes sure I have access to my vehicle and funds to pay the impound fee.

"You sure you're okay? You're shaking." I can see the concern on her face. Susan embraces me and holds me for a minute. "Hang in there, Darla. If you need me—for anything—don't hesitate to call."

"I will. Thanks so much for driving me." We say our goodbyes and Susan drives back to catch her next masters class at the university.

I'm about to pay the fee and drive off in my car, when I realize it's down to the wire, and that my sister could still be in the warehouse, however unlikely that is. I could at least find a clue to her disappearance if she isn't. The officer's voice comes back to me regarding the first 48 hours. If that's true, I only have a few more hours until she's moved. Maybe Justin was mistaken that she was long gone, or lied just to get me out of the building safely. I don't know what to think.

I tell myself that the thought of going back to the building has nothing to do with hoping to run into a particular tall, blue-eyed handsome stranger. *Nope, nothing at all. No interest there.* But my body betrays me, and it takes all my focus to avoid thinking about him and about how I feel so drawn to him.

I sigh. *I don't know what to do—I'm so tired I can't think straight.* Before I have time to talk myself out of it, I impulsively leave the impound office with resolve. I stealthily navigate the few blocks from the impound lot to the warehouse, climb through the hole in the hedges Justin revealed, then walk the thirty steps until I get to the window to the men's washroom.

I'm in luck! The window hasn't been shut. I jump up and hook my hands on the sill, then scramble up the wall, using the protruding burgundy bricks as footholds. I listen carefully and don't hear a sound, so

pull myself over the sill and drop down on the other side, again in the men's lavatory.

I crack open the main door and listen. Hearing nothing, I glance both ways down the corridor and see I'm alone. I head to the left this time, away from the private rooms and club. After a minute, the corridor branches off and I have the choice of going in several different directions. I decide to take the stairway and search downstairs for Natalie.

I descend one level, and find myself in a room with a large, curved convex window that covers an entire wall. The room itself is pitch dark with no lighting, but there is plenty of light shining in through the window. Enough for me to take in the strange sight below.

I must be in some sort of viewing room. All thoughts leave me as I take in what I see through the window. Below me is some type of huge sports arena, with surrounding seats filled to the maximum. I stand off to the side as I stare into the stadium and at the immense creatures fighting there. I watch as a rhino battles against a lion and a huge wolf, each taking swipes with claws, fangs, or horn.

I see the crowd erupt in applause, jumping up and down, as they cheer on their favorites, yet I don't hear any noise, I just feel vibrations and low reverberations. The booth I'm in must be soundproof. I note a line of similar raised booths around the arena, some with lights on and more patrons inside. I can see the closest ones in discussion while they carefully watch the carnage below.

How horrible—to pit animals against each other for sport. The thought makes me sick. I wonder if the tiger from last night somehow escaped from this place. Although it was a few miles away from here, I can't think of anywhere else it could have come from. Part of me worries for the human population and part for the well-being of the tiger.

I wonder then if experimentation is taking place here as well. I still haven't come to terms with last night and the glimpse I had of the part-feline, part-man creature. I was thinking that maybe the trauma of my sister going missing and more than twenty-four hours without sleep may be responsible. Or that somehow being drugged may have been the reason for my hallucination. *I really don't know what to think.*

If animals are being bred in captivity for the purpose of fighting each other, they may have stooped so low as to engage in genetic modification. *Ethically depraved monsters.* I'm referring to the human creators, not their creations as monsters. I snap some photos on my phone so I have some proof of what goes on down here to present to the authorities.

I watch as the rhinoceros uses its horn to gore the lion which is mid-flight in its attempt to pounce on the wolf. The wolf narrowly escapes the lion's pounce, and takes a swipe at the lion, raking its razor-sharp claws along the underside of its belly. I can't bear to watch any more, and I turn my head away.

I walk back to the stairwell, and realize that going any lower would lead me to the level of the crowd or even where they store the animals. Into the lions' den, literally. So I opt to ascend one level to the original floor. I stay hidden below the top of the flight in the shadows while I debate whether to ascend another floor, take another branch in the corridor, or just find the men's washroom again and skedaddle on out of there. Of course the last one's not an option, since I need to find clues about Natalie—or Natalie herself, if she's still here.

It's a tough call, because often offices would be on the second floor in a place like this. I find myself struggling to think, I'm so exhausted, but I can't see kidnapped girls being kept on the same level as executive offices. *Where would they keep prisoners?* I figure I'll have to keep exploring to find out, but I'm guessing they would be kept separate from

the captive animals and away from prying eyes of the crowds below. *Maybe on the main floor in some obscure section?*

I suddenly hear a bang from far below, accompanied by crowd noise. *Yikes!* I take off running down one of the unknown corridors, wondering if I should have aborted my mission for now, and if I've just signed my own death warrant.

CHAPTER THREE

I scramble down the corridor, hoping the patrons will take a different direction. I can make out loud voices quickly rising to the surface of the stairwell.

"Wish we could have stayed for the half-time show."

"Break's over. We have to get back to work. We can watch it on the monitor."

"Yeah, but it's not the same."

The voices are now behind me, but there don't seem to be any distance gains between us. *Shoot! They chose the same corridor, and must be walking at the same pace as myself.*

"Carlisle was doing pretty well this time around, don't you think?"

I speed up, jogging, yet keep my footsteps light.

"He's definitely improving. His motivation to train is intensifying."

"Haha! No wonder, since the stakes are so high for him. I'm sure you'll be pretty *desperate* when your time comes." I hear a grunting noise, as though someone has been hit.

The voices are still keeping pace with me. I try not to panic. I wish I had the brain energy to analyze their conversation. I'm too focused on debating whether to find a good hiding place and wait for them to pass, or to keep fleeing, with the possibility of running into someone else coming the opposite way.

I'm forced to go right at the end of the hallway, then at the last second I choose another right instead of going straight, thinking of doubling back to get back to my little exit window and steering clear of the club. My heart's pounding so hard, I'm not in a place to make rational decisions. I'll have to retreat for now and come back later once I'm calm again. If I

have the guts to return. But the voices follow me with each turn I make. By this time I can make out three distinct voices, which means the possibility of three pursuers.

"I definitely think Justin should get in the game."

My ears perk up at the mention of Justin's name.

"Oh he will. I have an inkling it will be much sooner rather than later." I hear a chuckle.

"Yeah, it's been three years, though." The voice sounds regretful.

"I have a feeling his interest may have piqued very recently."

"Haha! Wonder why you'd think that."

I hear more chuckling.

"So what should we do about the wild goose, then?"

I hear a pause in the conversation, and hope I've finally lost them.

"I say we chase it. See what Justin does."

"It might pull him out of his funk."

"Hehe. Sounds like fun."

I find myself back at the original corridor and make a left in the direction of the men's washroom. I pick up the pace. The voices go silent, and I think I must have finally lost them. After all, why would anyone who knows the complex purposely take a long route to get to a washroom that's just down the hall?

I'm back in the lavatory, scaling the wall with some difficulty and yanking myself up to the sill. Right when I'm about to swing my leg over the side, the main door opens, and I'm sure I look like a deer in the headlights. The bare-chested man opening the door spots me, and dashes over to grab me, as a couple other familiar men pour through the door.

Oh no. It's the twins and the guy from yesterday! There's no talking my way out of this one.

I quickly swing my leg over and jump, not bothering to flip around and hang by my hands first. It means a longer fall, but I need to get out of here ASAP! The first man has already lifted himself to the top of the window by the time I land, but thankfully his shoulders won't fit through the window.

"Hey, come back, little mouse! We don't bite!" I can hear the amusement in his voice and the other two guys laughing behind him.

I don't hang around, but hightail it out of there, making a beeline for my car at the impound lot. *Damnit! I should have paid the fee and moved my car before going in!* However, I was afraid my car would be impounded *again* while I was snooping inside the building. The delay is going to cost me, but I'm hoping to get my car and leave before anyone in pursuit catches up with me.

My hands are shaking when I get to the lot. I enter the small building, run up to the impound officer, pay the fee, and grab the receipt. I run out to my car, clicking on the door unlock button, and jump inside while turning on the ignition. I drive to the exit, the impound officer raises the bar to let me through, and I'm out of there.

I've just started to breathe a sigh of relief, when I see something bizarre in my mirror, coming my way. *Oh no! What are* those? I get a glimpse of feline heads on powerful musculature. My mind seems to focus on a strange but insignificant detail, considering the circumstances. *They're wearing* pants?

I make a left turn and peel out of the parking lot onto a side street. My car starts accelerating, but the creatures following me are incredibly agile and have almost caught up to me. *Am I hallucinating due to sleep deprivation? Wake up, damnit!* Oddly, I feel that physical speed will lead me from this strange fantasyland back to reality, where my feline friends don't exist.

I press the pedal down harder, and leap ahead of "them", the creatures that surely are strange figments of my imagination. But they are relentless. I keep glancing back through my mirror, and suddenly only two are there. *Maybe I lost the third?* I barely have time to process that thought when I hear a "thunk!" on the roof of my car. *Oh no! It's above me!*

I try zigzagging my car to get it off, but instead, I see sharp claws pierce through the roof, riveting the creature so it won't be thrown off. In the mirror I only see one of them now. *Where did the other one go?* I look forward, expecting to see more empty side streets, when I see the missing one leap from a tree on the far right. I scream as I swerve my vehicle to avoid it, but it leaps again in front of my car.

This time, there's no way to swerve. My car keeps going forward while the feline creature pushes against the front of it, slowing me down. I hear the metallic groaning sound of solid steel being bent. *What crazy amount of strength is this?*

I'm shocked at the physical power of this beast, but have no time to dwell on it. My car finally jerks to a stop and deploys the airbags. My doors are locked, but with that kind of strength, it will be easy for one of them to break a window, or worse.

The creature that was running behind my car walks up and taps on my window with a claw. Having one of the creatures this near, even with glass between, is a frightening experience. I can see it panting from the run, and see the black rosettes on its fur coat now that it's close up. At any other time in my life, I would have taken the time to gawk and admire the creature, but right now, I'm panicking for my life.

It taps on the window again and growls, "Out!"

I feel partially immobilized due to shock and fear. I stiffen, shaking my head briefly but defiantly, my mouth in a thin line. The feline human

rolls its eyes, and nods upward. I hear a creaking and jarring sound as though something is slicing through metal. I scream as the creature on top of the car rolls back the metal as if my car was a can of sardines. I gulp. *And I'm the sardine.*

A claw reaches down to slice through my seatbelt, and splits my cross-body handbag open along with its strap, causing it to tumble. My taser spills out, eventually resting underneath my seat. Another claw punctures my airbag. *Pop!* The airbag deflates and I'm plucked from the car by the back of my sweater. Except my sweater slips over my head and I bounce hard on my seat.

I start to scramble across to the passenger side, but there's no use opening the door to escape because one of them stands directly in front. Before I can even think straight, the door's ripped from the car. *Okaaay. So much for not opening the door.*

I dive down onto the floor beneath the passenger airbag. A few seconds later I hear a deafening *"Pop!"*, and the shadow above me dissipates. I start coughing and feel dizzy as residue disperses around me. Then I can no longer breathe. At first I think it's because of the airbag residue, then I realize I'm being strangled with my shirt. I've been plucked from the floor of the car and pulled from the mangled mess. I'm dropped on my bottom on hard pavement. As soon as I can catch my breath I cross my arms, pout, and mutter, "Car-murderers."

I panic as I see one of them move in my periphery. Out of instinct, I cover my head with my arms for protection, even though I know it won't protect me from its killing strike. All three of them now surround me, and I wait, my eyes squeezed shut. I wait. And wait. I open one eye to peer up at them and they are just looking at each other, as if they're having a conversation without moving their mouths or making a sound.

I've read that some types of animals communicate in unique ways. Giraffes make subsonic noises, the frequency too low to be heard by human ears, but audible to giraffes miles away. Bees communicate by leaving scents which have specific meanings. I wrack my brain to remember details about cat communication but come up blank. But as my thoughts are on animal senses, I think of an idea for a getaway.

It's a terribly embarrassing thing to resort to, but I can't think of any other options. I thought I'd die before doing it in public, but now when actually facing death, I've changed my mind. Cats have 200 million odor sensors in their noses, whereas humans only have 5 million. So before they break from their strange communication ritual—likely the equivalent of putting on a bib and grabbing cutlery—I do it.

Hands and feet on the ground, I stick my little tush up in the air, wiggle my butt...and fart. And while Mr. Cat-man and his two cronies are keeling over, I zip out of there, running as fast as I can.

If the streets around here weren't so desolate, I would jump in front of a car and try to get picked up. The only other way to lose them is to mask my scent and noise. Right now their systems are so overwhelmed they can't track me, but I know it's only temporary.

I never dreamed I'd be wanting to jump in the sewer so badly, but it's the only idea I have. But the culverts are all sealed with grates. I'm out of ideas, so I just keep running. To where exactly, I don't know. But I'm headed west, and having a heavy dose of déjà vu.

I feel regret that I wasn't able to locate my sister, and that regret, as well as exhaustion and cramping, starts slowing me down. I feel myself limp-hopping along since the cramping is getting so bad, and I have to slow to a walk for a few minutes. Then I'm back to jogging in a state of near-delirium, putting one foot in front of another, while staring at the cement in front of me.

As the rhythm of my limp-hopping reverberates through my body, my mind is involuntarily chanting in time to the beat. *I'm-dreaming. I'm-dreaming. I'm-dreaming. I'm-dream...*

Suddenly, my skin prickles and I'm on high alert. I glance in every direction, but don't see anyone. But my instincts tell me I'm not alone. Sure enough, a minute later, my pursuers close in on me again.

They saunter up to me lazily this time, surrounding me, and I take a swing at the closest one. I connect with hard muscle, and the feline human jerks back. My confidence rises as I pummel Cat-man with my fists, and I'm surprised he cowers as I strike him. I put in all the effort I have to scare him away or incapacitate him, but each time I try to run around him to escape, he blocks me.

Oddly enough, the other two feline-guys don't participate. I'm not sure I understand what's going on, but I seem to be making some headway with the leader of the group. Yet the other two just keep standing by, snickering.

Why aren't they helping their leader? It's good they aren't, or I'd be sorely outnumbered. I'll take any help I can get, so whatever "rules" their kind has, I'm relieved they're keeping to them.

A few minutes later, one of the secondary cats yawns and looks at his watch. "C'mon, Chet, we don't have all day. I'm hungry."

The other one sighs. "I'm hungry, too." He eyes me.

I fight even harder, knowing if I lose I'm on the menu.

Chet, his hands over his head, crouched down in a near-fetal position to protect himself from me, suddenly bolts upright. He looks unphased by my attack on him.

Huh? I don't get it? I thought I was being effective in my strikes on him.

"Cut me some slack, okay, this one's a lot of fun to play with. Look at her try to fight. I had to at least let her think she was making progress. Build up her self-confidence."

Then one of them bats me gently with a paw, not enough to hurt me, but enough to shake my confidence. The others chuckle at this new "game", and close in around me. They take turns batting me with their paws while I try to punch, kick, headbutt and do everything I possibly can to make some kind of impact. Every time I try to escape their triangle they just block me, and nudge me back into the middle.

The fact that they're so tall makes it impossible to knee them "where the sun don't shine". I can't reach their eyes to gouge them, and I'm not sure I'd want to risk attacking there anyway. To get to their eyes, I'd have to pass their sharp teeth.

I see they've retracted their claws, and have a sudden realization. *Oh God. They want to toy with me before they eat me. The leader's been toying with me this whole time!*

Dread settles into my stomach, threatening to squeeze bile up in surges. Adrenaline pumps, triggered by desperation. As a result, my actions become more flurried. I snarl like a rabid wolf, fighting for my life.

"Woo, yeah! Look at her go! Keep it up, girl!"

What the hell? They're actually cheering me on?

I feel my energy depleting after the running, fighting, and my final bout of flurried desperation. But adrenaline only goes so far, and I find myself starting to stumble. Each time I do, I get nudged back into the middle of the circle by soft but firm paws.

"It's kind of heartening to see one of *them* fight for once, even though a baby cub hits harder. A nice change." The cat-guy sighs as if reminiscing over the thought of a baby cub.

"Have to admit it was amusing while it lasted. But we're on a deadline."

What the hell are they talking about?

I start keeling over from exhaustion, and this time I can't stay on my feet, even when they try to stand me up. I fall down, but am caught by soft paws.

"Whelp, looks like she's ready to go. Too bad." I hear chuckling.

"Good. Let's go eat."

"She lasted longer than I thought, though." I feel myself being effortlessly hoisted over one of their shoulders.

I hear a couple more phrases before I pass out completely. "Yeah, man. You owe me twenty bucks."

Chapter Four

I wake up in a small white room, and wonder if I'm in the afterlife. I must be. But then I realize my muscles are still so very sore from all the escaping and one-sided fighting hours before.

How am I still alive? Maybe the beasts plan to cook me first? That thought is interrupted as a small door opens and a young woman in a white lab coat walks through.

"Hey there, you're finally awake."

"Uh, hi?" I sit up in my bed with trepidation over what comes next.

"I'm Joanne." She holds her hand out to me and we shake.

She doesn't look very threatening. Is she helping the catmen?

"I see you've met Larry, Joe, and Chet. We call them the three stooges around here."

I can see why, after today's fiasco. I try to get information from her to clear up my confusion. *This whole day has been beyond bizarre.*

"Hi Joanne. I'm Darla." I speak cautiously. "Could you tell me where I am and why I'm here?"

She smiles at me sympathetically. "Well, basically there's a shortage of humans..."

Oh God, I was right. A shortage of their food supply. The beasts really do want to eat me.

I'm trapped inside my own head in a panic, and can't comprehend what Joanne is saying. My eyes dart around, looking for an exit.

Should I bolt? No, not a good idea, there's just the one door and it's likely guarded. I'll bide my time and escape when I see an opening and they're least expecting it. Then I'll avoid this place like the plague.

Joanne is still talking. "So since it's your last night here, you get to choose whatever you'd like for dinner. There is a banquet being held in your honor. Well, not really a traditional banquet per se, more of a meet and greet..."

At least I'll have a lot of new acquaintances at my funeral.

"Then after the entertainment tonight, we'll see you off. I've picked out a gorgeous gown for you for the banquet and your send-off..."

Oh great. At least I'll be a pretty corpse. "Umm, Joanne?"

"Yes, what is it?"

"Why am I being dressed up when all they're going to do is strip me and eat me anyway?"

Joanne's eyes grow wide and her face blushes beet red. "Uh, I actually don't know anything about that end of things. You'll have to ask your benefactor."

My what?

"I'm going to go now, to uh, get you something to eat. Be back in a few." As she opens the door I catch a glimpse of a couple big guys standing outside my room.

Yup. Just as I thought.

After she's gone, I examine the room I'm in to see if there's another option for escape. Unfortunately, the air duct is too small. *Otherwise, it would have made a great intro-duct-ion to my escape.*

Inwardly I groan. When under stress I use humor to make light of my situation. *My terrible puns will be the death of me.*

I guide my attention to my current situation. *If they're doing some type of ritualistic ceremony tonight and I'm a major part of it, then I'm safe for a while longer because they need me. I'll have to find a means of escape later.*

I flop back down on my bed and wait for Joanne to return, planning to recharge my energy. I'm still not in the greatest headspace after so much lack of sleep. I partially doze off when I hear the door open again. Joanne brings a tray of fruit in for me.

Yeah, fruit of course—that way I'll taste sweeter.

"So, Joanne, any chance you could, umm...let me out of here?"

Joanne pushes her dark glasses up on the bridge of her nose. She really could work the sexy librarian thing if she tried. "Ah, sorry, we have a strict program here and keep to protocols."

"But surely you could *beeend* the rules once in a while?"

Joanne laughs. "Well, can't blame you for trying. At least you have a sense of humor about the whole situation."

Yeah, I was only half-kidding.

"Some people just freak out."

Hmmm, I wonder why? If you were on the menu, wouldn't you freak out?

I push my plate away now that it's empty.

"Wow, you were hungry."

"Yeah, I skipped breakfast, then ran for miles trying to get away from the three cat-guys."

"Ah, that's rough. Well, are you ready to be dressed up for the dinner tonight?"

You mean trussed up?

"So what, am I going to be dipped in honey glaze and presented for dessert?"

"Umm." Joanne's all red and flustered again as she clears off a counter and unlocks the drawers. She coughs. "I think you'll need to ask your benefactor. I'm not privy to those kinds of personal details."

"What do you mean by benefactor?"

"Oh, whoever wins you." I can't help but feel a bit confused at all of this. But before today, I was never truly aware that beast-men existed. I'd just heard vague rumors of strange beasts.

I try to get more info out of Joanne over the next hour as she does my hair and makeup, but she won't bite. She just deflects questions and I become even more confused about what's going on.

"I really can't tell you more. I've already said too much as it is."

Instead, she tries to make small talk about girly stuff like fashion. She pins my curly locks half up, making a rosette with curls that tumble down my back.

She dresses me in a floor-length cream gown with golden shimmer, which enhances my skin color. It has a fitted bodice, is loose around the shoulders, and has delicate lacy sleeves that travel down to my wrists. There's a long slit up the side, and underneath the airy gown are layers of filmy gossamer fabric. The dress is so light, I'm afraid a gust of wind will pick me up and blow me away.

Actually, that might not be a bad thing.

Once I'm ready, Joanne snaps a few photos and asks me which I like best. I pick one of me standing tall that I believe shows strength and determination. She sends it off somewhere.

"Great! Well, time for you to choose your dinner. Just check off what you'd like on the list here." She hands me a card with a list of entrees, sides, and desserts. I make my selections mindlessly, then hand the card back to her.

Joanne sighs with something that sounds like regret. "I wish circumstances were different, you know. It's been a fun afternoon, and in a different life, maybe we could have been friends. Usually my clients are in hysterics by now, but you've been remarkably calm."

If she only knew how freaked out I am...but I need to act calm to catch them off guard if I'm going to escape.

I nod. "I wish things had been different, too, Joanne."

"Well, time to go. I'll escort you as far as I can. I hope you at least enjoy your last supper here."

"Thanks, Joanne."

As she opens the door, I become hyper-alert, watching for any means of escape. Unfortunately, the guards at my door take up the front and rear. So much for an easy escape.

As we walk down a hallway with raised ceilings, Joanne gets excited. "See! How awesome is that?" She points up to the ceiling where the photo she just took of me has been projected on a large screen. "Your photo goes up on multiple screens in this and other buildings, as well as out on our app. That ensures everyone who wants to bet can do so here or online. And...anyone who wants to be in the running will have time to get here to compete!"

I think back to the girls' images that looked out of place during my meeting with Justin. They must have been on the menu. I feel insignificant as I'm one of the masses marching toward my doom.

On the other hand, as people stop to greet me along the hallways, I feel singled out. All attention seems to be on me tonight. Dying here seems to be an honor, according to the vibe I'm getting from these people.

Maybe these people are part of a cult?

We stop at a set of curved, elaborate double doors. Joanne embraces me. "It was so nice to meet you, Darla. I wish we had more time together. Just enjoy yourself and have fun. Enjoy the meal and meeting new people."

She drops her voice to a whisper. "When the painful, bloody stuff comes later, don't worry—there will be an end to it. Just close your eyes and try not to feel anything." I bid her farewell. Then she waves as she walks away with a sad expression on her face.

Two new guards throw open the double doors and I enter a beautiful rotunda with high ceilings and chandeliers. White tulle wraps around off-white lights strung toward the center of the room. If I had a wedding during this lifetime, this is how I would have envisioned my dream reception. That is, apart from my photos being projected on large screens hanging from the ceiling. I wouldn't be so vain as to have those at my reception.

Oh right. And apart from it being my last supper on this earth.

My original guards escort me to a raised square table with two seats, one with a full place setting and the other facing nothing on the tablecloth. It seems I am to dine alone, facing a full banquet hall of people. What the second chair is for, I do not know.

Although I'm served first, I'm unaware of the customs of the gathering, so I sit there, tummy rumbling due to the wonderful aroma of the food. My stomach is at odds with itself, as the stress of the situation takes away my desire to eat. A few minutes later, a lady comes by with wine, and I ask her what the appropriate manners are for the gathering, since no one is eating.

"Dear, you are the Guest of Honor tonight. No one will eat until you begin. Would you like white or red wine?"

After raising my utensils, cutting a tiny bit of steak and putting it to my lips, I see that everyone else in the room follows suit. My medium-rare steak is so delicious my eyes close and I make a small moaning sound. Whatever I'm about to go through, I'm determined to enjoy my last meal in this world, and take some pleasure before the pain.

However, I'm unable to swallow, due to the lump in my throat. I drink some water to stop myself from choking. After emptying my glass, I start on my wine. Thankfully, the wine helps calm my nerves and relaxes me, and I feel the stress dissipating.

The looks I'm being given from the main floor are friendly, and some even seem adoring. Several men wink at me from their places at their tables, and one even blows me a kiss. Although I'm feeling more at ease, my face feels heated. I'm sure I must be blushing because of all the attention.

For a moment I wonder if I've misconstrued my whole situation. Everyone seems so friendly. *I feel so confused. I wish I understood what was really going on.*

There is a lot of discussion at each table, phones are out, as are pens and notebooks. There's a lot of calculation going on. But the odd thing is the guests are looking at me, as if I'm being the one discussed.

The servers come around with dessert and coffee. "Come on, Dear. You've barely touched your plate. Try to eat something." I try to comply, so as not to attract more attention. I close my eyes and drift away on the wings of triple-layered chocolate mousse. At least it's a beautiful ending to a short-lived life.

After a short reprieve, I return to the reality of my situation. *If I truly am in danger, and my instincts are telling me I am, I need to keep my wits about me and get out of here.*

I see an opening. *Time to make my move.* One of the servers comes by with more wine. I try to project innocence. "Excuse me, could you tell me which way the ladies' room is?"

"Just off to the right corner, down the little corridor."

"Thank you." I slide my chair back, and start walking toward the corridor, noting the "EXIT" sign above. I try to be as nonchalant as

possible to avoid notice. *As if I can avoid notice with all these people in here.* But I give it a shot.

When I get to the corridor, I hear footsteps following behind me. *Just great. No easy exit, I guess.* I turn to the door of the ladies' room, glancing back in the corridor, and see my guards have followed me. *Even better.* I roll my eyes, sigh, and open the door, knowing they'll be waiting outside.

There's no window. I check each stall to make sure. I spend a few minutes in the ladies' room, then exit into the corridor. I would have considered running for it, but one of the guards is waiting between myself and the exit. They escort me back to my table, and I take my seat.

A few minutes later, a middle-aged man with a lapel microphone steps onto the platform, one level down from where I am seated. Noise from the room falls to a hush, while faces look up at him eagerly.

"Good evening! As you all well know, we have gathered here in celebration and honor of our newly acquired lady. In keeping with our traditions, each person participating in tonight's festival will have time alone with the lovely Lady Darla at the head table. The time will be divided evenly among all participants with our Time-Master keeping track of each increment. From reports, we know the young Lady Darla is intelligent, spirited in her attempts to escape, is quick on her feet, and would be a worthwhile match for anyone looking for a headstrong opponent."

Suddenly I'm hit with a realization.

Oh. My. God. They mean to hunt me.

CHAPTER FIVE

The emcee continues, speaking to the hundreds of people in attendance. They sit in rapt attention, focused on every word he speaks.

"As a number of you have anticipated, there are more participants tonight than ever before, and the betting is already off the charts, in the millions!"

And that's what it all comes down to. Money and entertainment.

Thunderous applause and excited cheers reverberate through the banquet hall, echoing off the rounded chamber ceiling.

"And those participating—well, let's just say history is about to be made, and tonight will be a night to remember for years to come!"

Applause erupts with a standing ovation, whistling, yelling, and cheering. I hear joyous laughter and watch as faces look up at me, enraptured. Although I don't really know what's going on in this strange society, the two glasses of wine in my veins keep me calm and my heart rate from exploding. I should probably be drinking carafes of coffee before tonight's main event, so I can be on my toes. But this floaty feeling is so nice, just tipsy enough to prevent anxiety from building up.

The emcee calms the room of applause. "It is now time for one of the most enjoyable parts of the evening. The time when the participants get to meet our 'Darling Darla'!" I hear chuckles from around the room at the new term of endearment.

"Protocol is the same as usual. Names will be called." The emcee then addresses me. "Darla, my dear, not all participants are in attendance tonight. Some have signed up via the app as well and won't arrive until after the meet and greet." He turns back to the crowd. "Let us begin!" Applause echoes through the banquet hall.

The emcee walks off stage, and I hear a disembodied voice over a speaker call the first name. A man ascends to the head table and sits in the empty chair facing me.

"Welcome, Lovely Darla. I'm David, but you can call me Dave. It's wonderful to make your acquaintance." He gently lifts my hand to his lips. "You are truly delectable."

I feel my face heat up and I feel a bit shy. "Hi, Dave. Nice to meet you."

And so it begins. Every few minutes the voice calls out a new name, and the previous man bids me farewell, saying how much he can't wait to see me during the next part of the evening.

"God, I can't wait to taste you. Don't worry. I'll be gentle."

I imagine Fredrique gently strangling me as he munches on my toes. *I think the wine is affecting me. Seriously.*

"I'm going to be the one to have you. Please be forewarned that it may be messy, but I'll make sure it's over quickly so there is no suffering. Sometimes a quick blow to the head is the best solution." Maurice taps me on the temple. "That way there is no pain."

I see so many faces and learn so many new names throughout the evening. There is no way I'll be able to remember them all. Not that there is a reason to remember any of them. But it just adds to my confusion and feeling of being overwhelmed.

"And now, we move on to the next part of tonight's exciting program! Participants, please make your way downstairs into the waiting wings and prepare yourselves. Audience, make your way to the stadium. And don't forget to bet! The stakes are continuing to escalate!"

The emcee gestures to my escort, and my guards lead me out of the rotunda, downstairs. We travel down three flights, a bit tricky wearing

stilettos, but the guards provide looped arms for me to grasp. My head is still high and my dignity intact. We reach the bottom of the stairwell.

"Thank you, Gentlemen." They nod at me, respectfully.

The wine is still working its way through my system. It mutes my nervousness. My guards direct me down a narrow corridor, up a flight of stairs, and to a door at the top. My imagination runs wild, thinking about what could be behind that door.

My escorts open the door for me, and I set foot on a platform in an arena. Except I'm not really *in* the arena per se, I'm suspended *above* the arena. I can see everything from my vantage point. I must be in the same building where I saw those poor animals fighting this morning. The noise is almost deafening.

Oh no. Although I'm still unsure what's happening, it can't be good. My "fight or flight" instinct kicks in, my natural drive for self-preservation. I whip around, surprising my guards, and make a dash for the door. Firm hands stop me from making it past three steps. They turn me around, and march me forward.

One of them points a few steps ahead to a wooden pole, seemingly in the middle of nowhere. I shake my head in dissent. Instead of dragging me, they easily lift me by the elbows and carry me the few remaining steps to the ordinary-looking pole. When we reach it, I notice there is something hanging from the top on the other side.

Oh no. The items hanging from the top—they are shackles. I scream and try to fight the guards, but they keep me suspended. *If I can just get in a few stabs with these stilettos, maybe they'll drop me!* I try kicking, and one of them rolls their eyes.

By now, one guard has me by the waist, pinning my arms, and the other has my legs. I struggle with them as they stretch my arms up and

shackle my wrists above my head, and my ankles below. I feel soft fabric lining the shackles. They aren't meant to feel uncomfortable or barbaric.

Why do I feel like I'm waiting for King Kong to show up?

I focus on breathing in and out. I feel like I've run a marathon. I'm choking for air.

Sensing my anxiety, one of the guards makes a nervous cough. He yells in order to be heard. "Don't worry, it's just theatrical. Nothing will happen to you while you are shackled to the pole. We will make sure of that."

The other guard speaks in a loud voice, trying to be heard over the noise. "The shackles also protect you. As long as you're shackled you're free."

As long as I'm shackled, I'm free? Now that sounds like an oxymoron if I ever heard one. I roll my eyes at my own double meaning.

"Nothing will attack me or eat me while I'm attached to the pole?"

The guard's lips quirk at the corner. "We promise. Nothing will harm you while you're shackled. It represents deep-rooted history steeped in tradition. Nothing to worry about. Once you're unshackled though—well, let's just say that's when you'll feel sharp teeth sinking into your flesh."

I scream in terror, and my vision becomes patchy with black spots. I fade in and out for what feels like an hour, but turns out to be less than a minute.

"Milt, stop scaring her." One of the guards holds an open water bottle with a straw sticking out. "Here, drink this."

I take a few sips of the cool water, and look forward. I can see myself up on the big screen. My image is being projected live, shackled to the pole. I feel a bit self-conscious, since my arms stretched above me make my breasts perk up. I look like the cliche damsel in distress.

I have more serious things to think about than how I look!

I take a few more sips and a deep breath. Then I take in my surroundings. My anxiety is so high that I'm hyper-focusing, becoming more observant and aware of small details than usual.

My guards are now holding poles with burgundy flags attached to them. They stand at attention. It's as if they've transformed into an honor guard.

I'm in an enormous, domed room, an arena of sorts, but with the ceiling of an ancient cathedral. I tilt my head upward to look more closely, and see the ceiling is embellished with an intricate bronze pattern. It looks like the arena has been here for a long time, as some of the decorations look worn. From the temperature and dampness, I'm guessing we are underground.

The stadium is packed full with people. They're cheering and I can feel the tension building up into a frenzy. Others are focused on their phones, no doubt on the betting.

I don't understand the betting side of things. *I thought I was going to be hunted and the bets would be on my captor?* Obviously, I have things mixed up. As usual.

Struggling isn't working. Maybe the guards will listen to reason. *I wonder if I could convince these guys to let me go.*

I yell to be heard. "Since I'm not really doing anything right now, is there any way you'd release me so I could do nothing elsewhere?"

One guard laughs while the other snickers.

Or not.

The guard named Milt answers me. "Right now you're providing inspiration. And you'll be involved in plenty once the next part is over. Rest and save your strength."

I try to appeal to their humanity.

"Please, don't do this. I came looking for my sister because she's missing and I'm worried about her. Please let me go!"

"Sorry, Love. No can do." The other guard does look somewhat sympathetic though.

I'm about to beg for my freedom, when the crowd noise increases. The emcee walks to a podium set above the arena on a different elevated platform. He gestures to the crowd and the cacophony dies down.

"It looks like we're just about to begin! We had a few late entries, but are all settled now. So folks, just to give you an idea how significant tonight is, and how special our honorary guest is, the most participants we've ever had has been a few dozen. We usually average a dozen in the battle for dibs on the 'princess'."

Wait, dibs? So this is a competition for dibs on me? My mind floats to the worst-case scenario. I morosely wonder who my executioner will be.

"Well, tonight, we have over fifty participants! Fifty!" The crowd cheers with wild abandon. "It's unheard of!" The thunderous roar of the crowd seems to shake the building.

"Now, you all know our Dear Darla." More cheers and whistles. The platform I'm on starts descending. Fear grips my heart. Thank goodness, it doesn't lower all the way.

"Well, it's time to introduce our participants!" Hoots and hollers come from the worked up crowd.

"Everyone, please welcome: Akhekh, Kholkikos, Druk, Fafnir, Kulkulkan..." The list drones on and on, but I'm more focused on what's happening in the arena than on the emcee.

One by one, filling the arena are large animals, bears, lions, wolves, leopards, rhinos, raptor birds, and various other large creatures. Except each of them is like a giant-sized version of their species.

If they aren't here to kill me, since my part is theatrical, what are they here for?

"Every participant will fight until submission. Traditional yield signs apply. Any going beyond will be disqualified. Assisting others results in immediate disqualification, as does ganging."

Oh no! Those poor animals! Their owners are making them fight. It's barbaric!

"Is everyone ready to see them fight?" The crowd goes wild. "Everyone ready for a bloodbath?" You can see the lust for blood in their eyes.

"Begin!"

After that, the most horrific sights take place. Animals are attacked, blood spurts all over, and fur and feathers are plastered to the ground, soaked in crimson. Dead animals are being dragged out of the arena by handlers who avoid being hurt in the fray.

I don't know when I started screaming, but I realize one of the guards is trying to calm me down. Although I can't hear him, I see him mouthing the words. "Breathe! Or you'll pass out!"

Passing out might be the best thing under the circumstances. Attacks and battles are going on all over the arena, and the crowd is as frenzied with bloodlust as those fighting on the field. The volume is that of a constant roar, so loud that nothing else can be heard, not even the emcee as he attempts to announce each casualty being removed.

Tears stream down my face. It's as though all those beautiful creatures are disposable. Disposable like myself. Just pieces of meat to be torn apart, with no care for life.

It's despicable. Disgusting. Inhumane.

The carnage continues until there are five contenders left. The rhino, tiger, and kodiak bear are in a standoff. The grizzly attacks the lion in a gory mess of claws and teeth, each vying for power.

Grizzly is a good name for this. All this waste. It's grisly.

One of the guards puts the water to my lips again and I sip. I feel so exhausted I can't scream anymore. If I wasn't secure on the pole I'm sure I would keel over.

The lion is down and the tiger approaches the grizzly victor. The rhino clashes with the kodiak and gores it with its horn, throwing the bear off balance and damaging it badly. Blood pours from a wound in its chest, and one arm hangs limply by its side.

The tiger attacks the grizzly and the two of them flip over in a tangle of teeth and claws. The grizzly tries to rise to a dominant stance and that's its downfall. Literally. The tiger uses the grizzly's own weight against it to throw it to the ground. The tiger takes a swipe at the grizzly's underbelly, and I close my eyes, waiting for the carnage to be over.

The crowd noise becomes deafening over the next few minutes as it underscores roars and grunts. I smell the metallic scent of blood from far up on my perch of safety. Then I hear a victory chant with music in the background. The crowd erupts in madness.

I open my eyes to see everyone on their feet, elated, screaming, howling. Neither bear is anywhere to be seen. The tiger has pinned down the rhinoceros and has it in a death grip, its thick, grey hide torn to shreds. I can see its internal organs and think I'm going to be sick.

I open my eyes again several minutes later. The rhino has been removed by the handlers. Men exit the arena with reams of blood-soaked towels.

The tiger, in all its majesty, stands proudly, basking in the roar of the crowd. It turns and faces me. Its awareness of my presence seems to be

heightened, as it focuses on me alone. Its eyes find mine and hold them. It's as if it has a soul.

I shake my head to clear my mind. Now that this part of the evening, this bloodbath, is over, my demise is imminent. Communication has been so poor I'm unsure what to expect. I can only guess.

The tiger's owner is the winner. Then it becomes clear in my mind. *I'm about to become food for his pet.*

CHAPTER SIX

I remember what my guard said. While I was shackled no harm would come to me. So I decide I want to stay shackled. However, the platform starts lowering me to the floor of the arena, my podium sinking beneath the floor. As we descend, the tiger looks up at me. It walks up to the shadow of the descending island, then stands on its hind legs, balancing itself against my lowering platform. It seems to know what it's won. That I am its prize.

The crowd continues to roar and cheer, egging the tiger on. I can see why they would have no care for life, after reveling in the carnage that occurred this evening. The platform stops at ground level. The tiger circles me and seems to be inhaling my scent. I can feel myself perspiring, just waiting for those huge jaws to clamp down on me and take my life. Tears are streaming down my face again. And I know it smells it on me— fear.

A strange thought pops into my head. None of the animals ate the others on the battlefield. *They must have been fed before the carnage started.* Which would mean this tiger is hungry now after all that vicious activity. *Why is it holding back?*

The tiger continues to sniff and explore me, ignoring my guards. It starts to rub its face on me, and then I see it's teeth ready to bite. But it nips me gently instead, moves its body close to mine and rubs its soft, sensuous fur on me. It puts a paw on the pole and balances, pressing its belly and chest against me so all I feel is a cloak of softness.

As it balances there, cloaking me, it looks down into my eyes. It leans down toward me, opens its mouth, and I brace for the worst. Then I feel its raspy tongue licking me. Licking up my tears. I know l must be in

shock. I'm numb with a floaty feeling. My eyes widen, not understanding or grasping what's going on. I just know it's a miracle I'm still alive. I close my eyes.

Then I hear the most horrible cracking sound. *Oh no. I'm being eaten alive, but I'm in shock so I can't feel it. Goodbye, cruel world.*

Then I realize the sound is coming from the tiger and not from me. *Maybe the tiger had internal damage from the bloodbath? Its bones—for some reason they're breaking now instead of earlier?* I close my eyes and shiver as the crackling continues.

I feel the soft blanket of fur dissipate until it feels as though human skin is touching me. I don't understand what's happening when I feel the paw that grips me be replaced by a hand. Instead of whiskers, wet nose, and licks, I feel a human face gently rubbing my cheek, a nose gently nuzzling me, lips tenderly brushing over me. I feel fingertips brush up the outsides of my arms then touch my wrists shackled above me, thumbs rubbing the back of my hands.

I stand there paralyzed, my body's senses too confused to make heads or tails of my situation. I don't want to open my eyes, for fear of what I'll see. If I ignore my surroundings, place myself in a cocoon of denial, then maybe everything will go away. Then I'll wake up, realizing it was all just a dream.

A forehead touches mine, then lips reach down and gently caress mine. They create a gentle explosion of pleasure. A diffused lightning bolt travels down through my most innermost parts and settles deep inside me. The face moves away from mine, and I can feel his body has stepped away. But he uses his finger and thumb to tilt my face up, prompting me to open my eyes. I open them, and I gasp.

Once again, I'm looking into Justin's eyes. I hear myself sound out a cry of relief. Deep emotions stir inside me. This time when he brings his

lips down on mine, I allow myself to fall into his kiss. His lips sweep mine, and he takes my breath away.

Even with all the confusion and cacophony going on around me, my only sense becomes touch. And I long for *his* touch. He sweeps his lips over mine again, and gently touches his tongue to my bottom lip. I part my lips slightly, and he gently sucks on my lower lip.

He flutters kisses along my jawbone to my neck, to my shoulder, and stops. He stands again, looking down at me, looking into my eyes.

I'm suddenly brought back to the present, to all the cheers and yelling, laughter and celebration from the crowd. And I realize, I don't know what comes next, what my fate will be. My anxiety returns, and my chest tightens.

My guard gives Justin the keys to my shackles, and he unlocks my ankles. He reaches up and frees my wrists, then gently massages them. He loops his arms underneath my legs and upper back, and picks me up, turning toward the crowd. The crowd goes wild, chanting his name. I'm at a loss as to what customs have taken place or the significance of what has occurred. I feel emotionally exhausted, so I turn away from the crowd and toward Justin's chest to find some solace there.

After some time, the crowd has finally hushed. Shifting my head to see, I can tell it's the emcee's doing.

"Our obvious winner tonight is Bagheshwar, Justin's tiger!"

The crowd roars. It takes a few minutes for the emcee to settle them down again.

"An amazing performance! But not a surprise for those of us who have seen him fight before."

The crowd laughs and I hear some happy cheers.

"And, of course, he's holding his prize."

And suddenly, I feel coldness grip my spine. I'm confused. Is Justin about to kill me? I don't understand the traditions and customs of this group.

Am I to be fed to his pet tiger? Or sacrificed to some unknown deity? Or worse? I wonder if this whole organization is a cult.

My eyes open wide as I stare at the emcee.

"And we're waiting..." The emcee uses a sing-song voice, and the crowd breaks into laughter.

Justin brings his mouth to my ear. "Darla, tradition states that I mark you as my mate so you're under my protection. It's the only way I can keep you safe. Otherwise, you'll be given to the second place winner, and from what I know of him, he doesn't treat women kindly." He pauses. "Can I mark you, Sweetheart?"

I'm speechless. I look up at Justin's caring face with wide eyes. I find peace there as the overwhelming noise and crowd fade into the background. I'm still in shock from what I've seen tonight, and from what Justin has just asked me. But he gently and affectionately strokes my cheek with his thumb and calms my soul with his touch. Clinging to Justin as I lay safely in his arms, I nod my head.

Justin smiles at me, and feathers kisses along my neck to my shoulder. Then I feel a sharp pain, hear myself yelp, and everything goes black.

My eyes flutter, and I feel gentle strokes on my cheek as I slowly move from the purgatory of sleep to awareness. I lean into the hand stroking me, and feel a soft kiss on my forehead. I open my eyes completely and feel the warm sunlight streaming down on my face.

"Hey." Justin looks into my eyes and smiles.

"Hey." I reciprocate his greeting and smile back.

He leans over from his sitting position, and cages me with his arms. "I just want you to know I'm so glad you're here. Nothing could make me happier."

I give him a shy smile, as I arch backward on the soft white linen sheets, stretching out my muscles. I let out a big yawn.

Justin's hand smooths over my forehead. "How are you feeling this morning?"

"I'm feeling okay. Just having difficulty focusing my thoughts. It's morning? What happened last night?"

"After I marked you, you passed out. That usually happens. It's nothing to be worried about." He kisses my forehead, softly. "I brought you home with me."

"Where are we, exactly?" I try to sit up, but am hit with a wave of dizziness. Justin cradles my head with his hand and helps lower me back on the bed.

"About an hour north of the city. I brought you to my house in the country so you could recuperate, uninterrupted, where it's quiet."

My head's still stuffed with cotton, but I know I should have questions. I just can't remember what they are. Instead of stressing over what I can't control, I let myself go, and just be in the moment. I smile as the warm sunshine meets the cool breeze, wafting the sheer eyelet curtains at the window.

Justin climbs beside me, on top of the duvet that is wrapping me in a cloud of softness. He gently strokes my cheek with his thumbs, cradling my head in both hands, and kisses me on the forehead again. I look up into his deep blue eyes. I feel so drawn to him.

"Now that I've got you here, I don't want to let you out of my sight. This all feels so surreal."

"I can definitely understand what you mean by surreal." This all feels so foreign. Cuddling up in a warm duvet beside someone I have such an intense connection with feels heavenly.

"Come here." Justin pulls me to his body, duvet still between us, and just holds me close. My head tucks beneath his chin and I can feel his warm hands on my back. The feeling of "home" overwhelms me. I hear his breathing start to even out, and my mind drifts off into the bliss of oblivion.

I feel someone stroking my hair as my eyes flutter open. Justin smiles at me through the afternoon shadows that have settled upon the room. My head feels clearer than before. And again I feel drawn to him, like a bear to honey...

Bears. Grizzlies and kodiaks.

Suddenly, my eyes flash wide open.

Justin sits up with concern. "What is it?"

"Last night. All those animals." My lip starts trembling. "They're all dead." Tears start making their way down my face.

Justin scoops me, duvet and all, onto his lap. "Hey. Shhh. It's okay. They're not dead. And they're not just animals."

Justin wipes away my tears with his thumbs,while planting gentle kisses on my face. I look up into his eyes, searching. "What do you mean?"

"They were all shifters. Shifters have the ability to heal rapidly. By now all the guys are fine, some feeling beat up and bruised I'm sure, but no one died."

I still can't fully grasp what he's saying. "So you're saying that not one of the animals in the bloodbath died?"

"Not a single one." Justin smiles at me and strokes my hair behind my ear. I feel relieved.

Then he takes a serious tone. "I think you've had a shock to your system, with everything you've seen during the last twenty-four hours. It's overwhelming for you and you can't wrap your head around it. But I'll give you the answers you need, as you can handle them." I nod, looking up at him with big eyes.

He breathes in sharply. "God you're so beautiful. How did I get so lucky?" He holds me closely to his body. "At some point we're going to have to talk about 'us', but for now, just know you're safe and protected, with all the support you need. Okay?"

I nod my head. "Okay." I can do that much, to trust Justin that I am safe and can count on his support as I recuperate.

"So your first question about the safety of the animals has been answered. No animals died, and they are all perfectly healthy. So no more tears about that." He gently touches his nose to mine. I still have so much confusion over the events of yesterday, but I can grasp little truths. Little statements like the one he's just given me.

Then my anxiety rises as my mind allows more to float to the forefront. "But what about those cat creatures? I was chased by them. And you speak about the animals like you know them as people. And...and..." I feel the place between my shoulder and neck, stroking my fingers over it. "You *marked* me? I don't understand." I'm starting to feel agitated, as thoughts start flowing again through the pathways in my mind.

"Shhh. It's okay. One thing at a time." He strokes my hair rhythmically. "The next thing I'm going to explain will be the most difficult to wrap your head around, but it will answer many of those questions floating around in here." He strokes my forehead with his thumb.

"Do you remember when the tiger was standing by you last night?"

I close my eyes. In the back of my mind I recall the soft fur and way I'd felt enveloped in its embrace, even though I must have been quivering uncontrollably with terror.

"I remember feeling I was going insane with fear. Yet at the same time felt such a softness that I wanted to cuddle up in its warmth, regardless of what it would do to me."

Justin nods. "Do you remember when you first felt me touching you? You felt my skin?"

"Yes."

"In between the tiger holding you and me being there with you, do you remember a cracking sound?"

"Yes! I thought the tiger was either eating me or it was injured from the fighting. I closed my eyes."

Justin held my face in his hands, brushing my cheeks with his thumbs. He looks into my eyes and smiles. "In this world there are people who can shift into the form of animals. They're called 'shape-shifters' or 'shifters' for short." I search his eyes, trying to comprehend what he's explaining to me.

"Shifters can change from human form to animal form at will."

I stare at him for a moment, question marks in my eyes. "Okay. Let's just say I believe there are shifters for now." I think of the animals again. My eyes open wide. "So the animals were all shifters?"

"Yes, that's right. And because shifters heal at an incredibly fast rate, it means—"

"—That's why everyone is okay and no one died." I nod, thoughtfully.

Justin puts his forehead to mine and breathes in my scent. Then he pulls his face back so he can look at mine.

"Darla, I'm a shifter."

Chapter Seven

Justin gives me a minute to absorb his statement while he searches my eyes.

"And your animal is a—tiger?"

He smiles gently, knowing I've understood him. "Yes, that tiger was also me."

"Wait a sec. You were the one who scared those men away."

He laughs. "Well, that's a whole other story, but yes, that was me, too."

"What happens when you shift from a human to a tiger?"

"Well, remember when you were being hugged by my tiger, and you closed your eyes? That crackling noise occurred when I shifted back into a human. My bones were changing and realigning."

I stare up at his face, wide-eyed. I don't know how to manage this emotionally. So I compartmentalize the information by putting it into a mental filing cabinet, and locking my feelings of incredulity, awe, and fear away with it. My mind will sort through that information as it gradually seeps into my consciousness. I reach up and pull Justin's chest down to me and we just hold each other, feel each other's warmth, feel each other's comfort.

As the shadows deepen in the room, I hear a low growling noise. Justin pulls me up into a sitting position and kisses me on the top of my head. "Follow me. It's time to do something about that growling tummy of yours, or it might get mistaken for a tiger." The side of his mouth twitches up and I giggle.

He takes my hand, and we walk out the bedroom door into a hallway with deep brown tiles that shine with opal reflections in the late afternoon

sun. We walk to the winding staircase where he offers me his arm for stability. I hold onto his arm, still a bit lightheaded, and descend with him to the main level. *I must have missed seeing all of this yesterday, because I was unconscious.*

Smooth cream accented with burgundy and gold adornments on the stair rail sets the tone for the room. The entranceway is decorated with cream crown moulding in an intricate pattern. The floor tile is the same iridescent brown as the upstairs tile, and a cream winged bench with burgundy seat cushion adorns the entranceway. The ceilings are high, and the walls are adorned with beautiful bronze sconces holding candles.

"What a lovely home you have!" I am taken with the beauty of it all.

Stained glass is inset into the double doors, and a large stained glass window above the doors provides colored light which enhances the beauty of the room. The room nearly takes my breath away. By his gasp and the look on his face as he stares at me with fascination, I can tell something is up. I give him a questioning look, raised eyebrows, an expression I've seen him make before.

He bursts out laughing when he recognizes my expression. He teases me. "You're such a copy-cat." I laugh at his cute pun.

Then he makes his confession. "I was just noting that the way the light falls on you makes you look positively angelic." I can feel my cheeks turning red for the umpteenth time.

I stare down at my oversized shirt that belongs to Justin and laugh. "You're so silly." I playfully bat him on the arm.

"I'm serious, Darla. You are an angel to me." I turn a deeper shade of red, and there is an awkward silence.

Yeah, with my flushed cheeks, I'm sure I look like a cherub.

"Come with me and I'll show you the reminder of the house." My tummy growls again.

"Oops, the neglected tiger-tummy needs her food before she eats us all up!" If I had a pillow at that moment I would have thrown it at him. As it is, Justin picks me up by the elbows and spins me around. I can't help laughing.

"Hey, I'm already spinny today. You're just making it worse!" My eyes are bright, and my mood is playful, even though I am darn hungry.

Justin returns my hungry look, but it's a different kind of hungry. He gives me a wolfish grin, and I can see the desire, the want, in his eyes. He reaches down and kisses my mouth, swiping his tongue down the crease between my lips. My lips part, and he uses that opportunity to dart his tongue inside, as if probing, a yearning to know me more. To understand me more.

Justin's tongue flickers in and out, setting mine on fire with every subtle touch. His hands cradle my neck as he tilts my chin upward for his kiss. His kiss is full of sweetness, but it also hints of things to come. I can tell his passion is bridled, and he's holding back. And I can feel the strain on him, the energy it's taking to hold himself back from devouring my very soul.

He breaks the kiss, gently placing more soft kisses on my lips, face, and collarbone. "We need to get you fed." He holds out his arm, and I take it as he leads me farther into the house.

He holds a door open to a large room with a mahogany dining table and chairs and waits for me to walk through. "So the dining room is also accessible from upstairs, without having to go as far as the entryway. Just take the middle flight of stairs for that. I just wanted to show you a bit of what you missed last night."

"Hmmm. What else did I miss?" I'm in a mischievous mood, but playing innocent.

He looks down at me with desire again. Then he rubs his hand through his hair and clears his throat. "I had difficulty keeping my hands to myself, so I asked one of the staff to change you and put you to bed. I didn't want to take any chances, after leaving my mark on you."

We walk toward the table. That brings up another subject I'm curious about. "What does it actually mean when you mark someone? Not just the symbolic explanation, but are there any physical effects?"

Justin stops dead in his tracks and turns to face me. He stares down into my eyes with honesty. "I regret that you didn't know more about the mark before last night and what it signified, but everything I said was true. I couldn't let you end up in the clutches of a misogynist like that rhino. He would have ruined you, and you'd be an empty shell by the time he discarded you. I couldn't let that happen to you." Justin's eyes are moist, and his kiss on my lips is tender.

He won't let himself be distracted though. "I'll explain more later. Right now, we need to get you fed." He pulls out a chair for me at the dining room table, then walks briskly out of the room, I'm assuming into the kitchen. A few minutes later he comes out.

"I checked on dinner and it's on its way. Now while we're waiting, we can talk more."

I smile at him. "Thank you for being so thoughtful, Justin."

"I enjoy being attentive to you. There may be times when we're both busy and pass like ships in the night, but I was hoping we could take some time to start things off on the right foot."

"So back to the marking."

"Yes, the marking. You were asking how it works, beyond just having symbolic meaning steeped in tradition."

Justin takes a deep breath. "So first of all, it used to be thought that the effects of the mark were due to purely mystical origins. It was only discovered recently that biology is tied directly to the power of the mark."

"The short version is the mark stimulates the release of two chemicals in the body that affect bonding and the desire to protect one's mate. The chemicals are called oxytocin and vasopressin."

"So how does a simple bite mark trigger the release of the two hormones?"

"Most people become very sensitive to touch at the site of the bite mark. That sensitivity in the nerve receptors stimulates extra oxytocin to be released frequently, resulting in faster bonding and attachment. Stimulation to that spot also triggers nerve cells at the base of the brain to produce more vasopressin, which results in a stronger drive to claim and protect one's mate.

"Those hormones trigger others to build up, which in turn causes larger production of pheromones. Pheromones affect production of oxytocin and vasopressin in one's mate. Then comes the snowball effect."

"So you're automatically drawn to your mate because of the effects of the mark, and the more time you spend with them, the more you're drawn to them?"

"Exactly. And the more you think about your mate, the higher the oxytocin and vasopressin levels become, the keys for bonding with and protecting your mate. It's why shifters and their mates fall hard and fast for each other."

"I have a question regarding our mark." *Ooo, I like the sound of "our"!*

"Shoot and I'll do my best to answer."

"Would you have fought for me if the misogynist rhino-guy in second place wasn't there?" I pause, trying to reword things so Justin understands

where I'm coming from. "I'm basically asking, did you fight and mark me just to rescue me from him? Or was there another reason?"

Justin hesitates, as he phrases his answer. My heart drops into my feet, waiting. Maybe he did it just to save me from a difficult fate, and not because he was actually interested in me specifically?

"Regardless of who was in that arena, I would have fought for you, Darla. I felt drawn to you and an undeniable kinship with you the first time we met. When I found out you were to be presented in the arena, I rushed over as soon as I could, determined to win you.

"If we'd had a normal courtship, I would have waited until all cards were on the table before asking if I could mark you. Which leads me to a question I have for you, Darla. Regardless of everything that's happened and with you being marked early without knowing all of the ramifications, would you be open to having a courtship?"

Chapter Eight

Just then there is a knock at the door, the staff walks in, and dinner is served. I can sense Justin's frustration over the interruption, but it gives me time to think over my answer. One thing I am appreciating more and more about Justin is he doesn't force me into making decisions or take away my options. Well, apart from the marking. But that was an exception since protecting me meant marking me.

I'm very attracted to him and he's kind, truthful, and fair. Entering into a courtship would mean we would be able to spend time together just getting to know each other with no pressure. But it would make our intentions clear. That we would value our relationship and not take it lightly.

After the staff leaves, Justin continues to look at me, searching my eyes for my answer. I smile at him from across the table. "Yes, Justin, I would love that."

His eyes light up, he rushes around to my side of the table, lifts me out of my chair, and kisses me, cradling my head in his hand. He pauses. "You've made me one happy man, Darla."

His lips are on mine again and I melt into him. I'm still holding back, but it isn't because I don't want him. I do. But I want to get to know him as a person.

Although the beginning of our relationship has been rushed, it doesn't mean this has to be a whirlwind romance. We need a friendship we can rely on if we are to have a future together. Our lips separate, and Justin holds me tight while I nestle my head underneath his chin. I feel so content being near him.

"Here, I'm going to move around to your side." Justin grabs his dinner and we sit beside each other.

"I sat with the table between us earlier so we could talk, without me acting on the need to keep touching you." He inhales as if he's taking in my scent. "But you need to eat and I'm distracting you from that."

Justin holds my hand and sits close to me while we share dinner together. I glance over at him shyly, and he can't help but kiss me, his hand in my hair. My first dinner with Justin is special, and it's the start of our new adventure together.

During the following days, I make dozens of calls, trying to figure out what happened to my sister. Thankfully, our parents are on a long European vacation. We usually don't communicate much, and the time zones means we talk less frequently than usual.

It's not that I don't love my parents, but telling them about Natalie would really complicate things. They're older, my dad has a heart condition, and my mother suffers from anxiety. The last thing they need is to hear of Natalie's disappearance. I'm determined to get her back before they realize she is missing.

Susan comes to visit me at Justin's home and offers support. She agrees that telling my parents isn't a great idea. I introduce her to Justin between his conference calls, and I show her around the place. I can tell she's impressed.

"Wow, I can't believe this place." Susan and I are walking in the garden in the backyard.

"Being away from the city helps me to stay focused. And being here helps settle my anxious spirit and keep me calm. Spending time with Justin is so soothing."

"I can tell. He seems to be good for you that way." Susan pauses and looks a bit uncomfortable. "But don't you think you're jumping the gun

a bit? I mean, you're practically living together and barely know each other."

I know Susan isn't aware of how the marking accelerates bonding—I haven't told her anything about shifter culture or my own experience.

"I can't explain how, but I know we're 'right' for each other. I'm positive he's 'the one'. I feel it."

"Well, I admit it wouldn't be hard to fall in love with THAT." Susan giggles as she refers to Justin. "He's like the ideal man. Supportive, considerate, compassionate, sexy..."

I smile as we walk. "I know. He's pretty amazing." I look over at her. "But about my staying here, I still have my own apartment. So it's not like I'm limiting my options. And I have my own room here at Justin's place. I'm staying like any other guest would. Otherwise, we'd barely get to see each other, with our schedules."

"I understand. I just want you to be cautious, okay? You're emotionally vulnerable, especially right now with everything going on with Nat. Just be careful."

"I will. Justin has been a gentleman, so there's no reason to worry that way."

"I'm concerned about your heart." Susan places her hand over her chest.

"I know. I promise you I'm going into this 'eyes wide open'." I sigh. "But sometimes we need to take a bit of a risk. And Justin is definitely worth taking a risk for."

A few days later, after commuting back to Justin's place, there's a knock on the front door. I've cut back my hours to part-time at the youth program for now, so I have time to follow up with Natalie's disappearance. Justin is fully supporting me in that endeavor.

It was easy to find out what initially happened to Natalie. However, it hasn't been easy to track her down or find out how she's doing. Justin had seen her photo on the app after she went missing. She looked distraught. We know she went through the same thing I did.

However, the victor of her fight wasn't a local patron. We discovered he left a false name. He could be from anywhere globally. We just don't know. Beyond that, I had reached a frustrating dead end. I hired a private investigator to discover the identity of the victor who marked her.

One of Justin's staff drives me to and from work, since sadly, my car had been buried in the scrap metal graveyard. However, the commute works out well this way. I can update my client notes during the drive, instead of spending equal time doing it at the office.

I've been staying with Justin so we can allow this special bond between us to grow. Even though the rate of our bond's increase may be affected by the mark, that doesn't mean the bond itself doesn't need nurturing. We both recognize we have something unique and precious together, and that we need to protect it.

One of the staff opens the door, and I don't think anything of it, until I hear familiar voices in the entryway. My anxiety level shoots up. I duck into the room in front of the dining area, wedging the door open slightly. This way I'll stay unseen, find out what they want, and determine whether I'm in danger. I'd know those voices anywhere—they are the voices of the three feline-humans that tore my car apart and took me, after toying with me.

The three of them wait in the entryway, but I know Justin is home and will protect me, so I try to breathe in and out slowly. I hear his footsteps coming from his office, down the corridor, and into the foyer.

I peer through the crack in the door and feel my face draining of color. They're the same three men Justin's lion scared away. I should

have put two and two together when I saw the men in the washroom and later was pursued by the three creatures. But I hadn't known about shifters at that time, so hadn't clued in. I'll have to ask Justin why they didn't shift completely into cat form, but I'll wait until he kicks their asses first. This, I want to see.

But instead of witnessing a confrontation, I'm taken aback as the men embrace as though they are brothers. My heart rate speeds up and I start to panic.

Is everything Justin and I have together based on a lie? Was Justin in on things from the beginning?

It couldn't be. I was sure I could trust him. There must be some explanation for this. Some confusion. Maybe he doesn't know they were my captors. I listen in on the conversation because my drive for self-preservation outweighs the shame of eavesdropping.

"Hey!" One of the men slaps Justin on the back with congratulations. "So you got her. I knew you would. Joe owes me another twenty bucks."

"Ha. Ha." Justin's voice is sarcastic. He is facing the other direction but I can imagine him rolling his eyes. "And you guys are *still* with the betting thing?"

"Yeah, Larry and I are about even though. We've never actually had to pay out. He wins, I lose. I win, he loses." That must be Joe speaking.

"You guys." Justin shakes his head.

This doesn't mean he knew they took me though, just that they knew he'd won me.

"We did make a killing off the fight though. We're all set up for a while, thanks to you." That sounds like the one they called Chet the other night. The one with the face of the jaguar. "Did you want a share of the winnings?"

My heart skips a beat. *Please don't have an ulterior motive for winning the fight. Please let it be just to win me, not money.*

"No thanks."

I exhale with relief. I'd been unaware I'd been holding my breath.

Joe, one of the twin leopards, smirks as he speaks. "You must be pretty happy that we snatched her, hey?"

My throat makes a little choking noise. *Oh no. Justin couldn't have known.* I stumble backward into a chair.

"Sounds like your little mouse has been spy-ing." Larry uses a sing-song voice.

I hear Justin angrily utter an expletive. Not caring about the noise I make, I run to the dining area, right as Justin comes in through the door of the front room.

"Darla, wait!"

But I continue running down the hallway, bursting through the back door, startling the tiny birds hopping around the stone birdbath. Tears slide down my face, and I run, barefoot, on the cold manicured lawn, skidding here and there as I slip on the short grass.

"Darla!" I glance back and Justin is following with quick strides. I can hear thunder rolling in the distance.

I continue to run past the gardens and hurl open the black metal gate in the hedges, dashing out of the backyard and toward the lake. The sky is getting dark, due to nimbus clouds blocking the sun, and the first sprinkling of rain begins. It's not a cleansing rain. It's an angry rain.

"Darla, stop!" He's almost caught up with me. Then I hear his voice change. "Please? We need to talk."

I whirl around so quickly to blast him with an angry retort that I overspin and slip on the grass. Justin grabs me before my butt has a collision with the ground. He stands me up, then withdraws his hands

before I can pull myself away from him. By now the rain is coming down in sheets.

"You lied to me!" My anger flares out of control. "Everything we're building together. It's based on a lie!"

Justin tries to explain. "Look, Darla—"

But I want to cut into him, I'm so hurt. My arms fly out. "I never should have trusted you."

When his eyes fill with sorrow I know I've hurt him. He closes his eyes and hangs his head, pinching the bridge of his nose. Then he lifts his head. Rain is running off the two of us, and every moment we're becoming more and more drenched.

"Darla, can we please go inside and talk about this?"

But my stubbornness kicks in. "No."

"Will you at least listen to me?"

I deliberate for a moment. "Fine. You have two minutes to explain yourself. Then I'm leaving and going home."

Justin's eyes look frantic. Everything comes spilling out. "I didn't know they were planning on taking you. I warned them away from you that first night when you saw me in my tiger form, and that's when they realized they could use you against me. Well, not really *use*, and not *against* me, but to influence events to help their cause.

"The guys figured there was something between us, and there was. That's why I tried to protect you from being taken. I didn't think you'd come back to the club, although part of me wished you would. The other part of me wanted you to stay far away, so you wouldn't be hurt."

"So who are they, and what's their cause? Why would they want you to fight in the arena?"

Justin looks more hopeful, because I'm not outright rejecting him. The rain is cooling me off, bringing my intensity down a notch, and I'm

not about to throw away what we have without understanding the situation thoroughly. The rain changes into a torrential downpour and a shiver goes through my body, from top to bottom.

"Darla, can we go inside and hash this out? You're going to get sick if we stay out here."

After a moment I nod my head. He holds out his arm for me to loop, so I avoid slipping on the grass. I can barely feel my feet, I'm so cold. After a minute, Justin scoops me up in his arms.

He catches me by surprise. "What are you doing?"

"Getting you back to the house faster. You can barely walk on those feet." He grips one with his hand and I can barely feel his warmth. "You're freezing!"

Justin rushes back to the house with me in his arms. My body tilts toward his in an attempt to steal some body heat, but my body is so cold it doesn't seem to make a difference. We enter through the back of the house, and Justin quickly finds one of his staff.

"Please direct the visitors to wait in the gaming room. We're going to be a while." He further directs the staff member, and she nods unphased, as though seeing us drenched through is an everyday occurrence. My teeth are chattering.

Justin jogs up the back flight of stairs, and takes me into one of the suites. He gently lays me down on the bed, not caring I'll get the bedding wet, and grabs a warm blanket to wrap me in. He gently peels my clothes off, snatches a towel from the ensuite to pat my body down, then wraps me in the warm, soft blanket.

The staff member from downstairs has brought up a warm mug of hot chocolate for me. I sit up and thank her, and drink the chocolatey liquid. Justin prepares the room's unlit fireplace with kindling and wood, and strikes a match to start a fire. Once the fire is going, he scoops me up

and places me in front of it. He then has me lie naked in front of the fire on the soft rug. I would object, but I can't feel my fingers or toes, and I'm chilled to my core.

Justin strips out of his wet clothes, drying himself off with a towel from the ensuite, and puts on a pair of boxer briefs. He lies down behind me, spooning me. Despite also being in the same downpour, his body is like a furnace. *Maybe it has to do with him being a shifter?* My teeth are no longer chattering, but my body still feels cool to the touch, and I have the occasional shiver.

I soak up Justin's warmth and the heat of the fire while we lay there. His hand props up his head while he gently rubs my body with his other warm hand. He gently kisses me on the top of my head. After a while, the goosebumps disappear, and I feel warm again.

Although we're in the middle of conflict, I can't help but be very aware of his body lying next to mine and pressing into me. It's the first time we've ever been practically naked together, skin-on-skin. I watch the hypnotic dance of the fire while my body relaxes, basking in the heat, and my eyelids get heavy.

"Are you feeling warm now?" Justin breaks the spell and my eyelids shoot open.

I turn toward him, and our bodies press up against each other. Justin inhales sharply. It's difficult to stay angry after Justin's caring actions and with our bodies so close together, but I need to know the truth. I look into his eyes, searching for answers.

"The truth, Justin."

He assists me and we both stand up, facing each other. Justin nods. "C'mon, I'll let those cocky bastards explain it to you."

One of the house staff brings us some dry clothes. Once we're both dressed, part of me wishes we were still lying down together. The feeling

of skin-on-skin felt wonderful. We make our way downstairs and meet Justin's guests in the games room.

"Hey man. We got in three games of pool while you were gone. Have a nice detour?" Larry winks at Justin.

"Very funny." Justin's voice reveals an edge of sarcasm. "Darla was freezing from being out in the rain, and she needed to warm up and change."

"Whatever you say, bro." Joe winks at me.

He has the audacity to wink at me after everything they put me through last week?

"We need to clear some things up for Darla. She thinks I had a part in her being taken."

"Well as much as we'd like to implicate the old guy, he had nothing to do with it. Other than showing a more than keen fascination with you, of course." Joe snorts.

Larry's grin is mischievous. "When we saw there was an *obvious* attraction between the two of you, we had to take advantage of it."

Justin groans. "You saw us kissing at the club."

"That was more than kissing, dude. I was about to tell you to go get a room. But then you did, didn't you?" Joe laughs.

Oh no, they think what we were doing at the club was real. Then again, it was, wasn't it? After a few seconds I gasp. *Oh God, they think we went into one of those private rooms together! They think we... Oh no— I'm so embarrassed!*

I can feel my face turn beet red. I'm about to interject to deny their insinuations, when I'm distracted with some new information Chet introduces.

"He's been mateless for three years and he closed off that part of his life. Wouldn't let anyone in, not even members of his own pride." There's an awkward silence.

I feel a wave of compassion toward Justin. Clearly he lost a mate. I know it's not the same, but the loss of my sister helps me to understand a bit of what he's feeling. Except I hope to find her. That's the difference—hope for the future, versus complete and utter loss.

I'm confused at first about the usage of the word "pride", but then I think I've caught on to what Chet is referring to. "Pride? Like a pride of lions?"

"Well it's kind of like a pack? You know, a pack of wolves?" Joe scratches his head.

Larry explains. "We call it a pride even though it technically isn't one, but you can think of it as a pack because other shifters refer to their social structure that way."

"Except there are a lot of differences between a typical pack or pride and us. Like some big cats like lions typically hang together, and others of us tend to go off and live a more solitary life." Chet gives Justin a pointed look and mutters under his breath. "Some more than others."

"It's really up to our human counterparts whether we live together in a pack-like environment or live apart."

"We had a great pride. Then three years ago Justin decided to go solitary." Joe says in a low voice.

Chet hits Joe on the arm and speaks in defense of Justin. "Hey man, it wasn't his fault."

Justin redirects the conversation. "Anyway, let's not get off track, Guys. She needs to know why she, specifically, was taken."

"Well, for three years, Justin hasn't interacted with our society."

"Yeah, it's a really messed up story why—"

"Guys, you know I'm not going there, so shut the hell up." Justin sits in one of the chairs, leans back, and crosses his arms. The rest of us sit together with him at the card table.

"Okay, man. Calm down."

"We thought if he had a mate again, it would draw him back to the pride, since his protective instincts would take over after the marking. Then he would take his rightful place as our leader again."

My eyebrows raised. "You were the leader of the society?" *Hmm...I could see that. He is fair, just, wise, and one hell of a fighter.* Justin nods reluctantly.

"Yeah. He was the best, which is why we need him now, more than ever."

"Actually, he technically still is the leader. He just hasn't done any leading for three years."

Larry looks at me. "We knew if you were at risk of being mated with someone else, especially a particular rhinocer-*ass*," the three of them snicker and Justin rolls his eyes, "he would step in."

My voice starts rising. I despise their carelessness. "But wasn't that putting his life at risk?"

I think of something else and become more irate. "And what about me? What if someone else had beaten him? You," I lean over and poke Larry hard in the chest, "could have ruined my life if that rhinoceros dude is as bad as you say! And what about Justin? He could have lost his life!"

"No, no way." All three of them have serious looks on their faces and are adamantly denying my charges.

"Firstly, the rules of the arena are strict. No one dies, otherwise there's disqualification. There has never been a death—of any competitor, at least—in the arena since the practice of mate selection started three centuries ago."

Chet mutters under his breath. "Yeah, no deaths of *competitors* anyway."

"Secondly, neither of you were at risk. It was a 100% win." Larry gives me a toothy grin.

I annoyingly mutter. "Why? Did you somehow rig the fight?" This time Justin surprisingly lets out a chuckle.

"No. Yes. Well, in a way?" The three of them can't seem to make up their minds as they deliberate over the answer.

I have no patience anymore. "What if something went wrong or you were caught? Didn't that occur to you?"

The corner of Justin's mouth is still curved up in a nearly imperceptible smile. But his twinkling eyes give him away and I give him an annoyed questioning look as the others are expressing their denial.

Justin sits forward and rolls his eyes. "Shush, you guys."

He looks me straight in the eyes in all seriousness. "The reason why they say 'rigged'," I lean forward and listen intently, "is because I have never lost a fight. Ever. There was never a chance of losing you. As they say, there was a 100% chance of me winning."

CHAPTER NINE

I plead with him. "But that's still manipulation! They manipulated you, basically, into marking me." By then I am standing. "How can you sit here so calmly with these—with these—scoundrels!" I gesture to the group of them.

I hear them muttering to each other. "Scoundrels? Who us? Been called a lot of things, but never a scoundrel? What about you?" *Sheesh.* I wouldn't put it past them to not know what the word means.

Justin sighs, running his hand through his hair, and looks up at me sheepishly. He makes an admission. "Sometimes you need the people in your life to build a fire under your ass in order to push you in the right direction."

"Yeah, he needed a swift kick--"

"Shush, you." Justin shakes his head.

The three of them start chuckling. They almost sound like a group of giggling girls. *Or gaggling geese.*

I start to calm down. I realize then I need to reframe this situation. Obviously, there's some type of long term relationship between the guys I'm unaware of. I know exactly what they are talking about. Both my friend, Susan, and I have done the same thing to each other many times. It's called "tough love".

However, coming from three jokers like these, it had seemed more like manipulation. Well, I guess it was, but not with malicious intent. They were thinking of their friend's happiness and the well-being of their society, which it seems Justin is also a part of.

"So how long have you all known each other?"

"Wow, changing the subject so soon?" Justin whacks Chet on the arm and he shuts up.

"Since we were cubs."

"Yeah, since *you* were cubs, Smartass. I was old enough to change your diapers back then."

"See, we were right to call you an old dude." Justin rolls his eyes at Joe's comment. There's a lot of that going around. Can't help the eye rolling with these stooges.

The longer I'm around these characters, the more I think I understand the situation. Although they may have acted rashly, their hearts are in the right place. They obviously look up to Justin as a big brother, and Justin sees them as younger brothers.

I sigh. I can't stay mad at them any longer. "Okay, so although I'm thankful Justin and I are together," they sit up straight and look up at me eagerly, "no more meddling or matchmaking. Got it?"

They nod their heads collectively. "Yup, yes. Uh huh. No more meddling." I can see how eager they are to please, and find I have a soft spot for them. A pang of longing for my sister grips my heart.

"Well, now we have that issue all sorted out..." Justin trails off, sitting up straight and ready to get down to business. "I can only *guess* what you came to talk about, but could you fill Darla in?"

Then he pauses, looking as though he's in deep thought, while putting his finger and thumb to his cheek and chin. "Or wait, maybe I should do that myself so you don't screw things up again."

They mutter with annoyance at Justin. "Hey man, don't embarrass us in front of her. Yeah, Dude, not cool." I'm beginning to find their antics somewhat comical, and my lips twitch with amusement.

"Okay, then. So what's up?" Justin gestures for them to explain.

"There's more going on than you think. It's more than the usual request by the *konseho* asking you to take responsibility for the leadership."

"Yeah, the packs have called a summit meeting."

"Sooo, why can't the Second-in-Command or a senior *konseho* member attend in my place?"

"Dude, this meeting's about humans."

By now I'm curious. "What about humans?"

"There's supposed to be something big going down. Something that will affect all the packs in the region."

"Renny and Gordy let it leak that going to war with the humans is on the agenda." Chet is all serious now.

"What? Those fools." Justin puts his head in his hand, then brushes his hair off his forehead. He looks over at me and takes my hand.

"Go to war with humans? What do you mean?"

Justin sighs. "In the past, some packs have suggested making a preemptive strike before humans decide to come after our larger society. The rhino shifter I mentioned to you, Gordon, has been a driving force behind that movement."

Chet scoffs, "Yeah, while leaving a long string of damaged women behind him as part of his 'legacy'." He then mutters to himself. "Misogynist human-hating jerk, trying to work his way up to fame."

"But why would they come after you? No one knows you exist." My breath catches. "Then again, when I was at the police station a while back, they said there was some type of investigation into the club. Do you think it's because of the girls and the arena fights?"

The four of them exchange glances. Chet answers. "Actually, the human government and authorities have been aware of it since it started centuries ago."

"They have an understanding with our society. They won't interfere as long as we don't take anyone high profile, and as long as the women are kept safe during the fights and marked at the end for their own protection."

Suddenly, I find myself standing again. "What? You mean they've known all this time and haven't done a thing about it?"

"Well, it's part of the treaty between humans and shifters. We have an overwhelming percentage of males, as they account for nearly all births. That's one reason males are willing to go into an arena bloodbath and endure major physical pain to acquire a mate."

"Yeah, before the arena it was done as an auction."

Chet mutters under his breath. "More like a slave auction."

"But there was so much corruption, and human trafficking was a major issue. With the arena, there's a real price in blood, and the human female has to be marked by the claimant in the arena. That way she can't be sold into slavery, and that way no one can claim two mates."

"Unless the first mate has died." Chet's voice is quiet and somber, and he is pointedly avoiding Justin's gaze. "Then he can compete for a new mate."

"The point is, there's nothing new there, and as long as we abide by the treaty, we keep the peace between us."

"Well, apart from that one accident in the arena that wasn't really an accident."

"Huh?"

"Don't scare her, man."

"No, I want to know. Tell me."

"Decades ago, they didn't use a raised platform for the human women, and one jealous competitor killed the girl when he realized he

wasn't going to win. He said if he couldn't have her, then no one could. That nearly sparked a war."

"Yeah, but then changes were made so the females are physically out of range of the immediate fighting, plus they now have guards." I thought about my two guards who vowed they would keep me safe.

"So why would the packs be considering going to war with the humans if there's a treaty in place?"

"Well, there are always ulterior motives behind what might look like a righteous or just cause. We just have to remove the smokescreen to find out what those ulterior motives are. Lust for power, lust for wealth, and revenge or hatred are the three biggest motives."

"How can we remove the smokescreen?"

"Well, first of all, I need to be updated by the *konseho* and by the other pack leaders on the status of things."

The three stooges are grinning from ear to ear.

"Secondly, I need to find out what the primary issue is that has made war a consideration."

"Thirdly, I need to rally some of the other pack leaders together who will take a stand against going to war unless it's absolutely necessary."

"So in other words, between running your company and this new list, you have your work cut out for you."

Justin sighs. "I sure do."

"Well, it's a good thing you have three go-fers and me to help keep you on top of things."

"Uhhh..."

My mischievous side takes over. "What, boys? You don't think you're up to the challenge? You know, some girls find a man who takes responsibility to be sexy."

"Really?" Their interest perks up.

Justin's clearly trying not to laugh. These guys are too much.

It's a Sunday, and we have several pride rounds to make. I've baked several dozen cookies for the families we're visiting, and Justin introduces me, while reintegrating himself into pride society. The relief on everyone's faces is as clear as day. After going three years without their leader, whom they referred to as *ikati* wherever we went, people are excited Justin is out visiting, and the reception toward me is warm.

While visiting the Second-in-Command's home, his mate pulls me aside while the men are in the office, going over the state of affairs within the pride.

"We are so thankful you're in Justin's life." Katie and I have tea together in the kitchen, while she prepares lunch. "He shut everyone out until you came along."

"That's just due to the physiological effects of the mark he placed on me, isn't it? Justin mentioned the desire to bond and protect is linked to chemicals stimulated in the person bitten, and their mate is influenced by pheromones released after the fact."

Katie laughs. "That's just like Justin, to strip everything down to bare bones science." She wipes her hands on a tea towel, and pulls her stool up to the breakfast bar.

"There's also a metaphysical connection that takes place when a person is marked. The best way to describe it would be to say it's like an imprint on your soul.

"Otherwise, if it was purely biological, then anyone could take a marked person's mate and the bonding and protectiveness would increase between whoever spends the most time together. It would also

rule out exclusivity. However, the metaphysical connection caused by the mark guarantees exclusivity to one mate."

I'm realizing there is a lot I'm still unaware of regarding how marking and mating works. The marking in the arena wasn't just symbolic or just physiological, but metaphysical as well.

"However, even before marking, if there is an initial connection between two people, if they were fated to be soulmates, they will feel drawn to each other. That's how some mates find each other, outside of the arena."

I think about the initial connection I felt with Justin when we originally met at the club that first night, and wonder if this is what Katie is referring to. The irresistible draw I felt toward him and still do.

Is it because we are actually soulmates? I've never felt a connection to anyone like this before. It goes far beyond anything I've ever experienced.

"Anyway, regardless of how it all came about, he wants to be back with his pride, his family. We didn't know if we'd ever see this day, but meeting you has helped to bring this all about."

I want to understand more about his role and responsibilities in the pride, and Katie is more than willing to answer questions. I'm thankful for her guidance.

"So what is his new role going to be and what does that all entail?"

Katie hesitates. "Well, technically, his title doesn't change. He's always had the *ikati* title, since it became his six years ago. Other packs acknowledge him as our leader; however, some packs have been noticing his lack of involvement in inter-pack affairs, and we think they are using that to press their advantage.

"Issues such as war with the humans would never have come to the forefront when Justin was heavily involved, since he commands the most

respect from all alphas of the other species. But since they've suspected his disconnect, some factions now see this as an opportunity to push their own agendas.

"Although our pride hid it as well as possible, having my mate, the pack's *kedi*, or a *konseho* member attend meetings in Justin's stead made it obvious after a while that he's been either disinterested or incapable of fulfilling the role of *ikati*. Now those who previously operated in the shadows feel immune enough to consequences to operate in the light."

Katie uses the tea towel and a pot holder to pull a hot pan out of the oven. "Just need to let this cool for a few minutes."

She continues. "We are fortunate that Justin agreed to retain the title of *ikati* for the protection of the pride. It's provided us with protection we wouldn't have had if he had stepped down and another had to take his place."

Katie looks directly at me, with significance. "Justin has extraordinary physical strength and agility, and every pack recognizes and respects his power. And by participating in the arena fight, he has just reaffirmed that power to each of the other packs. The fact that he has marked you will now strike fear into those who oppose his ideals, since they know now he hasn't been broken psychologically, but has been healing from past grief."

I'm about to ask a question about that past grief, when I hear male voices coming down the hallway, toward the kitchen.

"The guys must be done. For now." Katie smiles.

The two of them tie up their conversation as they walk into the kitchen.

"Wow! That smells sooo good." Katie's mate inhales the aroma permeating the kitchen. "Smelled so good, we couldn't stay away." Nelson puts his arms around Katie and gives her a kiss, while Justin comes up to me.

"Hey." He puts his forehead against mine.

"Hey." I breathe in his masculine scent. Our lips connect, and we give each other a squeeze.

We take our lunch, cutlery, and plates into the dining room and are each seated beside our mates. Justin and I look at each other shyly, as he strokes the back of my hand as it sits on my thigh. We serve ourselves, and get down to discussing more about the inner workings of pride hierarchy.

Katie explains how the pride's been operating. "So Nelson has been looking after decisions usually made by the *ikati* and *kedi*, and our *marjari* has been in charge of regular operations and programming." I notice Justin has a guilty look on his face.

Nelson sets his utensils down as he explains more. "Some of the *konseho* members came out of retirement to provide extra guidance and extra support as needed over the last few years, mainly for event planning, fiscal direction, and any domestic emergencies. So things have been stable, and we haven't been flying by the seat of our pants or anything like that.

"Looking at the bright side, we're set up so Justin can ease back into duties, rather than have everything dumped on him, which sometimes happens during sudden leadership transitions."

Justin clears his throat. "After going over everything with Nelson, I'll be lessening my business hours and hiring more staff. That way I'm not overloaded and we'll still have 'us' time." Justin smiles down at me and I reciprocate.

I won't deny I'm relieved to hear Justin will continue to balance things. I was concerned his leadership duties may take away from our time together, but that doesn't seem to be the case.

Nelson continues. "The priority right now is to deal with inter-pack relations and relations with humans, especially anything that could signify the threat of war between the pride and either of those groups. That's where Justin comes in.

"Firstly, he'll send a message that he's actively involved, and will begin attending all meetings right away. I'm bringing him up-to-date with any issues that can't be dealt with by the *marjari* or *konseho*, and we'll start from there. Kind of like a crash course on current events."

We continue to chat during lunch, and I'm all ears, learning what challenges the pride is dealing with.

"So, what is my role in all of this?" I can suddenly feel tension invade the room.

There is a pause before Nelson speaks. "Well, traditionally, the mate of the *ikati* takes on the role of *ailouros*, similar to the position of *luna* in other species' packs."

"What does that role entail?"

"Whereas the *ikati* looks after protection of the pride as a whole, the *ailouros* looks after the well-being of the individual members of the pride. She makes sure pride members are being nurtured."

Katie jumps in. "She also provides support for the *ikati,* and represents him within the pride when he is absent."

"Is there any role to be played outside the pride?"

Nelson explains the role further. "The *ailouros* provides support for the *ikati* at outside functions, and becomes his eyes and ears. Her role is one of observation and discernment when outside the pride, and to report that information back to the *ikati.*"

Justin hesitates. "How do you feel about accepting the role of *ailouros,* Darla?"

"I think it's a role I would enjoy and be very good at."

Justin's eyes sparkle and he looks proud of me. The sense of relief in the room is evident once I've expressed willingness to take on the role.

Nelson observes me as he speaks. "In a couple weeks we have a formal meeting of the pride scheduled. How do you feel about going through a ceremony that will accept you into the pride?"

"What is involved?"

"Some formalities, and a small cut to your hand which is instrumental in creating the pride bond."

"What will happen once the ceremony is complete?"

"You should be able to feel our cats. Some humans are able to hear commands, and other humans can communicate through the pride bond, although that is rare."

Katie jumps in to explain further. "Again, it's a metaphysical experience, even though it takes mixing your blood with the blood of the *ikati* to occur."

"I'd be honored to join the pride."

"What about accepting the position of *ailouros?*"

I look demurely at Justin. "I would be happy to serve in that role, my *ikati.*"

The atmosphere at the table goes from relaxed to excited and overjoyed. It's nice to be part of something positive that will make a difference in the lives of others.

"Next meeting, we'll perform both rituals." Justin takes my hand.

"It will be wonderful, having you as part of the pride." Katie looks thrilled.

"Thank you for accepting me with open arms." I look shyly at Nelson and Katie.

Katie beams at me. "You're welcome. It will be so exciting to welcome you to the pride and induct you as *ailouros!*"

CHAPTER TEN

Over the next while, we do our rounds, meeting with the pride members. My heart goes out to some of the families on our list. In one family, the children's eyes are hollow and clothes hang off them, highlighting their gaunt figures. I wonder if my *ikati* notices. I plan to send an emergency food hamper, then probe into the source of their malnutrition or illness.

I wonder if this is a result of being deprived of an ailouros *for three years? Children slipping through the cracks because they've been overlooked by those who could help them?*

Determination seeps out of my bones and into the rest of my body. *This is my opportunity to start making a difference in the lives of people Justin holds dear, people I will soon come to love and call family.*

By late afternoon on the day of the ceremonies, we've been welcomed to the pride hall of the lions. I say "of the lions" because the majority of shifters on the vast property are lions. The remaining shifters are social cats who've opted to live with the group, rather than in isolation.

Tonight will be different than their regularly scheduled meeting. The entire pride has been invited to the celebration hosted by the lions. When we arrive, Justin goes to an early meeting, while I'm swept away in a wave of ladies and deposited in a large dressing room. For the next two hours, the ladies dote on me, setting my hair, perfecting my makeup, and dressing me in a fitted gown of royal blue, with sequins that sparkle as I move in the light.

As they prepare me for the ceremony, I start to realize what a big deal tonight is, and what it means to the pride. I begin to really understand its significance, and the weight of what is to happen tonight increases, as does

my heart rate. I need to calm myself, to breathe slowly, one breath at a time, in order to tamp down my anxiety.

Once my fairy godmothers are satisfied with the results, I am taken to Justin. I keep my eyes downcast, watching my step, and raise them for the last few feet. As I walk in three inch heels to meet him, I can see the admiration on his face. He is dressed in a black tux with matching royal blue cummerbund, bow tie, and pouf.

He draws me to himself with his hand around my waist and speaks to me, gently. "Stunning. Absolutely stunning." He cradles my head as he softly kisses my lips in a romantic gesture, stroking my cheeks with his thumbs. He gently touches his nose to mine, then pulls me in and holds me tightly to his body. At that moment I am lost in him and never want to let go.

Taking my hand, we walk toward the great hall where the ceremony will start shortly. As we pass by the front of the building to get to the side entrance, I see a line of people being welcomed.

I didn't realize there would be this many people! The nervousness in my chest grips me tightly.

"Welcome to each of you." The hostess stands by in a violet satin and black lace dress. Her brown hair is piled on her head and curls down the sides. At the tall double doors to the hall, she welcomes all those who have arrived, grasping hands with affection.

Justin and I walk by the main entrance and enter the hall from the side. We wait together in the wings for the ceremony to start. Justin squeezes my hand, kisses me softly on the cheek, and whispers, tickling my ear. "You're gorgeous."

Then he takes his cue and walks from behind the curtain to stand before the pride. The noise dwindles quickly as they recognize their *ikati*

is about to address them. There are gasps, and some eyes in the crowd become glassy. There is hope on each face, as they look up to Justin.

"We are gathered here today to welcome the newest member of the pride, Darla." Justin looks over at me and beckons me toward him.

That's it? No lengthy introduction? I thought I'd have a few more minutes to collect myself!

I carefully walk toward him, and he gently takes my hand. He picks up the ritual knife and pierces his palm with the sharp blade until a trickle of blood flows. Then he pierces my hand and we put them together, forming a blood bond. I look up at Justin through my lashes, and see nothing but love and admiration in his blue eyes.

"I hereby welcome you into our pride, Darla. I hope you will feel secure and content, and that your life will be filled with special memories of love and kindness."

I know entering the pride is a very important event, but this feels like so much more. I can tell Justin wants to be the one to grant that security and to fill my life with special moments. His eyes show he's personally committing to giving me those things.

Suddenly, I gasp. Hundreds of candles, each lighting quickly, have permeated my mind. They have always been there, but I wasn't aware of their existence before. I look out at the witnesses to my induction, tears shining in my eyes, gratefully. *I will never be alone.*

Each of those candles represents a life at varying stages and levels of brightness. I'm in awe, as I can sense the entire pride and they now sense me. Collective, diffused emotions are coming through the bond, and I turn toward Justin to keep myself grounded. I hear the applause and feel overwhelmed by the sincerity of the welcome.

Justin keeps formality as he makes an announcement to the pride. "As most of you know, I recently claimed and marked my new mate." He looks at me with tenderness.

"I believe she is a woman who will bring to this pride's members the nurturing that has been missing, and provide what I cannot.

"I must ask you, 'Do you, Darla, accept the role of *ailouros* in our pride?'"

"I do."

"We accept your assent and I hereby declare Darla the new *ailouros* of this pride." Justin swipes his finger along his palm, and places a drop of his blood on my mark by my neck.

Suddenly, the largest candle in my mind flashes to blinding proportions. I feel myself falling into a never-ending abyss, being consumed by Justin's light, surrounded by his arms of love. Now that candle burns brightest, not just in my mind, but in my soul. I can feel the energy radiating off it in waves, waves crashing around me, permeating me, soaking me with affection.

As I begin to return to reality, I find myself floating in his arms, his eyes filled with tears of joy. He's looking down at me, then touching his nose to my nose, his lips to my lips. He rests his forehead on mine, and I feel we are as one.

The crowd is still and silent as Justin carries me out of the hall. He carries me along a short path, enters the pride house, and takes me upstairs. In an empty guest room, he lays me on the bed. He lies beside me, his head resting on his hand, looking down at me. He strokes a wisp of hair behind my ear.

His voice is soft and gentle. "Hey."

"Hey."

He continues to stroke my head then my forehead. After a few minutes, the floaty feeling starts to dissipate.

"Can you move your limbs yet? It may take a few minutes to recuperate."

I'm surprised at his question. I try wiggling my fingers and succeed, but there seems to be a delay between me thinking about moving them and them actually obeying me.

"My fingers aren't behaving. See? They wiggle too late."

Justin smirks. "My fingers don't want to behave either. See?" He gently strokes down my side from under my arm to my waist, then repeats his gentle caress.

A delightful shiver runs through me each time he brushes down from my sensitive under arm area, over the side of my breast, and to my waist. I close my eyes and gasp when instead of continuing down to my waist, he drags his finger below my breast, following its curvy line. He draws his fingers up between my breasts and strokes underneath my chin with his fingers until my face tilts up.

He draws his lips underneath my chin, and slowly across my collar bone. I savor every brush of his lips, every touch he makes that makes me quiver. He tenderly picks up my wrist, and slowly kisses my fingertips, one by one. I'm finally able to unfurl my fingers on my other hand, and I open my eyes and place my palm on his cheek. He leans into my hand, and his lips start caressing my palm, slowly planting gentle kisses all over the surface.

He pulls my body to his and rocks me gently, kissing me on the top of my head. Then he tightly holds me to himself. I close my eyes, wanting him to absorb all the affection and care I have for him. And all this time, his candle burns brightly, pulsating and throbbing, threatening to catch fire and set us both alight.

He sits me up, and we smile at each other. He cradles my head with his hand. "Ready?" I nod, and we both stand up beside the bed.

Justin offers me his arm, and I wrap mine around his. We walk out the bedroom door, downstairs, and outside, toward the reception. The hall itself has been transformed. The room is now lit, not with electric lights but with candlelight. Instead of row on row of benches facing forward, those benches are now situated alongside the edges of rectangular tables.

Royal blue, gold, and silver decorations have been raised to the high ceilings. The mobiles of stars and moons dance in the gentle air exchange. The decorations reflect the candlelight from the tables below, creating ethereal patterns on the walls of the hall. The young girls who live at the pride house float around daintily, making sure the food is set out and everything is ready.

I'm seated in the middle of one of the long tables. Justin sits on one side of me and Katie sits with Nelson on the other side. The center pieces are blue and gold, and glass vases contain water with floating candles. The setting is beautiful, just as the gesture of welcome and acceptance is.

As we're served, many eager faces have questions for us. I'm asked about my background and Justin is asked what his plans are, now he's becoming reacquainted with pride life. People show compassion when they find out my parents live on the other side of the country. My sister and I had branched out on our own before our current situations befell us.

One elderly lady grasps my wrist with her leathery skinned hand, and looking into her eyes, I feel hope emanating from her. I realize I'm so much more sensitive to people's emotions because of the pride bond. Becoming the pride's *ailouros* has heightened my intuition related to their

well-being. Feeling the elderly woman's touch, I can tell she has experienced much sorrow and multiple losses of those closest to her.

So this is the power of the bond of the ailouros.

I now know I've been given an extraordinary gift that will help me nurture members of the pride, grieve with them through heartache, and bring healing to the broken. The responsibility that comes with my role weighs even more heavily on my heart, now that I have enhanced sensitivity and insight.

It's incredible. This power is... I shake my head for lack of words to describe this overwhelming feeling.

Justin squeezes my hand and looks at me. I can tell he's asking me if I'm okay, not with words, but through concern that flows through our bond. I smile at him with tears in my eyes. I know he senses I'm overwhelmed and in awe, being drawn into a swirling ocean of emotion. I'm experiencing a connection with others on a level I never thought was possible. He cups my cheek and rubs his cheek on mine, and affection sprouts through our bond.

I ask him a concerning question. "Can others feel what I'm feeling the way I'm sensing them?"

He kisses me on the cheek then lets go of my face, taking my hands in his. Sitting up, leaning slightly toward me so I can hear him above the mingling crowd, he explains more about the pride bond.

"The first bond that was made ties us all together as a pride and brings awareness of the others who have the same bond. For a few, it also brings sensitivity to others' emotions, if they are intuitive beings to start with."

He then goes on to explain about the *ailouros* bond. "The *ailouros* bond is a one-way bond that heightens the ability to feel others' emotions, amplifies intuition, and increases sensitivity regarding their well-being. The intuitive value of and control over this bond can be increased with

time, experience, and practice, making the *ailouros* more effective in her role.

"From what I'm sensing through my own bond as *ikati,* you already have intuition and sensitivity heightened beyond what is normal for an *ailouros.* Because of that, gatherings like this one may be overwhelming at first, but you will be able to hone your skills so you can focus on or block out specific individuals in the future."

My eyes contain unshed tears. "It's an incredible gift you've given me. That the whole pride has honored and trusted me with." I lean forward and tenderly brush his lips with mine. "Thank you, Sweetheart."

Justin kisses me more fully, holding me in his arms. After coming up for air, I realize where we are, in a hall full of people at the center of attention. My face flushes. But our public display of affection doesn't seem to phase anyone. In fact, through the peacefulness of the pride bond, it feels like it was expected.

Justin strokes my nose with his. "Most of the time, human females make the most effective *ailouroses.* One reason why the arena rituals are so sacred and the women are treasured."

As we engage in discussion with pride members, partaking in a meal together, I have a flash of reality that calms my underlying fears. I realize that my sister may be somewhere acting as an *ailouros,* every bit as happy as I am. The thought comforts me and gives me hope. Hope that she is alive and well.

Chapter Eleven

The following day, I wake up with a splitting headache. I hear light tapping on wood and assume that's what has awakened me.

"Come in!" I regret calling out as soon as I do, as the volume causes an eruption of stars behind my eyes.

The wooden door opens quietly and Justin enters, carrying a tray. He's wearing a white dress shirt and black trousers. His voice is soft and low. "Good afternoon, Darla."

"Afternoon?" I sit up quickly, but immediately regret it, now feeling pounding pressure at the front of my head.

Justin sets the tray down on the white linens. He pours me a cup of tea, drizzling a spoonful of honey into the dark liquid.

"Here, drink this. It will help with the headache."

I take the floral patterned china cup from him and sip some tea. It has a refreshing scent to it that reminds me of jasmine. The honey blossoms into sweetness on my tongue.

"What type of tea is this?"

"It's a special tea that should help get you back on your feet."

"Is it normal to have a headache like this after the rituals?"

He nods his head. "Mmhmm. My induction as *ikati* put me out for half a day, then it took me another day to recover fully from the headache. The pride bond ritual doesn't usually have side effects, but the *ikati* and *ailouros* bond rituals do."

Justin slides closer and his hand smooths over my cheek, playing with my curls by my ear. He looks into my eyes and I see an ocean of sincerity. "Have I told you yet today that you are beautiful?"

His other hand gently grasps my arm covered with frilly cotton, the nightie I vaguely remember myself slipping into last night, before I descended into my slumber. He strokes me through my nightie, from my elbow to my wrist. The headache starts to subside a bit, and I'm able to offer a small smile. He reciprocates with a smile and eyes that dance in the afternoon light. Then I notice that it's a mischievous dance.

Justin dips a small spoon in warm cereal, cradles the back of my head with his other hand, and draws the spoon to my lips. Because he's babying me, I pout. He laughs with sparkling amusement. He touches my pouty lips with the spoon, but I don't budge.

"Please, do this for me. Humor me." I continue to pout, until I realize I could use this to my advantage.

I sigh as I give in. "Fiiine. As long as when you're sick, you give me the same luxury."

"Hmmm." He pretends to ponder.

"Deal?"

He looks at me, and I can tell the wheels are turning. Then his eyes sparkle again and he smiles. "Deal." He mock-shakes my hand, enveloping my small hand in his larger one. He drops his voice to a whisper and leans in, as if to tell me a secret. "Psst, by the way, I never get sick." He impishly smiles at me.

Well, after that revelation, my quest is to get even. He puts the spoon to my mouth and I take a tiny bit of the warm cereal from the end of the spoon into my mouth. He looks at me, as if to say, "Really?"

Once there's a bit of space on the spoon, I swirl my tongue around on the metal, while looking up at him with doe eyes. His jaw drops. Then I take more of the spoon into my mouth, and create suction with my lips as I suck the rest of the porridge into my mouth, keeping my cheeks indented.

I can hear Justin swallow. He sits there, frozen and fascinated, until I speak. "More please."

He quickly spoons up more porridge and touches my lips with the spoon, looking on as if entranced at what I'll do. I sweep my tongue over the top of the cereal and around to the bottom of the spoon. I slowly drag my tongue toward me on the bottom of the spoon. Then I suck half the porridge off the spoon. Justin moves on the bed, and I can tell he's adjusting himself.

I open my mouth and envelope the spoon past the head and take part of the handle into my mouth, closing my mouth on the spoon, sucking on it and pulling my mouth back toward me with pouty lips. My lips open then clamp down on the head of the spoon, as I suck in the porridge. Justin seems to be at a loss for words. He spoons more porridge for me, and I continue to move my lips, tongue, and mouth over the spoon, with my eyes fluttering.

I let out a tiny moan. "Mmmm...so good."

I continue to build up my slow torture until the porridge is gone. He doesn't seem to notice until he attempts to scoop it up without looking and there is nothing left in the bowl.

Justin clears his throat. "So, how are you feeling now?"

I yawn and stretch my arms slowly above my head, subtly watching his eyes as they are drawn to my breasts as they perk up, and I know he can see the outline of my nipples through the thin white material.

"Mmmmm. I feel *much* better now. What about you?"

He tries to nod casually. "Yeah, I'm—uh—doing just great. I'll just take this tray downstairs." On his way out, I hear him mutter under his breath. "That was *totally* unfair."

Once he's left the room, I break into a small laugh, satisfied that my temptation was ample punishment for him trying to baby me. I slip out

of bed to get dressed, pulling on a cute pair of yoga pants and a matching black and pink top. I grab a pair of sunglasses, to lessen the impact of the light on my headache.

I find Justin in the kitchen downstairs, just finishing up the dishes. Although he protests, I pick up a tea towel and start drying. Once the dishes are put away, we retire to the living room, and cuddle up beside each other on the couch.

"So what's the plan for today?"

"Well, I took the afternoon off so I could be here for you after you woke up, in case the side effects were really bad. And you, my dear, are to stay at home and rest."

I look at Justin coyly, "Hmmm...are you sure you didn't take time off to be with your helpless mate in order to take advantage of her? Tell the truth now."

He smiles at me, with a hungry look in his eyes. "Well, I can't deny that it's been on my mind. I know you might not be up to anything today though, due to side effects from the ceremony."

"I'll be the judge of that." I bump him with my arm playfully, while leaning into his side. I see the hunger intensify in his eyes, and he leans over to kiss me. He cups his hand around my face and rubs his nose to mine. His lips challenge mine in a bold embrace, and after sweeping my upper and lower lips with his tongue, his lips slowly and gently pull away. Now I'm left hungering for more.

He pulls me sideways onto his lap and we snuggle up closely. "Sooo, I have a question about shifters."

"Sure, Hun, what's on your mind?" Justin strokes my hair and kisses me on the top of my head.

"I've seen you shift into your tiger, and have seen other shifters as half-human and half animal."

Justin nods, understanding what my question is before it's even asked. "We can shift partway or fully. If we shift partway, we retain certain abilities such as the ability to talk and move as bipeds, on two legs. If we shift fully, we gain immense power. That's why in the arena, for example, you saw that everyone was fully shifted. It's our most dominant position."

"Ah, okay." He nuzzles my hair, kissing me along the back of my neck. "Speaking of 'dominant positions'..." I giggle.

"Hmmm?"

"Yesterday, one of the elderly ladies took me aside and asked me when our mating ceremony will be. I was at a loss for words. What did she mean? I thought I was already your mate because you marked me?"

"Symbolically, the mark signifies that we are mates, warning any other unmated males to stay away. It also causes a spiritual and physiological draw. I've already explained about the biological effects. I'm not sure exactly how the spiritual bond works, other than it ensures the person marking and the marked one are drawn together, instead of the biological bond attracting random males or females.

"As we're drawn more deeply to each other, there may come a time when we want to take the next step and share a mating bond. The bond creates a more potent spiritual connection between mates, and we may be able to hear each other's thoughts and communicate that way, instead of just understanding each other through feeling and intuition. It's similar to the type of spiritual connection we made when you became *ailouros.*"

"I see. Are there any biological effects?"

Justin smirks. "Maaaybe." I can tell what kind of physical effects it must have, by the way he's eyeing me. "It increases the mates' sexual hunger for each other, making it very difficult to resist your attraction to your mate."

I can feel my cheeks flush.

Justin takes on a serious tone. "Which is one reason I want us to take our time, until you feel ready to take that step. I don't want us to feel like we need to rush things. A lot has happened in a short period of time, and you need a period of adjustment. I didn't want you to feel any pressure, so I didn't mention it to you earlier.

"The other reason is because I didn't want you to feel obligated to be with me because I marked you."

I sit up from my reclining position in his arms and look directly into his eyes. "What do you mean?"

"There is a way to break the effects of the mark. If you were marked and truly didn't want to be mated with me, someone else could mark you directly on top of my mark, breaking the original mating draw. I'm telling you this because I want you to know you have options. Even though I've marked you, you aren't obligated to choose me.

"Or you could choose me to be a companion instead, if you didn't want to go through with the mating ceremony. But it would be very difficult to stay platonic because the physical draw of the mark will eventually become so strong it will be nearly unbearable if not sated."

I snuggle back into Justin's lap. I've never felt like I was being forced or controlled by him, which is another thing I love about him. Having freedom is important to me. Justin has never asked me to quit my job and I'm free to stay at my own apartment if I want. But I choose to be with him. It's nice to be able to choose him and have freedom in my life to pursue my dreams, instead of being pressured and suffocated.

My eyelids begin to feel heavy, as Justin's rhythmic rubbing of my back spreads warmth through me. I now understand why he wanted me to stay home today. The exhaustion is forcing me into Lala Land. I snuggle up even closer to him and drift off.

CHAPTER TWELVE

The next few days are filled with pride departmental meetings, mainly debriefings discussing the inner workings of the pride. Since I am welcome to attend, as *ailouros,* I've transferred my clients for the week. I dive right in and go to as many meetings as I can. The quicker I understand how the pride operates, the more effective I will be in my role. Just from his glance, I can tell Justin is proud of me.

After the round of debriefing presentations, spotlight being on the here and now, the next step is to brainstorm for improvements. We will be looking for ideas that will reinforce the good or change a department's direction to get more positive outcomes. One of the issues I've prepared to talk about is the issue of cubs being malnourished.

During a meeting with the head of cub protection, I bring up the issue.

"During my visitation of the various groups and families within the pride, I noticed some of the families didn't seem to be able to take care of their cubs' basic needs."

"I'll take down names, and start the process to remove them from their families right away." A woman named Marriot Riley stands shorter than most of the pride, and her face always looks like she's eating a sour lemon.

"Mary, let's not be so hasty." One of the members of the group, Colin, tries to calm her and change her mind, unsuccessfully.

She sneers at him. "If they can't look after them, they don't deserve to have them!" Marriot launches into a tirade about the cubs' families, but I cut her off.

"Mary, we all know you're very passionate about the cubs and their care. We are all very concerned." I look around and my statement is verified with nods. "However, I know of those families' situations, and they are doing their best to get by. Some have fallen on hard times financially and can't find work, whereas others are too sick to work."

"So what do you propose to do? Leave them in an unhealthy environment where they remain high risk?" Although Marriot's face goes blank and unreadable, I sense there's something else going on under the surface. She may care for those kids, but I'm wary of any other motives she may have.

"I'm thinking that in order to solve a problem, if we get to the root of the problem it won't keep popping up in the long run." A few members slowly nod their heads in agreement.

"How would you go after the root of the problem?" Marriot looks impatient as she taps her fingers on the light table.

"We already have plans to combat the issues of hunger and poverty within the pride. I would suggest we put our resources and energy there, and help get those families on their feet, rather than letting them fend for themselves. The faster the parents can get the medical care they need or the employment they need, the faster the kids will have the stability they need."

"And you let the children suffer until that time?" She shakes her head. "Not going to happen."

"Until that time, we use excess emergency relief funds to help those families with basic needs and give them extra assistance at home. That way you could focus more on families who purposely neglect or abuse their cubs, or put their children in harm's way due to their lifestyles."

I hear Marriot mumble something. The rest of the committee dives into open discussion about the issue, and my concerns are taken

seriously. Instead of automatically removing cubs from families that are in those types of situations, it's agreed that giving in-home support is a better strategy in the long run. It's a better strategy for the cubs' well-being, the health of the families, and for pride distribution of finances. Of course abuse, purposeful neglect, and harmful lifestyle choices would still warrant immediate removal of cubs.

I can tell Marriot isn't too pleased. She has a scowl on her face which makes that obvious. If we can affirm her and let her know we're all on the same team, she may ease up on things. I have a feeling she may have issues due to the feeling of "loss of control".

"Mary, we all appreciate very much what you are doing. The work you do to ensure cub safety is invaluable. We're hoping to ease up the workload you're carrying because we know the caseloads in your department are higher than they should be."

Marriot slowly nods her head.

"I would also like to suggest the home support team works closely with Mary, since she knows many of these families and circumstances. Mary could refer any current cases she thinks would be successful with emergency funding and ongoing home support. What do you think, Mary?"

Mary loses her scowl and brightens a bit, as she realizes we're not trying to take her job away from her or micromanage.

"I suppose that would work. It would free us up to focus on the tough cases."

"Great. I'll leave you and the committee to vote and work out any logistics. Thank you for including me in your meeting." I pack up my folders and prepare to leave the room.

The committee members smile and utter their thank yous. Marriot is one of those, and her small smile really makes a difference to her

countenance. It seems to take years off her appearance. I leave the committee room and sit at my office desk to jot down notes before writing up a report of my observations, which will be attached to the final meeting minutes.

Each report I write up frees Justin from extra paperwork duties. He lets me know if he'd like me to add additional notes to my reports, and between the two of us, we're getting a lot done. Once we're through the initial meetings with each department, we won't need to attend every meeting, and the *marjari* will resume those duties.

By Friday I'm feeling exhausted, between the meetings, work, and anxiety of hearing my P.I. has hit a bunch of dead ends regarding my sister. Justin and I enjoy a quiet meal together by candlelight, then he sits on the couch with my head in his lap. I stare unthinking at the ceiling, tracing the moulding patterns with my eyes.

"Any news about your sister?" Justin is stroking my cheek and our eyes lock. I sit up, and slide backward onto Justin's lap. I lean my head sideways against his chest.

I sigh, breathing in his scent. "Nothing yet. I hired a P.I., but all his leads have been dead ends so far. It's so frustrating. We haven't made any headway."

"Where did you hire him from?"

"Some detective agency I found online. It had great reviews."

"What's their specialty?"

"They specialize with spouses—you know, when one spouse doesn't trust the other..."

Justin sighs and speaks reluctantly. "Let me hire another P.I. He is the best I've ever known." Justin starts muttering. "Even though he is a dick."

"Who?"

"You've met him before. He calls himself Dick."

"Oh! He's that good?" I think for a minute. "Then again, he did have info on my sister. He led me to the club—and to you." I unknowingly flutter my eyelashes at Justin.

"When you do that, my heart starts to pound."

"Do what?"

"That fluttering thing with your eyelashes."

"Oh, I didn't realize I was doing that."

"It's okay, I don't mind at all. As long as you don't mind me doing this." Justin slowly cradles my head in his hand, stroking my hair with his thumbs. I lean into his hand. I feel his other arm around me as he pulls me in for a tender kiss.

"Are you okay with me contacting him? He's a wealth of information. He hyper-focuses on details so much and gets so absorbed in following up on them that he does a thorough job. I don't know how he packs so much info into that tiny brain of his."

"Sure. It couldn't hurt. And if he's that good, maybe he'll find something."

"Okay I'll fire him a text."

Justin: Darla is still trying to find her sister. Are you for hire?

Dick: Okay. I'll start following up on leads. Same rate as usual.

"Done." Justin gives me a squeeze.

I kiss him on the cheek. "Thank you." Then I laugh.

"What is it?" Justin looks at me curiously.

"Well, the first time I saw Dick in his trench coat, I thought he was an exhibitionist or a streaker."

"Hahaha! Believe me when I say that he's the farthest thing from that. He's always so uptight."

"How long have you known each other for?"

"Oh, a long time."

"How did you meet?"

"Well, I've actually known him since he was a baby kit."

I clue in. "You're related? No way."

"Yeah, I don't usually let people know this, but he's my cousin."

"You guys are completely different. I wouldn't say polar opposites, but different enough."

"Mmhmm."

"So do you guys get along okay?"

"We've always got along as cousins, but aren't as close as we were as kids. Not like my other cousin and I who've always been like brothers. In a professional context, Dick doesn't always seem to have the discernment of when to withhold info. Like when you first met." Justin sighs. "I know he was trying to set us up with each other romantically in the process, but he literally sent you into the lions' den."

"But I wouldn't have met you if he hadn't given me that info."

"True. But he still needs to get it through his thick skull not to give info like that to someone who will run headfirst into trouble."

"Heyyy!" I pout at him.

"Put that lip back in your mouth before I lose control and kiss it." His voice is teasing, with a touch of warning.

I continue to pout and cross my arms, making a huffing sound, to accentuate how I feel about his comment regarding me running headfirst into trouble.

"Now you've asked for it!" Justin quickly leans in with a smile and sucks on my lip while tickling me at the same time to open up my closed posture. My arms are involved fighting off his tickles, and he now has me lying on my back on the couch, straddling me so he has better access to my ticklish zones. I can't stop laughing.

He's laughing at me, too. "Gotcha! Now for the real torture!" He has me pinned down on the couch, my arms to their sides, and leans down to my face and kisses me on the lips. He kisses me again and takes his time, gently sliding his tongue through my startled open mouth, drawing me into the kiss. I try to move my arms, but instead he takes them in one hand and pins them above me on the couch armrest.

Justin uses his other hand to cradle my head, then brings it closer to himself, pressing me more intimately into our kiss. He then gently rests my head down again, drowning me in his growing passion as he sweeps his hand down the side of my body. I shiver as his hand brushes softly over the side of my breast, and he smiles into our kiss.

He did that on purpose! Inwardly I pout, while he chuckles a bit then sucks on my lower lip, pulling my lip out into an actual pout. *Grrr! Two can play at that game!*

The next time he darts into my mouth, I catch his tongue and start sucking on it. I hear him moan. I swirl my tongue around his, then around the tip of his tongue, then suck on it some more. He groans, and I feel him put his knee down to balance himself so he doesn't press into me at his waist...or below. It's my turn to smile and giggle.

His voice sounds playful as he hugs me. "You little minx. Or should I call you my little edible lynx? Tigers sometimes eat lynxes, you know." His eyes twinkle and I blush. We continue kissing, now more passionately. His arms wrap around me, pulling me up and holding me to him, and my arms wrap around him now they are free.

I slide my hands up his back and he moans as my fingers hook over his shoulders. His hands dive underneath my shirt, gently massaging my back. It feels *so* nice having his hands on me, skin on skin. He strokes each area of my back, daring to slide around and run his hands up and down my body, over the sides of my bra.

His arms encompass me and his fingertips lightly run down my spine, making me shiver. I can sense his hesitation as he hovers around the hooks on my bra. I smile because I sense his inner conflict.

I'm finding it amusing how much restraint it's taking him to not unhook my bra, even though I'm aware that once he does, I'll be literally putty in his hands. If he undoes my bra and slides his hands to my chest, I will be in the same position he's in. I'll need to exercise copious amounts of restraint to avoid going further.

I think he senses this, and lets the gentleman inside overrule the animalistic urges that could easily escalate if he let them. Justin has amazing self-control. I shouldn't be surprised, since he's usually laid back and balanced, not impulsive or aggressive. I have a feeling he could become aggressive if I encouraged him to, but we are both trying to take things slowly, even with the marking and bonds. We've been showing respect to each other, allowing ourselves to adapt as changes occur in our relationship, and as we are drawn more closely together.

Our kiss moves from fast-paced and passionate into sweet and drawn out. In between kisses we touch noses, cheeks, and foreheads together. We sit back slightly and look into each other's eyes.

"You are so beautiful." I blush as Justin pulls me back into a sweet kiss, his hand cradling my head. Then we just hold each other. I feel myself lying down again, and we're cuddled up together on the couch, Justin dragging his lips over my forehead and kissing me there. Then we both drift off to sleep.

CHAPTER THIRTEEN

Now the initial planning meetings are finished, I dive into my training as *ailouros*. The challenge I'm facing is I cannot tell one "candle" from another, in other words one pride member from another. The only one I'm able to identify is the *ikati's*. His candle is the largest, and I feel the strongest emotional surges from him.

Justin and I sit on the living room rug on the floor together, in a meditative posture. We are trying to connect within *merak,* also known as the "inner world of oneness". The candles fill my mind, and I identify and sense the intensity of his candle easily. Today we are working on feeling each other's emotions without being overwhelmed by them. I am learning how to avoid the potential snowball effect that can occur from "emotional feedback" between the *ikati* and *ailouros.*

"Which emotion am I feeling now?"

"Grief, loss." My lips quiver slightly as I am overwhelmed with a wave of sadness, all-encompassing loss.

"In my mind we're all attached by rivers, whereas yours are candles. The way I deal with overwhelming emotion coming through my bonds is by creating a distributary, a river that carries excess water from the main river. That water then runs off the edge of thought, as if falling off a flat earth. I'm not sure how you would visualize it with candles."

"Hmmm." I allow my mind to relax and not stress over the issue at hand. Instead I stay in a meditative state. We both sit in silence for several minutes.

After our long silence, my voice sounds foreign. "Current. Yours is water current, mine is electrical current. When the current splits, it

weakens. One branch goes to absorptive material, the other to the candle where it ignites with emotion."

"Good job, Darla. I wouldn't have thought of splitting current. But it works!"

My eyes are still closed and I smile.

"Back to the emotion."

I feel the grief come through our bond again, threatening to overwhelm me because of my sensitivity to other's emotions. This time I visualize splitting the heat into currents that run along wires, from one destination to another. One of the wires ends at my candle, whereas another ends with a resistor that absorbs the current. As a result, I only feel half the strength of the emotion.

Justin can sense the strength of the emotion I'm feeling. "Great! You've split the strength of the emotion to make it more manageable."

I try splitting off a third current to a resistor as well, which reduces the energy even more so.

"I can sense that. You've reduced again. Okay, let's take a break."

We both change our positions and I grab a water bottle.

"So you've learned one of the most important skills, how not to let yourself become overwhelmed with the emotions of others. Now the next important step is to work on the speed of diverting the flows from the other candles."

I set my water bottle down, and we go back to our meditative poses, with Justin forcing strong emotions toward my candle, and me diverting flows more quickly. We work at it for the remainder of the afternoon. With each surge, I'm able to keep on diverting. By the end of the afternoon, I feel a light sheen of perspiration on my face and those other areas not covered with my moisture-wicking track suit.

"Well, I think we're done for today." Justin gives me a smile and a kiss as we walk to the kitchen to get more water.

"Whew! Well, I think I'm getting faster."

"Definitely. Still lots of training to do, though. We've only scratched the surface."

"I can tell. I can sense the potential for enhanced understanding between myself and hundreds of pride members eventually."

"Yes, eventually you'll be able to identify every candle, just like I can identify every lake in my head. Right now you're just feeling the main collective feelings from the entire group which are pretty neutral and should be subtle compared to the flow between the two of us."

I smirk, feeling mischievous, and let a feeling of desire flow through our bond.

"Better be careful, or I might not divert the flow of that one. It could snowball and overwhelm us." He winks at me, and I feel a surge of desire from him.

"Maybe that's something we could have fun with in the future." I flutter my lashes, like he warned me not to. I send the surge back to him, knowing that neither of us are diverting the flow.

He speaks in a gentle voice, saturated with amusement. "You're pushing it." He faces me, and cradles my head. "You know, you're playing with fire." He starts to softly kiss my face and lips."

"Mmmm. I wouldn't have it any other way."

The following week, I'm scheduled to work three days, and with the *ailouros* training and getting to know pride members better, I'm kept busy.

Later in the week, Justin gets a call from Dick. He puts it on speaker phone.

"Dick. Nice to hear from you so soon."

"Justin. I have information on Darla's sister."

"She's with me, listening right now."

"Yes. Well, as you know already, the name was false. However, through facial recognition, I was able to narrow it down to three shifters, from two different clans, both local."

"Great. You take one clan and we'll take the other for the sake of expediency?"

"I'll take the clan with two potential shifters, since my investigation has brought me to that area."

"Okay. We'll take the other clan. Text me all the details you have on the shifter and his clan."

"Will do."

I feel torn between listening for further information about my sister and rushing around to get ready to leave. It takes a significant amount of self control, but I stay to listen, to ensure I know all the details. Justin looks up from his phone at the sound of Dick's voice on speaker again.

"Done. Info's been texted to you."

"Alright, fill us in on the fly, if you know anything else that could be helpful."

"Will do."

We throw together what we will need in an overnight bag, Justin grabs our jackets, and we both hastily pull our shoes on. Within minutes, we find ourselves in Justin's black SUV, travelling north, toward one of the bear colonies several cities away. A security detail follows us in another vehicle, and I feel relatively safe in case there should be some type of skirmish.

As we drive, I arrange for a different therapist to take my client load for the remainder of the week. Since I'm technically "on contract", I set my own hours. However, my current clients need appointments on a weekly basis. Thankfully, a newer therapist at the clinic is happy to help out.

Four hours later, I startle as a cold blast of air hits me. Reluctantly, I open my eyes and see it's dark outside. We've arrived at our destination, and Justin is at my door, unbuckling me. I try to step out of the vehicle, but because I'm groggy I miss the step and stumble...right into Justin's arms.

He chuckles. "Whoa, someone's anxious to get going." Then he smirks as he sets my feet down on the pavement. I yawn and stretch. "Either that or you've finally decided to throw yourself at me." My face crinkles and I fake-slap him playfully on the arm. He laughs. "Well, I'm glad you're awake. Now that it's time to sleep."

"Ha. Ha." I'm slightly sarcastic, slightly daring him to tease me more, while the side of my mouth is pulled up in a grin and a semi-pout at the same time.

He smiles down at me. "You're adorable." He puts his forehead to mine, and sweeps my cheek with his thumb.

I playfully stick my tongue out at him and he chuckles with a glint in his eye. "Don't give me ideas, now." I blush, willing my mind to not go into dangerous territory.

Being close to Justin keeps my anxiety under wraps, so I don't become an emotional wreck. The calm flowing through our bond definitely helps.

"So where are we?" I look around and see we're in an unfamiliar city, surrounded by tall buildings, lit up with thousands of lights. We're

standing in front of one of those buildings, but I'm unable to see the building sign above us because of the angle.

Justin hands his keys and some money from his clip to a young man in uniform. "We'll be staying here overnight to rest, while my guys do some scouting and information gathering. Once they're back, we'll make a plan, and tomorrow we'll act on it."

He holds open the door to the entrance for me, and I walk into the brightly lit, expansive hotel lobby. One of the men in our party checks us in, the others survey the area and people, while Justin and I walk past a tiered fountain to the hotel restaurant. We are seated, the waiter takes our orders, and I look around, enjoying the ambiance. I start to relax, knowing my glass of white wine is helping.

I look across the round table at Justin, asking for reassurance. "She'll be okay, right?"

He slowly nods his head. "They haven't found any evidence of abuse so far, when it comes to the system. Not since the victors were required to mark women in the arena, and participants were limited to one victory. However..."

I sit up straight in my chair. "What? You know of a loophole?"

"Well, remember, another male's mark can be placed over the original mark if the couple haven't been fully mated."

I think of the implications and I shiver. It's not something I want to dwell on in the context of Natalie's situation.

"Out of the thousands of arena fights that have taken place over the years, there have been few cases where it's occurred..."

I'm alarmed. "You mean it's something that's been done?"

"It's only been in cases where, for example, a stronger brother or friend might fight in the place of a weaker brother or friend. However, a participant can't be mated already, and they only get one victory in the

arena, unless their mate has died." Justin's voice quivers a bit and he pauses to drink some water. At that moment, the waiter arrives with our salads and fresh rolls.

"So it really only makes sense to go that route if they've found their own mate already and haven't marked them yet, or have decided they 100% will never want a mate. And, any exceptions to the norm are investigated thoroughly to prevent abuse."

I lean backward into my chair again. "I see. So if everything is monitored, then she should be fine, working as the *ailouros, luna,* or equivalent in a colony." I sip my wine. "It's not like her to limit her contact with me though."

"I know. That's one thing that worries me."

"You're worried about other things, too?"

"Well, the fact that someone used a false name indicates they want to make it difficult for anyone to monitor them. It could just be for privacy reasons, or due to control issues, or for other reasons. It's the last two I'd be concerned about."

"Yeah, someone with control issues who doesn't want to be monitored—that would definitely set some red flags off in the relationship department." Justin nods at me. "What other reasons would someone have to not want to be monitored?"

Justin looks thoughtful. "Right now I can't think of any other reason why, apart from protest. You know, like 'big brother paranoia'?"

"I see what you mean. That would still fall under the desire for privacy though."

"Then I can't think of any other reason for now."

Our main courses arrive, and we start eating in a thoughtful silence, then progress into some lighter subjects. By the time we've finished dessert and cappuccinos, we're both ready to retire to our rooms for the

night. Justin settles the bill, then offers me his arm, and we walk to the elevator together.

We get out at our floor, and Justin uses a key card to open the door to our suite. Our security detail, secretly shadowing us this evening, goes in first to check all the rooms. Justin and I stand in the hallway chatting. Once the rooms are clear we enter the spacious suite.

Justin and I take the master bedroom and decide to get some rest while waiting for the team to return. After I slip into a satin nightie and cuddle up under the covers in bed, Justin joins me, bare chested, and spoons me. He kisses me on the back of my head. We lay there, heartbeats slowing until we sync in a rhythmic sleeping pattern.

A few hours later, I open my eyes and realize Justin is sitting up in the dark.

"Come." Justin's voice is at a low volume. The door opens quietly, and one of our security lets him know the rest of the team has returned. Justin slides out from under the sheets as if trying not to wake me, and I sit up, startling him.

"Oh, you're awake." Justin pulls on a shirt, then walks into the ensuite and brings back a robe for me. I'm grateful I don't need to waste time getting dressed, and the robe is squishy-soft and warm.

We walk into the common area, complete with couches, table, chairs, and more. One of the team members places a cup of coffee for me on the patina and glass coffee table. I glance around the room, taking in the light blush-toned walls, looking for a clock. My eyes settle on a standing clock on the mantle that shows it's just after 3 AM. Justin dials Dick's number and puts him on speakerphone.

"Dick."

"Justin."

"Our team uncovered some important info in their recon tonight. You're on speakerphone."

"Good. Your shifter's two cousins over here generated no leads. Nada."

The team debriefs as they normally do after recon. When they get to the part where the "target was present but is now missing", I butt in.

"What do you mean she's now missing?"

"Sorry, *ailouros,* but she's no longer with this sleuth of bears."

My anxiety is causing my stomach to feel like it's ping-ponging around in my body. "What about her mate? Is he gone, too?"

The team locks eyes with Justin, not used to speaking freely with anyone besides him. "You can speak freely in front of your *ailouros.*"

"The shifter is still here—Parker saw him with his own eyes. But Derby's source disclosed that the shifter has apparently come into a very large sum of money lately and hasn't got a mate...anymore."

I whisper. "So she was sold then." I feel despair. Justin senses my desperation, and seeks to comfort me. He pulls me to his side and holds me tightly to him. When he sees my eyes, he pulls my face to his chest.

He whispers, placing a kiss on the top of my head. "It's okay. We're going to find her. Hey." He tilts my chin up with his finger and thumb and looks into my eyes. "I'm here for you." He gently kisses my lips then pulls me into an embrace, rocking me gently. I feel comforted by his gestures of warmth.

One of the team members, Derby, clears his throat. "She may have been sold, but remember, she would have had to be marked again, which provides some protection."

"What do you mean?" I find myself sniffling a bit.

Parker answers. "It means she would still eventually become someone's mate. And believe me when I say this. She's actually better off

with someone else. When I observed this shifter, I found his disposition to be cruel and vile. It's obvious he doesn't have the temperament to take a mate and treat her properly." He resorts to mumbling. "His only priority is cold, hard cash to match his cold, hard heart."

His voice returns to its regular volume. "And if someone was willing to pay that amount for her, they obviously place a high value on her life."

Derby speaks up. "What we're trying to get at, is that she would be safe until she arrives at her final destination, and when she arrives there, she will end up with a mate. One male, singular. She couldn't have been sold into the sex trade."

The fourth security member mumbles under his breath so I can barely hear him. "Unless the 'mate' transporting her conveniently dies." Justin glares at him. My anxiety level, which was starting to abate, increases again.

Parker elbows the guy and speaks up. "That wouldn't purposely happen, or it would affect her state of mind for months because of the marking. Believe me, the mate at her final destination would not be pleased. She will be well-protected. I can guarantee you that."

But I wonder to myself. *Even if she's relatively safe on her way there, what if her mate at her final destination doesn't treat her well?*

125

Chapter Fourteen

"But couldn't the one marking her take advantage of her before 'passing her on'?"

Justin takes my hand. "I know I haven't explained everything about the actual mating bond yet, but there are two parts to it. One is the ceremony I've already mentioned to you. The other part involves the biological tying together of mates."

"Y-you mean sex?" I can feel my face flush, asking the question in front of a room filled with males, but I need the point to be clarified. Then I notice everyone except Justin is looking in different directions, studying their hands, the floor, the table, the ceiling. *Wait, the* ceiling?

"Yes." Justin sits back on the couch, still holding my hand. I sit back, turning toward him, my knee on the couch, so it feels like just the two of us having a conversation.

"Either the mating ceremony or physical bonding of the couple with a marked female will create a heightened awareness of one's mate, or the initial awareness if they aren't bound together by pride or pack.

"Completing the mating bond with the second part increases the awareness and drawing together. The ceremony increases the physical desire to be bound together, and the physical binding increases the emotional draw. Both parts of the mating bond increase the spiritual awareness they have of each other, to the extent where they can locate each other geographically and communicate with each other. For some mates, if the bond is strong enough they can communicate thoughts through telepathy, in the same way that some family or clan members can."

Parker clears his throat and I turn back to my original position on the couch. "So as you can see, if someone has the intention of turning a marked female over to someone else, they won't be able to complete either part of the actual mating bond, since both are dissolvable only by death."

"Okay, that does make me feel better, having all of that explained to me."

"Everything was well-thought out before starting up the arena system. It was tailored to the way the markings and bondings work."

I know in my situation, I'm very fortunate Justin and I met before the arena fight, and he felt so compelled to fight for me. I've chosen of my own free will to be with him. However, I originally thought for some women, being marked like that was akin to sentencing them to slavery. Until Justin explained how the marking actually works.

Becoming an *ailouros, luna,* or the equivalent is a position that demands respect, including respect from the *ikati, alpha,* or pack leader. Those are the positions the majority of the women won in the arena would be fulfilling, positions in packs where the male leader believed in and would respect a female counterpart in leadership.

But still, there is a major flaw in the system. *Women don't have the initial say in whether to enter the system to start with!* I see the difficulty the society faces, obtaining enough women in a demographic where most births are of males. Keeping vital secrets, such as that of their existence, are of utmost importance.

It's not like they could come out and recruit willing volunteers—unless all the clans globally decided to go public. That would create an explosion of new potential problems, including the one many shifters worry about. Fear and envy of their power make them targets for genocide.

There must be a better way to rely on getting mates, besides through an antiquated system acceptable in the 1800s, but not acceptable in today's world. Well, at least not acceptable by human society. I sigh, knowing this conversation will come up again, because of my support of human rights. There has to be a better solution overall. I just have to find it.

"What's got you thinking, Darla? I can see the wheels turning."

"Just some things about the way human mates are obtained in general. But that's a conversation for another day. Today, the priority is finding my sister and ensuring her safety and well-being."

Justin nods. He likely knows what I'm alluding to, but doesn't bring it up. "So what's the plan?"

"The bear shifter is a dead end. He won't talk. He's as stubborn as they come."

Justin thinks for a moment. "Let's work on the financial angle, and Dick, think you could put the squeeze on his two relatives in the other pack?"

"Will do. I'll let you know if any info pans out."

"Great. We'll see if we can find out where the large transfer of cash originated from."

"Thank you, Everyone. This means the world to me, finding my sister and whether she's safe or needs help." I smile, grateful for all their help.

"Any time, Darla. You're not alone in this. We're here for you." Justin sweeps back the hair that has fallen in front of my eyes.

I suppose I could dwell on the negatives and play the "blame game" regarding my sister. I could lay the blame at the feet of the shifter community for their actions toward human women. But I'm not like that.

Blaming is counterproductive, unless you're pinpointing the root of a problem to prevent future occurrences. Then it's more like attributing responsibility to a party so they can be accountable in the future. So instead of "canceling out" Justin's statements due to the troubling practices in their society, I choose to accept the current circumstances and the help being offered.

Justin and I grab some sleep while the others keep working, delving for more information. When we awake a few hours later to a knock on our bedroom door and the smell of breakfast, we find our guys have hit another dead end. It's Dick who's come through for us again.

Okay maybe he's not a Dick-wannabe. He's the real deal, a fully-fledged-Dick.

The guys have him on speakerphone, and we quietly grab some breakfast from the carts as we listen. It's still dark outside, and moonlight spills into the room before it's swallowed up by the light from the dimmed lamps.

"His cousins let it spill that she was transferred a few days after the win. The payment came in the week after the transfer, which means the person who paid has a lot of pull, or our 'friendly neighborhood bear' was part of a joint contract with the next person up the line.

"So that gives us three routes to pursue. The first is known associates trusted enough to take on a joint contract that relies on both people's performance of duties. Secondly, deposits made around the same date from the same account would indicate others involved in this who we might be able to lean on for info..."

Derby interjects his thoughts. "And the final avenue would be the account itself. Our guys weren't able to recover any info on that end because they hid their tracks well by transferring the money internationally. Our not-so-smart bear didn't bother to set up a foreign

account, which is how it was discovered so quickly that he received the funds."

"That's right. I'll follow up with my undercover network, then try to get a couple hours of shuteye while they do the legwork."

Dick has an undercover network? I'm starting to think he might be King of the Dicks. *The Dick-King.*

"Sounds good. We'll follow up with our contacts as well."

"Alright then. Until we hear something."

"Talk to you soon, Dick."

As soon as we are off the phone, our guys head into the den to follow up, giving us a bit of privacy to finish our breakfast.

Justin puts his hand on my knee and turns to me. "How are you holding up?"

"I'm torn between relief and anxiety. Relief because of the way everything was explained to me regarding my sister's safety, but anxiety over knowing that anything could go wrong between Point A and Point B. Like what if human traffickers killed the guy who marked her?"

"Yeah, you're right. It's not one hundred percent foolproof when you look at factors outside the shifter community. But to be honest, it's really difficult to kill a shifter."

"Then there's concern over where she would end up and who she'd end up with. What if she ends up in an emotionally abusive situation? Heck, I don't even know if she had a boyfriend when she was taken. We were close, but she was shy about disclosing that stuff to anyone, including myself.

"I feel so fortunate I'm with you, Justin. But she might not be so lucky and her mate might not have the same level of empathy and understanding as you do."

Justin sighs. "It's true that many of our kind in the *alpha* role tend to be more controlling, if they don't learn to harness their animalistic instincts from a young age. I understand your concern. In fact, during your own personal experience with shifters, you've been more than patient and fair, giving us the benefit of the doubt."

"Thank you for understanding where I'm coming from, Justin. Sometimes it's difficult to not let my worry push through the roof and control me emotionally, but I'm really trying to 'go with the flow'. Some things can be changed and some can't. To me it's about having the wisdom to tell the difference between the two, and letting that wisdom guide my actions."

"You've got great discernment, Darla. That's one reason why I know you're going to be an exceptional *ailouros*."

I smile at Justin and kiss him softly on the lips. "Thank you, Justin. That means a lot to me."

After our early breakfast we retire to our room and lie in each other's arms, hoping to catch a few more "Z"s while our team works their magic. I'm grateful Justin suggested getting Dick involved. He has quite the "interesting" personality, but he sure as heck gets the job done. My confidence in him increases with each revelation he brings to the table.

Later in the morning, we sit with the team for a debriefing on their progress. Parker was able to pull some strings with local law enforcement. They had been willing to liaise with him regarding known associates of Mr. Bear. As a result, there is a list to follow up on.

One of those creeps may have taken my sister and know her current whereabouts.

The team figures the fastest way to narrow down the list is through financial records. They are hoping anyone relevant skipped getting a secret account.

Dick's network is still tracing the owner of the account that dispersed the funds. So far the result is uncovering account after account, convoluting the origin of the funds. For all we know, the funds could eventually link back to a local account, however unlikely that would be. Dick, again on speakerphone, has a hunch we're not dealing with someone close to home.

"There are so many more convenient ways to disperse local funds than running them through this kind of system. So logic follows that we're looking at a foreign destination and someone wishing to remain anonymous."

My heart clenches. *That means she could be hidden anywhere in the world!*

We check out of the hotel, and the team continues to work through the day as we travel back to the pride. We've uncovered everything we can locally, and it's best to regroup at home. Justin and I need to tend to any pressing pride duties in case we are required to travel again for the investigation.

From my experience yesterday and today, I see I'm not really needed for the follow up—the team is adequate for that. I have a feeling Justin and I would miss each other too much if I travelled without him. I realize if we both stayed unnecessarily, it would just take us away from our duties and eventually increase our workload. So until we have some tangible evidence or I'm needed, staying in the loop via teleconference is adequate.

But I'm glad Justin and I went along with the team on the first run. It gave me insight as to how they operate, and the best way to bring my ideas to the table. Most importantly, it shows Justin's sensitivity to my need to find my sister. It means the world to me that he recognizes how important

it is to me, without minimizing the danger she could be in. He reassures me, but is also realistic.

I slide back into work and my pride duties. I realize Justin and I will need to have a discussion about a future mating ceremony and bonding at some point, but thankfully he hasn't mentioned anything more about it. I just don't feel it's a good time to talk about it, with everything swirling around in my head. So many things have changed from the time I met him that fateful night to the present that it's kept my head spinning.

Days go by while the team investigates all the financial angles and those of the bear's known associates. Just when they think they're about to make a breakthrough, records go missing overnight, lips become sealed, and our group is at an impasse. Informants clam up, and other records become "classified". In other words, someone high up isn't happy with us investigating, and a threat has come down the line that has halted our investigation.

I cuddle up beside Justin that night, needing his comfort. I don't have to say a word; he knows exactly what I need. He strokes my back, while kissing the top of my head, and holds me until I fall asleep.

CHAPTER FIFTEEN

The following day, we're doing a teleconference with the team. Parker admits they've run into a brick wall.

"So what's the next step?" I ask cautiously, but no one answers. I wait a minute, watching each of them look down and avoid the camera. The only one looking forward is Dick, and his gaze seems to be weighing me.

I see Justin give the most subtle shake of his head beside me. I wouldn't have noticed if we hadn't been on camera. I know something is up between Dick and Justin.

Parker breaks the silence by clearing his throat. "So we're back to square one. We have a better idea of what went down though, and of the overall situation. We just need to find a different way to pursue leads." He's looking down as he speaks, glancing up on occasion.

"Okay, so if the victor and that trail is dead, then what's our next avenue of investigation?" An uncomfortable silence reigns. Dick opens his mouth and I see Justin jerk his head, a bit more noticeably this time.

"That's enough, Dick and Justin. If you have an idea of how to pursue this, please share it."

Justin's expression changes from resistant to reluctant, and then to resigned. He sighs and lowers his head.

Dick speaks. "We could replicate the original circumstances and look for leads that way."

I'm curious. "How would we do that?"

"Well, we would need bait..."

Justin sounds forceful as he speaks. "You're not using her as bait, and that's final!"

Dick flinches and nods.

"What are you talking about? You need me to act as bait?"

Justin is adamant. "No! We're not risking your safety and well-being..."

"This is my sister we're talking about—someone I'd lay down my life for! I deserve to at least hear the plan before it's nixed. Even if we don't use it, it may contain crucial ideas and we can formulate a better plan."

Parker speaks up again. "She's right. Maybe we can figure out a plan involving less risk, based on Dick's original idea."

Justin nods reluctantly. "Darla, whatever is decided, your safety comes first."

I nod. "Okay, let's hear it."

Dick shares the details. "I know a guy who's in tune with the growing 'mate request' market..."

I'm confused. "Why didn't you tell us this before?"

"Because although he's an older, reliable informant of mine, I only put feelers out regarding 'mate transfers' a couple days ago. Anyway, he has access to a growing list of requests for mates—made by VIPs, of course.

"If there was someone willing to pose as one of these mates, they could go undercover and possibly glean some information, both on how these guys operate and specifically on your sister."

Justin asserts himself, and I can feel his *ikati* forcefulness pushing through. "I'm not letting Darla go alone. There's no way I'll allow her to go unprotected into that kind of situation."

"Hold on, Justin. You're so opposed to the idea, you didn't let me finish explaining the second part of the plan earlier."

Justin relents and allows Dick to continue.

"The system requires someone to hold her marking, remember? That 'someone' would be you."

I track Dick's ideas. "Which means you'll be the one protecting me, Justin. And it's expected, right? That Justin would be protective even though he's posing in a position as if he's giving me away?"

"That's correct. Justin would also be acting undercover to get more info about the operation and your sister's whereabouts."

I can see Justin's wheels turning as he relaxes a bit.

"You'd be with me the entire time. What do you say, Justin?"

There is a pause, while Justin considers the idea. He looks into my eyes and speaks to me softly. "I'm willing to do this with you, Darla, if you promise not to do anything risky and to stick to me like glue."

I nod, elated at his agreement, and fling my arms around his neck. "Thank you so much, Justin. This means so much to me." I pull back and my eyes connect with his. I mean, really connect. I feel so captivated by him, and my lips gently land on his. He pulls me close to him as we kiss deeply.

"Ahem." Derby clears his throat. Justin and I slowly pull away from each other, but remain seated closely together. "So what's our part in this, Dick?"

"We'll, we're at a huge advantage, as Justin and Darla have the perfect cover. Records show she was won by him in the arena, so all good there. We'll need documents that show Justin has some large debts, in case anyone decides to check. It helps to have clear motivation so everything looks legit."

Justin nods. "The documents won't be a problem." For some reason, Justin looks at the floor.

Is there something he's not telling me?

"Her *ailouros* bond will keep you both connected. There's been no mating ceremony or permanent mating bond if I'm correct?"

Justin chuckles. "That's correct, otherwise I would have stopped you at the beginning as it would have made the plan impossible."

"Is it well known that she's *ailouros* of the pride?"

"No. We haven't had any meetings outside the pride with Darla acting as *ailouros.*"

"Good. Because that position connotes permanency. We need your relationship to look as transient as possible on the outside. At the same time, Darla needs to be resistant to being transferred, and you need to be seen as resisting the natural urge of falling in love with her."

Justin clears his throat and his face looks a bit flushed. *Could he be...?*

"Anyone watching will expect that of both of you, as the mark draws you closer together. So it shouldn't be difficult for you guys to play your roles in the situation."

"So any thoughts on the overall plan?"

Parker comments. "It seems pretty solid. We've got the initial contacts, good cover, low risk. Makes for a good operation. I take it we'll be standing close by in case we're needed for an extraction?"

"Yes, the five of us will be close by. Justin, I'll need to rejoin the pride for the operation so we have a stronger link than just our familial one, and a connection to Darla."

"Sounds good, Dick. Darla, I'll teach you how to identify these guys' signals through the bond as we prepare everything."

"That's great, although there is a little problem."

"What's wrong?" Justin looks at me with concern.

I feel a bit sheepish. "Well, I never did get everyone's names. I think of you as Security Guy #1, Parker, Derby, Grumpy Security Guy #4, and Dick, of course."

I can see everyone's mouths twitching upward, except for Mr. Grumpy Guard, who doesn't look impressed.

Justin chuckles and introduces the other two guys. "Guy #1 is Carey, and Guy #4 is Scontroso."

"Alright, nice to be formally introduced, Carey and Scontroso."

Carey answers while Scontroso mutters. "Same here."

Dick makes arrangements with his contact to have a handler start a secret mate transfer with Justin. He specifically asks for someone who had recently transferred a woman with similar characteristics as myself. His contact was able to attract a handler who, after seeing my photo, had joked about handing off my "twin" recently to something called "The Circle".

The handler said he knew exactly who to contact, the same guy who dealt with the other girl—said it was already a done deal. I'm excited because we're definitely in the best position to find my sister. Maybe fate is smiling down on us.

The next couple of days involve arranging for a leave of absence and transferring clients. I delegate some pride responsibilities, and train to recognize our team through the pride bond. I'm anxious to get going, but neither Justin or I are in control of the timetable.

Justin assigns tasks to other members of his staff so his company will run smoothly while he's away. His *kedi* and mate assume leadership responsibilities, similar to how they carried the pride during the years when Justin was inactive. I'm particularly concerned about the needy families who need the extra care right now.

"Don't worry, everything is in good hands. Katie has your reports and will follow up with those families. She's good at that type of thing."

I sigh with relief. I'm thankful I have a partner who understands how important both these missions are to me—looking after those in our pride family while searching for the missing member of my human family. I'm glad everything will be taken care of on all fronts while Justin and I are away.

Today Justin and I travel. The handler agreed that Justin himself could take me directly to my final destination. This is instead of another shifter marking and accompanying me for the next leg of the journey. A second handler, aware of the final destination, would join us part way and the first handler would leave at that point.

Apparently, being marked only once isn't normal. However, Justin exaggerated, saying a second marking would force me into an extended coma. He would only agree to the transfer if it was on his terms, so eventually the handler caved. Apparently, the money was exorbitant enough to accept the unusual request.

After a thirty minute road trip, we find ourselves in a large private hangar. We meet my handler there in person. He laughs when he sees me, mentioning something about déjà vu. I know he is referring to my sister, but I refrain from asking anything, although I'm dying to. He would be unaware of her final destination, since he would only have taken her halfway. Otherwise, the guys would have just extracted the info from him. Apparently, info extraction is Scontroso's forte.

The handler addresses me with a smooth accent. "Name's Slice, Honey." He takes my hand and kisses it. I can hear Justin's faint growl.

Slice seems to be in a good mood. "Possessive are we? You've been around her too long, Justin." He slaps him on the back. "Happens to the best of us after the marking."

He reminds me of a snake oil salesman. In my mind, I nickname him "The Snake Handler".

Snake Handler stands in front of Justin. "So the rules have changed." Justin tenses up. "We'll only be taking you two."

Justin isn't about to back down. "You said we'd also be allowed two more companions."

Snaky guy laughs and shrugs. "Actually, it's not up to me. It's up to the pilot. He says there's limited capacity and the plane can only take six, including the pilot and co-pilot. That means you, the lovely lady, the flight attendant, and myself."

I have no idea when it comes to plane capacity. Neither does Justin. He hesitates.

The Snake sighs. "Look, you can ask the pilot about it."

I can tell Justin is calculating. If there are only six of us on the plane, we should be alright. The main concern is he can't safely shift without jeopardizing everyone. However, if anything goes wrong, he should be able to overpower Slice easily. I imagine what "Sliced Snake" would look like. *Ewwww.*

"Alright." The two of us board the plane, while Parker and Derby remain standing by our black SUV.

Once on the plane, Justin asks the pilot about its capacity.

The pilot is politely formal. "Six is the max since we have a lot of cargo in the hold this trip. Sorry your friends can't come with you. But there's enough to keep you entertained on the way."

Justin nods, and we find seats near the middle of the plane. The flight attendant comes over immediately, introduces herself, then offers us drinks. I take one to help settle my nerves. Justin thanks her but declines.

We wait for several minutes until the preflight routines are finished, then buckle up and prepare to take off. As we taxi on the runway, my drink starts to take effect, and I start to relax a bit. Slice sits facing me, a table in between us. I think that puts Justin at ease, not having anyone behind us.

I start to fall into my role. "So where are we going?" I give Justin a cutesy look.

"Just on a little trip, Love. I thought we should get away for a few days." Slice chuckles at Justin's comment.

With innocent eyes I look over at Slice. "Do you know where we're going?"

He smiles at me. "I wouldn't want to spoil the surprise." I can tell he's not going to give anything up, so I don't push.

I lean back in my seat, feeling the alcohol's effects calming me. Justin starts looking through a magazine, but I can tell he's very alert. I relax more into my seat, placing my head on Justin's shoulder, and start dozing off. I feel so safe with him.

I don't know how long I slept, but I'm awakened by arguing. My nodding head jerks up. Slice is still sitting opposite me. His eyes gleam as a broad smile covers his face. "Ah, nice of you to join us. I hope you rested well."

We're surrounded by a group of men—two are unconscious on the ground thanks to Justin—but Justin's movements are slowing down. *Oh no! Where did all these goons come from?*

"Looks like the 'cargo' wanted to come out and play." Slice snickers, watching Justin take on the men as they attempt to restrain him.

I realize why Justin's moves are slowing, after someone grabs my head to keep me still. I feel a prick in my neck, then liquid is forced through the syringe into my body. *They must have drugged him, too.*

"What are you doing? I don't understand?" Slice just sits back, smiling at me.

Justin tries to stay focused, but stumbles, losing his footing. "We had a deal, Slice."

"Yes, that deal's still on. You'll get your money..." I can no longer make sense of the conversation.

Through the *ailouros* bond I feel Justin's light shimmer and flicker, then as he falls to the ground his flame becomes small, even though it is steadily burning. I feel so alone.

I sense the plane descending, and my ears pop. I feel nauseated. Slice continues to smile at me as my head starts spinning and my eyes droop. Then everything goes black.

CHAPTER SIXTEEN

I wake up in a dark room, lying on something soft, under a cozy duvet. My head feels like it's stuffed with cotton. Something feels very wrong.

"Well, Dear, it's about time you awoke." A low light burns from an antique lamp, and I see a matronly woman in an old fashioned nursing uniform approaching me. I'm lying on a soft bed with comfortable sheets. I know they are clean by the scent.

"How are you feeling?" She touches my forehead with the back of her hand, then takes my wrist and starts counting while looking at her watch.

The dim room swirls. "Where am I?" My voice is raspy. I try to sit up on my elbows, attempting to grasp why I'm in this place and not at home with Justin. *Justin. Why can't I sense him?* Physically I'm unable to support myself. *I feel so weak.* I collapse onto my back.

"Don't overdo it, Dear. You're dehydrated."

Then I remember. My voice sounds like I'm croaking. "I was on a plane. Then someone did something to put me to sleep. Justin! Justin was hurt—he fell!" I start panicking. "Where is he?"

"Shh, shh, shh. It's okay. The man who marked you is absolutely fine." She smiles at me.

I start to calm down. "Where is he? Can I see him?"

"So many questions." The woman looks at me affectionately. "All in good time."

She walks to a chest of drawers and picks up a tray I didn't notice was there. "First, let's get you hydrated and some food in you. You've been out for over a day!"

"What?" I take the water from her, gulping it greedily.

"Not too quickly, Dear, or it might just come right back up." I realize she's right as I feel a wave of nausea hit me. "Just little sips."

I sip on the water, then am able to handle some of the broth she brought me. It feels like I'm getting over the flu. As long as I take things slowly, I can manage to keep it down. After a few minutes, I feel like my nerves are a bit more steady. *Just like the sipping, ask one small question at a time.*

I act with as calm a demeanour as I can manage. "Could you please tell me where I am?"

"You're at 'The Circle'. It's an 'in between' place. There's nothing to worry about. You're at the safest place you could possibly be." She continues to help me with the broth. "The security is exceptional. The place is built like a fortress, and here no harm comes to any of our girls. Think of it as a respite. A break from the troubles of the world."

"If you don't mind me asking, why am I here?" I continue to sip the broth and feel a bit of strength returning.

"You're here to rest and get stronger. It may take a bit longer in your circumstance since they must have given you drugs as well...the two together knocked you out for longer than is standard."

The two? What does she mean by that?

"I don't want you to worry about any of that, though. You're safe here and looked after. Everything will work out for the best in the end."

I think I can trust her. So far she's given me the information I've asked for, and she is helping me by bringing me water and broth.

"What is your name?"

"Oh, dear me. I'm so sorry I didn't introduce myself. You can call me Molly." She smiles at me as she clears the tray and places it on the

dresser. She brings over a bottle of liquid and hands it to me. "Vitamin water."

"Thank you." I open the bottle and sip, a little at a time. "My name is Darla." She nods and smiles at me.

"When you're ready, you are welcome to take a shower." She points to a doorway behind me that opens into a bathroom. "There are clean clothes in the drawers for you."

"Thank you, Molly. You've been very kind."

"Think nothing of it, Dear."

Once Molly leaves, I make my way to the bathroom and remove the nightgown she must have dressed me in while asleep. I notice a large bandage on my neck area, and assume it's related to the injection they gave me on the plane. I carefully shower, so as not to get the bandage wet.

When I'm done, I step into my room and open the chest of drawers. It holds the basics: nightgowns, underclothes, warm socks, a couple of cute tracksuits, a cardigan and a robe. Similar to the idea of 'comfort food', it holds 'comfort clothes'. I pull out a track suit, underclothes, and some warm, cozy socks.

After dressing, I walk to the door Molly left through. I expect it to be locked. I'm pleasantly surprised when I find it isn't. Perhaps they don't mind if I roam around and take a look at the place.

The door opens into a large common room with dark brown flooring. There are three steps down to a lowered TV room with couches, cushions, and throws. On the main level, there is a large, dark brown kitchen with cream marble countertops and stainless steel appliances.

Right next to the kitchen is a large dining table with a dozen chairs. Behind the dining area is a wall of glass, and sliding doors that lead to a glass sunroom. Although I don't see a door to the outside, beyond the sunroom is a beautiful flower garden with fountain, benches, and stone

walkways, all surrounded by high hedges. It's like something out of a dream.

I startle, hearing someone walk down the corridor toward the kitchen. I suppose the corridor leads to more bedrooms like my own. I wonder if I should be here. I wait because I need to understand my circumstances. I'm also remembering my original reconnaissance mission.

Although Justin and I are separated, I can still look for information about my sister. *In fact, if she was taken to 'The Circle', all the answers I need may be here!*

I see another woman, younger than Molly, also in traditional nursing dress. She's carrying folded linens in her arms.

"Oh hello. You must be Darla. I'm Sally. Welcome to 'The Circle'." She smiles at me, warmly.

"Nice to meet you, Sally."

She walks over to a linen closet and places the items on the shelf. Then she turns to me. "Would you like something hot to drink? Maybe some tea?"

"Sure, that would be nice." I smile back at her as she walks toward the kitchen and sets the kettle on. I seat myself at the table, and she sits opposite me.

"So how are you doing?"

"I'm feeling okay, just have a lot of questions on my mind." I decide to cut right to the chase.

"Okay. I'll answer them as best as I can. What would you like to know?"

"Firstly, where is the man who marked me? Is he okay?"

"All the men stay in another area in the compound. Only women are allowed in this section. It's like a sanctuary."

"So the man who marked me is well?"

"Yes, last time he inquired about you, he looked well." I am relieved he's well and asking about me, but still feel something is terribly wrong. It's like a sixth sense. I can't make heads or tails of it because I know Sally is being truthful.

"I have another question." I have no idea how to bring it up.

"Shoot and I'll answer it if I can."

"I don't really know how to ask this, but..." I take a deep breath. "Is there a woman who looks similar to me here?"

"There was, but she moved on to her final destination a while ago. Are you related? You have a strong resemblance to each other."

"Yes, she is my sister."

"Oh, that completely makes sense."

"Do you know where she is now?"

"I personally don't know where she went, but I wouldn't worry. Everyone at the receiving end of a mate transfer has been thoroughly vetted." She gets up and turns off the kettle as the water hits the boiling point.

I feel a wave of sarcasm coming on. *Yeah, I wonder what "thorough vetting" involves—a physical?* I stop my mind from making a stupid pun about shifters' animals and veterinarians. Then I feel a bit ashamed of my tendency to stereotype. The tea steeps, and I ask Sally questions about my sister, hoping she won't clam up.

I fumble with my teacup. "How was she doing when she was here?"

"She was really tired at first and quite scared, but after recovering for a couple days she seemed okay under the circumstances. It's a lot for anyone to process though, being drawn into a whole new world of shifters. Then going through the mate transfer on top of that...well, it can be overwhelming for some. She seemed a lot more introverted than you."

"I tend to be pretty outgoing at times. She's always been much quieter than me."

"She seemed very sweet, and I wish her well."

I smile at her. "Thank you. I appreciate that."

Once we finish our tea—I rush a bit and burn my tongue—Sally goes back to doing whatever it is she does. I begin my quest for information, searching for anything that could help me determine Natalie's whereabouts. I walk down corridor after corridor, checking the signs on the doors, until I finally see a door labeled "Records". I can barely contain my excitement, but also feel my heart start racing. I desperately need to get into the room, and am determined to do it.

I walk by, casually trying the doorknob, and of course it's locked. There is a curtained window, sealed to the wall. *No way can I break that without alerting them in a big way.* Then I see a card slot, meaning the door has an electronic lock. Sally or Molly must have a key card for the door. *I need that card!*

I find my way back to the women's quarters, cognizant of the offices I pass. I see the light on in the office closest to the women's living area. *What the hell—might as well try.* I knock on the door, thinking of an excuse to talk to Molly or Sally so I can scope out the office, but there is no answer. No noise either.

I try the doorknob, and to my surprise, it turns. I check the corridor, then quietly slip into the office, closing the door gently behind me. Then I scout the room.

I need to keep my search down to the seconds if possible, and my eyes scour the office quickly. The desks are tidy. *No key cards.* I check under the desks. *Where else might they keep a purse?* That's my best bet.

There are no lockers, and no purses under the coats on the rack. I quickly walk to the desks again, and start checking the drawers. I'm starting to lose hope, when at the last desk, I pull open the large bottom drawer. *Score!* I see a fern green purse, grab it, and quickly unzip it, kneeling on the floor.

Just then, I hear noise in the hall. Someone's talking. I hear the handle turn, and scoot underneath the desk before I'm seen. I hold my breath as someone walks into the office, hoping they won't come around to the side where I'm hidden. I hear a drawer open, some rustling, and something metal being collected. Footsteps make their way toward me, and I can smell the fresh scent of moisturizing lotion.

My heart is pounding, and I'm hyper-aware. I hear running in the hallway, and the footsteps nearly beside me stop. The door bursts open.

"We need your help. We have a situation in the men's quarters. I'll grab the med kit."

The footsteps scramble away hurriedly, as I hear items being gathered, and I hear rushing as the door slams. As soon as they are gone and I can hear them running down the hall, I widen the purse pocket so I can see inside. My heart drops. *Nothing!* I feel so disappointed. It means I'm going to have to steal a card from right underneath their noses. I halfheartedly check the last thin pocket on the side of the purse.

Oh my God! I pull out a set of cards attached together. *Thank goodness they didn't have this on a lanyard.* I saw Molly with hers around her neck, so I know they aren't her master keys. I mentally cross my fingers, hoping one of the cards will work.

I quickly rezip the purse, stash it in the bottom drawer, and make my way to the door. I listen, and it seems the hallway is clear. I quickly exit the room, and make my way back to Records. I try not to walk too quickly as I don't want to attract attention, but I'm fighting myself the whole way,

trying not to hurry. I use self-talk. *Just walking around, taking a stroll, relaaax...* It takes a lot of self control to abstain from rushing.

I find the Records room again, check the corridor, then start trying the key cards. The first one makes a loud buzz and the red light flickers. *Not that one, obviously.* I try the second one and the same thing happens. My anxiety rises. Third time, I get a beep and a green light, and quickly enter the room.

As I close the door behind me, I hear distant shuffling. I freeze, standing right inside the door. The shuffling gets louder, it's right outside my door, then I hear something bang against the door. I nearly jump out of my skin. I hear a whirring sound, then the shuffling, whirring object continues down the hall. I try to even out my breathing so my heart rate lowers. *Must be someone cleaning.*

Regardless of how modern The Circle's compound is, they have a large filing cabinet. Hoping they don't store details about our destinations strictly electronically, I try my luck there. My heart pounds as I locate and open a filing drawer labelled "Placements". I flip through the files, until I find one with my sister's name on it. I pull it out, lay it on the desk, and try to decipher it in the hallway light, dimmed from the curtained window.

Inside are standard items one might expect: large photo, medical information, other details about her. *Here!* I stop at a page about her placement. I scan the page and read the name of her benefactor. My jaw drops. Seeing his name and the photo of her destination, I can tell she will never want for anything. *That may be true, looking from the outside, but does she really want this? Does she feel secure and happy with him?*

Now I have Natalie's information, I can leave with Justin. I'm curious to see my own file about where I'm headed, but I need to get out of here before I'm caught. Besides, I don't need details, since we'll just abort our

current mission and go after Natalie. I can't wait to tell Justin the news! He'll be very happy, since he didn't want me taking unnecessary risks.

I carefully put the file away, making sure all the contents are still intact, and close the drawer. Suddenly, I hear someone in the hallway, coming closer. I wait on pins and needles. Then I hear them walk by. I see their shadow through the light curtain.

Whew! I try to calm myself. I wait until there is no longer any noise, then quietly sneak out of the office. I stalk down the hallway, nonchalantly. I was never told anything was off limits, so even if I'm seen here, it won't matter.

I just don't want to get caught with the key card on me. Then I realize, in horror—*I left the key card in the office! They'll know I broke in!* I try to stay calm. *I'll just have to feign ignorance if they find it before I leave this place.*

I walk back to the common area. I've withdrawn into my mind, thinking about my sister's situation. Now that I have the information needed, I can inform Justin and we can leave The Circle. Then we can plan reconnaissance, assess her situation, and visit her if it won't be disruptive to her new life. I ask Sally to arrange a meeting with Justin before we travel to my 'final destination'.

"You mean the man who marked you?"

"Yes, please. I'd like to see him as soon as possible." I look shyly at her as my face flushes a bit.

She smiles. "Sure. I'll make the arrangements." Sally pulls her phone out of her apron pocket and shoots off a text. "Done." She smiles at me.

At 2:00 pm, I'm ready to meet with Justin to tell him the exciting news. I follow Sally's directions to the co-ed lounge. I walk through the doorway, hoping to see Justin in the recreational room, but he hasn't arrived yet. Instead there are three other people sitting on couches, two

men and a woman. The woman throws a brief glance and a troubled smile my way, then goes back to her conversation with one of the men.

I sit on the only empty couch, beside the sofa where the second man lounges, and reach over to grab a magazine from the coffee table. I hope reading will fend off the nervousness as I await Justin. The man turns down the TV remote and looks as though he wants to chat.

"Uh, hi, there." He seems a bit self conscious. "The name's Mike."

"Hi, Mike. Nice to meet you. My name's Darla." He nods at me in acknowledgement.

"So, how are you doing?" It seems he wants to engage in conversation, so I set down my magazine. Not that I mind. It will pass the time while I wait.

"I'm doing okay. Just waiting for someone to meet me here. Do you know a man named Justin? He should be staying with the men."

His eyes look at me with confusion. "Justin? No, I haven't heard that name. Although a lot of people use aliases around here."

"I'm guessing the guys' area is packed with men because of all the guards?"

"Yeah. It's a bit of a madhouse over there. A lot of guys packed in rooms full of bunks." He chuckles.

After several minutes of casual conversation, I wonder what's taking Justin so long. Not that I mind talking with this stranger. He seems oddly familiar though.

"Have we ever met before, Mike? You seem familiar somehow."

Mike has an amused smile playing on his lips as he contemplates me. "We've never actually met, but I've definitely seen you before."

"Oh, okay. Do you remember where that was?"

He pauses for a moment. "Actually, it was here, at The Circle. You don't remember?"

"Oh." I vaguely remember him in a hazy way. "Must have been when I was in and out of consciousness."

"It was when you first came in."

"Oh, I must have been disoriented at the time. I apologize."

"Nothing to apologize for. They mentioned you aren't the greatest flyer, so they had given you something during the flight to help."

"It's true I'm not the greatest flyer." I feel confused at the explanation of their motivation for drugging me. *I doubt they did it to help me.*

We chat for a bit, and I'm starting to become antsy while waiting. My feeling of unease is growing stronger.

"Excuse me for a minute."

I go and look through the window in the door, but don't see Justin. However, I do see a guy in a military uniform standing in the hallway, so I knock. The soldier pokes his head into the room, and I hear a faint growl behind me.

I direct my question to the military guy. "Hey, could you ask for Justin, please?"

"Sure, ma'am." He walks back down the corridor. I go and sit back down.

"So who's this Justin guy, anyway?" Mike looks a bit irritated. I realize I may have come across as rude.

I'm unsure how to answer that, as I'm supposed to stay in character, but this is a stranger, irrelevant to my situation, and I'd rather not share details.

"The man I've been travelling with."

He looks genuinely surprised. "Oh, I didn't realize someone came with you. I didn't see anyone arrive with you."

That's odd.

"Justin and I are together." He can translate that however he wants. I'm anxious to hear back from the soldier who was at the door.

Minutes go by, and I don't hear back from him. Surprisingly, I feel drawn into conversation with Mike and we start going beyond small talk, chatting about our families.

"Yeah, my brother and I are pretty close. We're wolf shifters, so value family highly, and are a close knit group. I'm from one of the smaller packs."

"My sister and I live across the country from my parents. At least we used to. Now my sister lives farther away." My breath catches a bit as I speak.

"Hey." Mike's voice is soft. "Things change. Life changes, and life changes us. But we go on, and we build our lives wherever we end up. Even if you're on opposite ends of the globe, you'll always be sisters. You'll always have that bond."

Mike's amber eyes are mesmerizing, and time seems to stand still as he brushes my hair off my face and behind my ear.

I'm yanked out of the moment when I hear a door loudly open. I look backward and see the soldier. "Sorry, ma'am, I couldn't find anyone named Justin, and he's not on the sign-in list."

"Are you sure? He's the man who marked me." He gives Mike a strange look, and I see Mike stir, through the corner of my eye.

"I'm sure, ma'am. I'll let you get back to your conversation."

I'm confused and don't understand. I thought Molly indicated he was here with me. I recall the conversation I had with her earlier.

"The man who marked you is absolutely fine." And, *"It may take a bit longer in your circumstance since they must have given you drugs as well... The two together knocked you out for longer than is standard."*

Oh no. It can't be true. She couldn't have been talking about...

In horror I come to a sudden realization. I dash to the washroom adjoining the rec room. I rip off the bandage on my neck, wincing as I do so. Looking at my reflection in the mirror I see what I dread more than anything. My heart sinks. This is why I kept feeling something was terribly wrong.

In between my neck and shoulder sits a fresh bite mark.

CHAPTER SEVENTEEN

I've been marked by someone other than Justin, and their mark has cancelled out Justin's original mark. Mike comes up behind me and his arms encircle my waist. I try to pull away from him, but he holds me solidly.

"It's okay." He sighs, speaking softly near my ear. "You're not the first one it's happened to. The guys realize how much money is involved and the temptation is too great. This Justin guy brought you here and I'll be taking you the rest of the way to your new home."

"No!" I struggle against him, but he's too strong and won't let me go. "Justin would never do that to me!" *He wouldn't, would he?*

Mike looks down, then looks at me in the mirror as tears stream down my face. His voice sounds full of sorrow. "But he has."

I start to panic, and I feel short of breath. Mike tries to calm me down. "It's okay. It's okay, Baby. I'll protect you. Nothing bad will happen to you. I'm here. Remember what I said to you about family. The mark strongly binds me to you, and I won't let anyone touch you." Mike speaks with sincerity. "You're safe. Shhh."

I calm down a bit, and try to get my rational mind to kick in, but it won't. All I feel is grief, loss, and like part of me has been ripped away. I may have found the key to the location of my sister, but at what cost? I've traded a piece of my life away for information which may or may not even be useful, now that I'm captive in a real mate transfer.

"Let's sit down on the couch and talk about this." Mike leads me to a couch as Molly bursts through the door from the women's quarters.

"Is everything alright? I thought I heard yelling."

I'm too dazed to say anything. My ears are ringing, and I can barely move my legs.

Mike responds. "Darla's had a bit of a shock. She wasn't aware of the transfer process. She thought the guy who marked her was going to keep her. I wish these guys would be straight up and honest with the girls. They're a bunch of cowards."

Molly looks at me with sympathy in her eyes and sighs. "Poor dear." She helps me to sit, and Mike slides right up against me, his arm around me. It's strangely comforting.

Molly takes my hands in hers. "I know it's hard to accept. It is for everyone at first. But sometimes things aren't in our control, and we can only change those things we have control over."

"It's a mistake. You're both wrong. Justin planned on keeping me. We were planning a life together." *We were, weren't we?*

"But sometimes plans change, Darla. He may have had debts you weren't aware of. How long have you known him? Days? Weeks?"

I shake my head. "That's beside the point. You don't understand the bond we share."

"I do in a way, since I marked you. It amplifies and accelerates your feelings for each other. But now that bond is broken, it won't feel the same for you or for him. He'll move on, no matter what his original intentions with you were.

"The thing about life is that you'll move on, too. It may take a bit of time, but the new marking will help you deal with your grief much more quickly than if you weren't marked at all."

"I don't want to move on." My tears keep pouring out, and both Mike and Molly encircle me in their arms. I feel like Justin is fading away from my life.

"Come on, let's go back inside, and have some tea. I have a type that is soothing."

Although I don't want to accept their version of events, I nod. Molly and I leave Mike in the co-ed rec room and go back to the women's quarters for some tea. She has me sit on the couch in the lower part of the open concept room. She brings the tea over on a tray, and pours me some after it's steeped.

"This tea is similar to chamomile, but with a nicer taste. I find it's much more soothing."

By the time I've finished my cup, I'm feeling drowsy. Molly shifts my legs up on the couch, tucks a soft cushion underneath my head, and covers me with a fluffy blanket. Everything fades away.

After some time, my mind starts drifting back to the present and I hear hushed voices.

"She thought this Justin character was here with her, not realizing he had given her up."

I feel tears prick my eyes. I must be dehydrated—the salt from my tears is irritating me.

"Poor dear."

"Shhh. I think she's waking up."

They know I'm awake, so it's no use pretending to be asleep to hear more of their conversation. Besides, I'm pretty sure they'd be honest with me if I asked them anything. Well, apart from my final destination. They are apparently close-lipped about it. Maybe it's so girls don't react after finding out. Much easier just dropping them off and leaving them to deal with the emotional aftermath on the other side. Or it could be due to security risks.

Think. What things would be security risks? Obviously, getting word to someone on the outside? Wait a sec—I'm still linked to the pack and

as ailouros! *Both links must still be intact. But why can't I sense any of the candles? Is it because of distance? Heck, I don't even know where I am right now.*

I try as hard as I can to feel a connection with any of the candles, but am without any luck. I can't sense them at all. I visualize a circle, and try to send that image out into the infinite universe to show my location. I doubt the image will reach anyone. If Justin at least knows I'm at The Circle it could help. He may have found out more details about its location by now.

That's if he's looking for me. *What if I misjudged him and he decided to accept the money, leaving me in transfer? I'm not the first one it's happened to. Does the bond from the marking fade that quickly? Do I mean anything to him beyond that, now the marking has been taken away?*

I try to reach out through the pride and *ailouros* bonds. I sense nothing. No candles at all. It's distressing. *Does that mean something has happened to all of them? Are they okay? Maybe it's based on geographical distance and everyone is fine?*

Then I have a heart-wrenching thought. *What if my links were dissolved? What if I'm no longer linked to the pack as a member or as ailouros? There must be a way for them to break the pride links.*

Oh my God. What if that's why I can't feel them anymore? Because the bonds no longer exist? Did Justin hand me over in exchange for money?

I feel a warm hand on my shoulder and open my eyes. Molly is crouched down beside me, smiling at me. "You ready to get up? It's time for dinner."

I sit up on the couch, rubbing my eyes. "What did you give me?"

"It's a natural herbal tea recipe that brings about sleep without the 'drugged up' feeling, if you know what I mean."

I definitely know what she means.

"How do you feel?"

"A lot better, thank you. Still a lot of anxiety, but I feel a bit calmer now." I say this, though every time I think of Justin I feel a painful pang in my heart. But just as frequently, Mike pops into my head and I feel a different type of pang.

"Although it's not something we normally do, we've invited Mike for dinner. He has permission to come into the women's quarters under our supervision."

I'm surprised at this, but part of me likes the idea, while another part dislikes it. I feel confused. "Oh, okay."

"We realize you're going through a period of transition, so this might help make these couple days go smoother, before you reach your final destination." I realize they purposely are avoiding using the term "mate", and instead refer to that part of the process as my "destination".

"When will I know what my final destination is?"

"Not until you arrive. Not even Mike knows. Just the pilot and your new handler. And even they don't know the name of your...home you're going to." Again, they're avoiding the word "mate". I know they're trying not to upset me.

I sit at the table with two other women, one from the lobby earlier, and there's a quiet knock on the door to the women's quarters. For some reason my heart leaps. Sally opens the door, and Mike walks in.

He greets Sally, then looks over to us at the table. "Hey."

"Hi, Mike." There's a cordial atmosphere in the room as everyone welcomes him to dinner. He takes a seat next to me as the remaining dishes of food are placed on the table. As we pass the dishes around the

table and serve ourselves, Mike looks at me and smiles. He really does have a beautiful smile and kind eyes.

Dinner is relaxed as we all chat, making small talk with people we'll never see all together in the same room again. Molly is a great cook, and although I'm still somewhat limited with what I can comfortably eat, what I do eat is flavourful with really nice texture.

After dinner we sit around and talk some more while having tea, coffee, and dessert, and Mike helps keep the conversation light and fun. Later we all say goodnight, and I head to bed, surprisingly tired since all I've done is sleep the last couple of days. I fall asleep as soon as my head hits the pillow.

Morning comes with the reminder that I'm another day closer to losing my freedom permanently, if Justin and I are unable to reconnect. *If he's still interested in reconnecting.* All that practice working on developing my skills, and I'm unable to reach him or the rest of the security team through our bonds. It must be because of geographical distance. *Please let it be due to distance and not a severing of the bonds.* If I was asked to pinpoint the country I'm in on a globe, I wouldn't be able to.

Even if I could reach them through the pride bond and knew where I was, I would have no way to communicate that info to them. My pride bonds with Justin aren't as strong, now his marking is gone. *If the pride bonds still exist.* And we couldn't read each other's minds even with the marking. No, the best chance we had of getting through this together was for us to remain together. But somehow we've been separated.

I'm not sure if he was drugged to prevent him from knowing the location of The Circle, or to separate us. Since no one saw Justin arrive, I'm assuming that's when we were separated, before I disembarked the plane.

God, I hope he's okay and no one has hurt him. At the same time, I hope I'm not in denial, if he's exchanged me for money. I try to think back. *Were there any red flags I ignored?*

I get out of bed and ready for the day, whatever it will bring. I walk into the kitchen where Sally is preparing breakfast for us. I feel hungry this morning. I think I can handle eating a regular sized breakfast, now that my stomach is catching up with the rest of me.

"Good morning, Sally."

"Good morning, Darla. How did you sleep last night?"

"I slept well. I've slept so much the last few days that I shouldn't need any more sleep for the rest of the week."

She giggles at my comment. "Help yourself to breakfast."

I smile at her. "Thanks, Sally." She smiles back at me.

"So, when will I know what day I'm scheduled to leave?"

"Once Molly gives Mike the all clear, you'll be free to travel to your new home."

"Any idea of the time frame?"

"Either today or tomorrow. Most likely today." My heart starts racing at the news.

I may only have until tonight before I'm mated with a stranger. Or I could have an indefinite number of days before Justin is cut off from me, completely and permanently. It depends on what plans my new mate has in store, once he's marked me.

I shiver, not knowing what is to come, or if Justin and my bonds will be able to survive it. After breakfast, Molly walks into the kitchen with a stethoscope hanging off her, seeking me out.

"Darla." She smiles at me.

"Good morning, Molly." I smile back at her.

"Would you mind if I took your vitals and gave you a quick exam?"

I reluctantly follow Molly down the office corridor to an examination room. I roll up my sleeve, ready for her to check my blood pressure. I'm hesitant, because I know it's just another step toward what could be a permanent ending for Justin and I.

I don't know the character of the man to mark me at my final destination. He may try to force the actual mating bond between us after marking me, whether by mandating a ceremony without my consent, or otherwise. If he does, it's a permanent bond and can only be broken if one mate dies.

But it's not Molly's fault, and I won't take my frustration out on her. She must sense my anxiety though, since she strokes my back affectionately in between each procedure.

"Everything is looking good, Darla." She smiles at me.

"That's...great." I weakly smile back.

"Have a seat, Darla." We both sit in facing chairs. "I'm going to discharge you today. But before I do, I want you to listen and take these words to heart."

Molly takes my hand in hers and looks directly into my eyes.

"Remember, whatever life throws your way, you will get through it and become stronger because of your experience. With every change comes discomfort, but it will pass. And real love, not lust based on shallow promises of temporary release, conquers all."

I'm deeply touched by Molly's genuine words, and only hope they come true. "Thank you, Molly."

She pats my knee. "Okay, Dear. Let's gather your things together and ready you for what comes next."

I know it might seem strange, but my time at The Circle has been regenerating and empowering. I feel more capable of facing what is to

come. I collect my bag of personal items from home that was left with me at The Circle.

I say goodbye to Sally, Molly, and the other few ladies in the women's quarters. I walk to the co-ed lounge where Mike meets me. He takes my bag and offers me his arm.

Before leaving the compound, a black hood is placed over my head, preventing me from identifying landmarks revealing The Circle's location. Mike takes my hand as we're transported by vehicle to an airstrip. Then together we begin the next step toward the end of my journey.

CHAPTER EIGHTEEN

I feel the deep rumble of the plane as it takes off. Once we're above the clouds, my hood is removed.

"There we go." Mike smiles at me as he brushes stray hairs back from my face. "Now we can see your beautiful face again."

I feel myself blushing at his words. I gaze out the window, at the sea of fluffy clouds beneath us, and endless blue skies light up with the sun's rays. The cloudscape seems to go on forever.

Before I have time to sink into deep thought or reverie, I'm being offered something to eat and drink. As I answer the flight attendant, I can sense Mike's eyes on me. He is very attentive to me as he smiles.

As she walks away, he gives my hand a warm squeeze. "I know that flying isn't your favorite thing. You're doing great, by the way." His voice is encouraging, and I can see smile lines on his face, obviously well used.

I glance backward, and for the first time register several additional passengers. I suspect they're here to ensure I get to my destination.

Mike whispers. "Hey." His eyes are locked with mine now. "Eyes up front. Don't worry about them." He pulls out a pack of cards. I find it very sweet, the way he is attempting to distract me so I feel less anxiety.

We play cards for a while, then I sit back with a magazine. I try to drift off to sleep, but can't. My nerves are on edge, anticipating what comes next.

Time passes quickly and the plane starts dropping out of the sky. My black hood is carefully replaced. With every second of the descent, I feel like a timer is counting down the seconds until my life will be cut short. At least, the life I thought I'd have with Justin.

It's a bit unnerving, descending while blind, but Mike holds my hand the entire time. Soon I feel the "thunk" of the landing gear. I hear the roar as the plane fights its own velocity with its wing flaps, decelerates, and comes to a stop.

Mike unbuckles me, gently helps me into a heavy coat and boots, then takes my hand to assist me out of the plane. I can feel the cold, crisp air as it bites into my fingers, and Mike flips up the hood of my coat before he walks me to a vehicle. We now continue our journey by land.

After driving for an unknown amount of hours, listening to the men in the front conversing in a different language, I begin to feel nauseated. "I think I'm going to be sick." Although I'm under a black hood, I see a wave of green.

I hear Mike's voice speak assertively, switching between English and another language. He gently folds up the edges of the hood so my mouth and nose are uncovered. "Hand me that, quickly." I hear shuffling at the front of the vehicle as something is handed backward to Mike. It rustles in front of me. Then I feel something cool and flexible being held behind my neck.

Although it's cool inside the vehicle, Mike unzips my heavy coat. I have a bad taste in my mouth. "Breathe slowly. In through your nose and out through your mouth." I try breathing as Mike directs me to. The coolness of the air and the plastic behind my neck is keeping things from escalating. No one talks as I try to get my bearings.

After what feels like another hour, but likely much less, Mike zips my coat and the vehicle stops. He slips warm mittens over my hands. He rolls down the black hood to cover my nose and mouth, and flips up the hood of my coat as the doors to the vehicle burst open. What should be an icy blast on my face is muted by the black hood I'm wearing. *I guess every cloud has a silver lining.*

Someone yanks me by the arm, and Mike objects. "Stop. You'll hurt her. I've got her." I hear grumbling as the unknown man slows down and walks beside us. Snow crunches beneath our feet. We walk up some steps—and I feel my feet slipping out from underneath me.

"Eep!" I feel two sets of strong arms grab me from either side. They assist me up several more steps, and I feel like I'm going to be torn in two by the lifting and yanking on my right side in opposition to gentle assistance on my left. I hear Mike growl to my left.

"Gentle with her." Mike sounds exasperated. "Byt' nezhnym." The yanking on the right stops with a grumble. Now I'm merely being pulled along, instead of being pulled apart. At the top of the stairs, the guy on the right lets go of me, and I stumble over what I think is a door frame.

"It's okay. I've got you." Mike stabilizes me.

I can hear people banging their boots on a rug, so I do, too. Mike sits me on what I think is a bench, and removes my boots and mittens. Once the doors have been shut to the outside, he flips down my coat hood, unzips my coat, and helps remove it. I feel cold wetness through my socks from the melting snow on what feels like a smooth, cold marble floor.

I hear men's voices, some rough, others speaking in greeting to each other in a different dialect. I stand still with my hands clasped in front of me, to avoid accidentally slipping on the wet floor or tripping over someone's boots. I hear a man's commanding voice ask a question, again in a foreign language, and everyone hushes. Mike answers in the language.

The first man speaks out with an accent, clearly addressing everyone. "But where are our manners? We must speak English. This is her?"

Mike responds. "Yes. She will need to be released from her marking, after which I'll be on my way. However, once she is released, she may fall into a deep sleep for a day or so."

"Ah, right. I'd forgotten about the after-sleep in my excitement to meet her. I had hoped to spend some time together with her this evening after her marking, but that doesn't seem possible." He sighs.

"Why don't you stay for dinner, Mikael, then be on your way? I can mark her tonight before she sleeps. Until that time I will attempt to get to know her better, as much as your bond with her allows."

I hear Mike's assent, and feel relieved he will be sticking around for dinner. Otherwise, I would feel completely alone. I cling to Mike's arm, trying to position myself so he's between myself and the man speaking.

"Let me see her."

Mike turns to me and addresses me. "Darla, I'm going to remove your hood now. It's okay, just stay still." He gently removes the dark hood, careful not to catch my hair in the process. When I can see again, Mike is standing in front of me.

He takes my hand and rubs his thumb gently over my skin. "Focus on me, okay." He's looking directly into my eyes, and my vision focuses again, after so long under the hood. "You may feel a bit overwhelmed, but it's okay. We're all here to help you adjust."

And Mike is right about feeling overwhelmed. My brain starts to register my surroundings. I gasp. From what I can take in, I'm in a marble entranceway that opens into a rotunda. Water surrounds the circular platform, as do colorful potted flowers. Small marble bridges stretch over the reservoirs of water, connecting the rotunda to various rooms hidden behind double doors.

Rounded spindled marble balconies give glimpses of open circular rooms, both on the bottom floor and one story higher. Everything is off-white marble, except for the walls of the short entranceway which are crackled chocolate brown marble, and the floor pattern, which is rectangular. The rotunda floor itself has an intricate circular pattern made

of varying shades of brown crescent shapes, set against the off-white marble. It creates an overall shape similar to that of a flower.

As I become acquainted with my surroundings, my pulse speeds up, and hope floods my heart. *Could it be...?*

"You ready?" Mike sets his hand on the small of my back. He speaks quietly. "This is your final destination, your new home and your future mate." I know my eyes must be huge, trying to take everything in. Mike watches me and gives my shoulder a reassuring squeeze. I walk around Mike as he moves out of the way, to get the first glimpse of my future mate.

I gasp as I study the man who addresses me with a thick accent. "Hello?" He takes a tentative step toward me. He looks worried he'll frighten me and I'll scurry off like a scared little animal.

The man stands regally before me, but with concern etched on his face. He has defined cheekbones with chiseled features and piercing blue eyes, thick, dark eye-lashes, and brown stubble on his face. His loose dark blond hair, all one length, stops part-way down his neck. It's long enough to be tied back. He speaks to me with questioning lips.

"Darla, is it?" I nod. "Welcome. I hope you will feel at home here." Although he's a few steps away from me, he holds out his hand to me.

I hear a growl from behind me. "I apologize, Your Highness, that's not a good idea until the marking is overwritten."

The man nods at Mike, then drops his arm back to his side. He looks at me and gives me a cautious smile. "Please call me Vaughn."

I muster up my courage, and continue to see things through. Things may have gone terribly wrong, but at the same time they may have gone terribly right. I would have to weigh the cost later. I look up at him. "Hello, Vaughn."

My acknowledgement of him causes his face to light up, and he gives me a genuine smile, causing the corners of his eyes to crinkle. His expression triggers me to return his smile with a heartfelt one. I'm in a strange country with people unbeknownst to me, but because of Vaughn I feel at ease. My anxiety level drops and I feel at peace. However, my sense of peace is short-lived.

Suddenly, I hear a bang to the left behind Vaughn, as the double doors are flung back and another man and woman enter the rotunda. Vaughn glances backward and I follow his gaze. The man who has just entered has short blonde hair, but otherwise looks like a copy of Vaughn. However, he carries himself differently, full of self-importance. His eyes are calculating. He hasn't offered his arm to the young woman beside him, and she seems to be struggling to keep up with his stride.

But once they come closer, my focus is no longer on the younger version of my future mate. My attention switches to the beauty by his side, dressed in an emerald green gown. I sense a grim sadness from her. She looks detached from the world around her and has a stoic countenance—until she sees me. She stops in her tracks, her eyes open wide, unable to hide the shock on her face. She gasps and puts a white gloved hand to her lips.

I step forward, my voice in a strangled whisper. "Natalie."

CHAPTER NINETEEN

My sister removes her hand from her mouth, glances at the man beside her, and attempts to smooth her face so it's expressionless. By the time the man beside her glances backward at her, all evidence of her reaction has disappeared.

Vaughn introduces us. "Waylan, this is Darla. Darla, Waylan. And you and Natalia are well acquainted with each other, I'm guessing." Vaughn smiles and winks at me. "The resemblance is remarkable."

I attempt to be friendly without going overboard, but inside I'm bursting at the seams at the sight of Natalie. "Hello, Waylan, Natalie." Waylan gives me a cursory nod as does Natalie, and she maintains her stoic mask without moving toward me. That's when I know something is terribly wrong.

So this is Prince Waylan. I know he is a prince, due to the document I read in the Records Room back at The Circle. *And from Mike's initial address to him, and the way he carries himself, it looks like Vaughn is king.*

Vaughn has one of his men take my small bag of belongings to my room. Mike escorts me behind the man, through a set of double doors to the right, then up three floors.

"I'm off to the guest wing, but will be back to collect you for dinner in an hour." Mike smiles at me then follows the king's man down a corridor.

I have just enough time to take a shower and prepare for dinner. As I walk around in my towel, I realize I have no idea what to wear, since my overnight bag contains just the basics. I'm unsure what to do, then check the closet in case they've left something for me to wear to dinner.

I open the walk-in closet and discover it's full of formal wear, semi-formal wear, and semi-casual attire. I select a cherry red sequined gown, assuming my sister is wearing her emerald gown to dinner. I'm guessing dinners are a formal affair around here.

I quickly apply some light makeup, rouge, and cherry red lip stain from the vanity. After blow-drying sections of my hair and curling them, I remove my clip and my hair pours in curls that frame my face. I find a pair of sparkly, black strappy heels with bows on the sides and slip them on. I touch up my red toenail polish in a few places, and am ready to go. A few minutes later I hear a knock on the door.

I open the door and Mike stands there, dressed up for dinner. He's rooted to the spot, staring at me. "You look amazing, Darla." His smile is appreciative, and he holds out his arm for me to take. This time, we walk down a different set of stairs, which brings us to an ornate lounge where we join the others.

As soon as we walk into the room, there is a hush as the others stand to welcome us. I see appreciation and open admiration on Vaughn's face as he looks at me. I can tell he has to hold himself back to not approach me, and instead gestures for Mike and I to be seated on one of the couches together. One of the staff comes by with drinks for us, which we take willingly.

Although I wish I could get Natalie alone with me to talk, between Vaughn, Mike, and Waylan's attentions toward the two of us, it proves to be impossible. I have a feeling I won't have a moment this evening to approach her alone, so I just go with the flow.

Natalie continues to act reserved, with limited emotional range. She always was more introspective than me, but not to this extent. I can see from her eyes she's wary. Instead of "fight or flight", she's using another survival tactic. She's "playing dead."

Although I see her plight for survival, I haven't been able to pinpoint the threat yet. I'm still trying to get my bearings and adjust, while following the social norms required in the presence of royalty. As a result, any undercurrents go unnoticed by me.

Dinner is announced, and we are welcomed into the dining room. Vaughn takes his place at the head of the table, I am to his right, and my sister to his left. Mike is beside me, as Waylan is beside Natalie.

Utmost respect is paid to Vaughn by his staff, while Waylan seems to jostle in competition with his brother for attention throughout dinner. The staff is naturally respectful of Vaughn, but Waylan seems to demand respect, which makes people reluctant to give it to him. Of course I may be wrong about that, as I am a newcomer, after all. However, I get the sense the staff pays respect to Waylan out of obligation rather than as an intrinsic form of honor.

Although Vaughn has an intensity about him, he is still able to relax and enjoy humor in a situation. However, Waylan never seems to let down his guard, even in times of silence. Waylan's posture is rigid, his jaw tense, whereas Vaughn has an easy way about him, and is warm and welcoming toward others. The conversation turns toward that of the current predicament we are all in.

"Well, after Waylan went through his connections to recruit a mate, I realized how difficult it has been, finding time to recruit new blood to our society, having both time and geographical limitations. Unfortunately, time is always an issue because of my duties to my people, and geographically, we are isolated from other large cats."

My attention perks up at the mention of cats. "So your species then— you are cats."

"Yes, our clan shifts into tigers and snow leopards."

"And you are needing an *ailouros*."

"Exactly." Vaughn looks pleased I am familiar with the term. "As those in the shifter community know, humans make the best *lunas.*"

"Then why not choose one of the many human women in the region? Why go through the difficulty and costs of obtaining an *ailouros* this way?" I'm curious to understand his way of thought.

"Well, for a few reasons. One being it's difficult to enter into a relationship with just any woman, not knowing if her interest in me is due to my power and wealth. Also, how would I explain the shifter aspect of our community to her without her frightening and running off to tell others?"

"We've had to kill to protect our community." Waylan says this as though it is just a statement of fact.

Vaughn looks saddened by this necessity. "Unfortunately, previous generations in particular clamped down to the point where they eliminated even rumors of shifters. It meant that a lot of humans died, their only crime being mentioning they suspected we exist."

"A necessary evil, Brother." Waylan waved it off as if it wasn't of importance.

"From my perspective, it moves us on the spectrum from 'compassionate' to 'heartless'."

Waylan argues. "Sometimes one needs to be heartless to rule with good decision-making."

Vaughn counters. "Being heartless removes one's worthiness to make those decisions."

"I'm sure we'll continue to disagree with each other, as we always have." Both brothers lock gazes. Finally, Waylan looks away.

Vaughn continues. "Back to the subject at hand, having someone already acquainted with the shifter community saves a whole lot of

difficulty. There's less explanation, an easier and quicker adaptation to the role, and certain expectations."

"I see."

"And besides." I'm surprised to see Vaughn blushing, as he scratches the nape of his neck and looks down at his dinner plate. "When I saw the beauty Waylan brought home, I asked him to request the same one for me. How is it said? Same characteristics?" Through the corner of my eye, I see Natalie blush.

I mutter to myself under my voice. "Like mail-order brides."

Vaughn's eyes twinkle with humor. "I guess you could say that." It's my turn to blush. *I forgot about their sensitive hearing.*

I address Waylan. "So you put the exact same order in and received me?"

"Yes, and having two beauties around the palace makes things a lot more exciting." Waylan is very direct, and openly eyes me with lust. I feel uncomfortable under his gaze, which I believe should be reserved for his mate, my sister. I appreciate Mike's growl, as his reaction confirms I'm not just imagining things.

The staff clears our dishes away and serves us tea, coffee, and dessert. I look across the table at Natalie then at Waylan. I'm not sure how to approach the next subject.

"So...are you two mated yet?"

Waylan answers me. "Once Vaughn decided to get his own mate, he suggested that we wait and do a double mating ceremony. Less trips for family overseas, and a bigger afterparty." He smirks as though it's an inside joke.

His brother eyes him with skepticism. "Bigger celebration before, you mean. Afterparties are restricted to two people. I want all the privacy with my new mate I can get."

I begin to blush at the thought of us being alone after the ceremony. My heart is being pulled three ways. It has pangs for Justin, yearns for Mike, and is attracted to the charismatic man in front of me.

My mind plays tricks on me. *Is Justin okay after what happened on the plane? Will he just take the money and not look for me, leaving me to my fate?* I start to doubt my own heart. *Maybe he didn't care about me the same way I cared about him? What if the injection was fatal?*

Thinking about Justin causes me pain, and that's not going to help me in my present situation. He is a variable I cannot control, so I can't focus on him. I need to focus on the current factors, talk to my sister, then formulate an escape plan to get us both out safely. *If that's what she wants.*

My first impression of Waylan is neutral. He seems a bit self-absorbed. He also seems to be distant and cold toward my sister, which is odd considering the marking. However, I'm going to give him the benefit of the doubt out of fairness. First impressions aren't everything.

For all I know, they may have had a lovers' spat right before I arrived. There may be more than meets the eye. I need to get her alone and secure so she can tell me how she feels, from the heart.

"Well, you ladies can plan the celebration together however you'd like it—sparing no expense." Vaughn smiles at me, gazing into my eyes affectionately. He nearly takes my hands in his, until he remembers Mike and the marking.

The cappuccino ice cream with chocolate rivulets is heavenly and melts on my tongue. I slowly savor the taste and coolness of it in my mouth, only partially listening, as all my senses drown in an oblivion of bliss. It's a taste of heaven.

The men throw out ideas for the mating ceremony for Natalie and myself to think about. Natalie answers questions showing no emotion,

and she is almost robotic with her responses. I am saddened that she is troubled and I'm unable to help her...yet.

Planning a double ceremony with my sister should be one of our most precious experiences together, a dream come true. But the problem is we have the wrong grooms. Fate has swapped out my perfect mate or husband for another. Although Vaughn seems genuinely kind and is regal and refined, a perfect male specimen, he's not Justin.

I really need to get Natalie alone and find out her feelings for Waylan. Whether she wishes to stay or leave him, I'll honor her wishes. It will break my heart if she wants to stay though, when I'm ready to bolt.

After dessert, I ask if Natalie can show me the ladies' room. The two of us walk toward the powder room, as we listen to the appreciative murmurs behind us. "...absolutely gorgeous. How could anyone let either of them go?"

The two of us walk in silence until we reach the restroom. As I open the door, I see it's similar in style to a ladies' dressing room. We walk in.

As soon as the door closes, I throw my arms around Natalie. "Oh, why didn't you call me? I was so worried!" Natalie's body feels rigid, but softens as I hold her close to me.

"You seem stressed." I step back a bit, searching her eyes. They no longer have the same liveliness they once had. "What's wrong?" I gesture to the plush stools set up before the wall-length mirror and vanities. She tentatively sits, a resigned look on her face.

I crouch in front of her and hold her hands in mine. "Please tell me your feelings in all of this. Are you happy? Do you wish to be mated to Waylan?"

"I don't seem to have a choice, do I?" I detect a note of bitterness in her voice.

"Say the word, and I will do everything in my power to get you out of this."

I see the faintest glimmer of hope in her eyes. Then her expression changes. "I won't leave, but I can't say more here. Anyone could be listening."

That's when I realize there's much more going on than meets the eye. I pull her into a close hug. "I've missed you so much, Nat. I'm just glad to be here with you."

Natalie responds by awkwardly placing her arms around me. I don't like her hesitation to speak her mind or her reluctance to show her feelings. She seems to have withdrawn internally and is scared to express herself.

"It's okay. I'm here with you." I brush a few loose strands of hair behind her ear, and smile at her. Her eyes don't seem responsive, and instead she is closed off. I wish I knew the cause so we could work things out. But for now, I'll have to go along with things. I'm thankful the men haven't insisted on an immediate mating ceremony. That gives me some time to figure this whole situation out.

There's a knock on the door. The door opens. It's one of the staff. "Ladies, are you ready?"

"Almost!" I call out, hopefully buying us a couple more minutes. It's odd they would check on us.

I put my arm around Natalie protectively as we walk out of the washroom. The staff member directs us to the lounge. As we enter the lounge together, Vaughn's eyes brighten and he smiles. Waylan just smirks as he sees my arm around Natalie, as if he finds something amusing. Mike has a resigned look on his face, and a look of longing. All three men rise, and we are then seated on the white and gold brocaded satin-covered couches.

Once we are seated, Vaughn brings up the evening's dreaded conversation. "Mikael, it's time to conclude our business. Thank you for taking such good care of my mate. I will be adding in an extra bonus for you, as I'm very pleased." He looks over at Waylan and Natalie. "Mikael, Darla, let's retire to another room for the evening. We bid you goodnight, Waylan and Natalia." I see a sparkle in Nat's eyes as Vaughn calls her by his unique name for her.

We walk upstairs, to a section of the palace that looks familiar, where Vaughn's rooms are. We enter his sitting room, the outer room attached to his bedroom. I feel a bit alarmed, and Vaughn must sense that.

"Darla, once the marking takes effect, someone needs to watch you until you awake to make sure you are okay. Once I've marked you, I won't be able to leave your side until I know you're alright. It's in my nature. I've brought you to my rooms which are also attached to your bedroom.

"Mikael, we'll talk afterward."

"Sure. Sounds good. Darla, it was an honor to protect you during the transfer. I must leave the room for this next part." He hesitates. "Take care, Darla."

"Thank you, Mike, for your protection."

Mike closes the door softly as he leaves Vaughn and I alone.

"Darla, are you ready? This will be quick, so as not to irritate Mikael's wolf."

Am I ready? How do I answer that? What kind of life will I wake up to?

I reluctantly nod.

Vaughn quickly scoops me onto his lap. A second later, I feel a stinging sensation by the side of my neck, then I'm out like a light.

CHAPTER TWENTY

I wake up to the singing of birds, but don't see the sunlight streaming in. Then I realize the navy blue and gold curtains have been pulled around the side of the canopy bed that is facing the window. Vaughn was thoughtful enough to block the sun so I wouldn't have a harsh awakening.

I sit up, noting the curtains are open on the other side, and I see Vaughn in a chair facing the bed. His arms are crossed and I can tell he's been nodding off, by the way his head jerks up at the sound of my sheets rustling. He gives me a sleepy smile and walks over to the bed, sitting on the side. For some reason it reminds me of being in a blanket fort, and I giggle. He slides closer to me, and kisses my forehead.

"Good morning, Sunshine." He casually slides his arm around me as we lean back against the headboard together. "You look beautiful today."

I look up at him doubtfully. "That must be the marking talking."

"No. Ever since I first saw you, even after hours of travelling, I've thought you had an indescribable beauty. You are truly breathtaking, Darla."

He takes me in his arms and I squirm a bit. He pulls me more tightly to him so I can't move. My face is squished up against him. "I can't breathe." He laughs, kisses me on the top of my head, and loosens his grip on me.

He looks at me sincerely. "Darla, I'm so happy I have you. I'm going to treat you like the queen you are."

Once I'm up for the day, Vaughn leaves and some house staff help me to get ready for brunch. It seems my body needs less time to recover than last time—at least this time I hadn't been drugged as well as marked.

I glide into the dining room, where Vaughn stands to greet me with a kiss on the cheek, and pulls out my chair. His face is beaming, and his smile bewitching. My heart flutters a bit, and I feel drawn to him. The marking is already taking effect. I'm seated opposite Waylan, as he sits between Natalie and Vaughn. Vaughn, of course, is seated at the head of the table. We are served brunch immediately by the house staff.

"So now that you're here and settling in, Darla, we have a special announcement for the two of you ladies. Tomorrow night we are throwing a ball in your honor. All the leaders from the prides in Primorye have been invited to attend, to introduce them to both their future queen and their future princess."

Wait...did he say "queen"? I thought he meant it figuratively earlier!

"Qu-queen?" I place my cutlery back down on my plate. *I guess I never connected the idea of being queen to Vaughn being a king. My mind must have discounted the idea because my heart belongs to Justin.*

"Yes. I tend to be informal when it's just family around, but I am responsible for all the prides in Primorsky Krai. I oversee their well-being and work together with the leadership to find solutions to any major difficulties that may arise."

"What will my duties be?"

"The queen's position is *prime ailouros*. It involves the regular duties of an *ailouros* plus arrangement of charitable functions for the betterment of the shifter community. The princess can assist you with these duties. It's ideal now that we have the two of you here. Our area has needed you for some time."

I nod my head with understanding. The shifter community as a whole needs the nurturing side of leadership. This vital piece seems to be lacking globally, since the male birth rate is extremely high.

My mind wanders. *I wonder why there are so few girls born into the shifter community?* It's an important question that I intend to ask at some point. However, right now I am focusing on Vaughn's words.

"At the ball, you'll be introduced to the leaders you will be working with in the future. The ball will have a similar atmosphere to future events and introduce you to some traditions of our country."

There is an event organizer looking after the ball, so Natalie and I don't need to focus on anything besides getting ourselves ready. And there will be staff to assist us with that tomorrow. So I don't feel too stressed about it, although Natalie, with her shyness, may.

During the afternoon I am taken to Natalie's dressing room, where staff has multiple gowns ready for us to try on. They help us select dresses for the ball, measuring and pinning anything that needs to be altered. Although we are together for the afternoon, there is such a flurry of activity we are unable to hold a proper conversation.

Dinner is the same that way, as Natalie and I aren't able to get in a private conversation with the men around, so I hope to have some time with her during the evening. I need to know if she's really okay.

Obviously, her material needs are being looked after, but what about her emotional needs? Is she happy here?

I sense she's struggling with something. I'm here until I know what and if she truly wants to stay or leave. Until that time, I will continue in my role.

After dinner, the four of us walk in the gardens, Natalie with Waylan, and Vaughn with myself. Vaughn is a good conversationalist, and very interesting to talk with, but my mind isn't fully on him. It's on Natalie.

We sit down on an elaborate stone bench by an ornate fountain. "You seem distracted, Darla." Vaughn gently takes my hands in his.

I was hoping he wouldn't notice, but I decide to be honest with him. "I'm just concerned about Natalie. I haven't had the opportunity to talk with her, and she's so much more reserved than she usually is."

"I've noticed that myself."

I'm surprised. "You have?"

"When she first arrived she was more vibrant, but as days have gone by, her eyes seem to have clouded over. I've actually been wondering if I should have a talk with Waylan, although he's not that forthcoming these days. It would be good for you to talk with your sister to see what's troubling her."

I feel relief, and my respect for Vaughn has gone up a notch. He seems to genuinely care for my sister, and he is not blind to her emotions. "Thank you for understanding, Vaughn. I really appreciate that you care so much."

Vaughn looks surprised. "Of course I care. You girls are family now. Family is precious and I don't take it for granted. In a split second, anyone could be taken away."

Seeing Vaughn's expression when he mentions losing family, I'm about to ask him about it, but instead he stands up and offers me his hand. We continue along the garden path until we catch up with Natalie and Waylan by another garden entrance.

"Well, I think we'll retire for the night. Waylan. Natalia." Vaughn gives them both a nod. I find it cute, the way Vaughn says Nat's name, and the way she responds to it. Her facial expression always tends to light up when he addresses her.

I give Natalie a hug. "Goodnight, Nat." I whisper in her ear. "We'll talk tomorrow." She nods, and Vaughn offers me an arm.

We walk inside and upstairs. Vaughn opens a familiar door and we walk into the sitting room where I was marked by him. I now notice there

are two closed doors, one on either side of the room. There is a loveseat behind a coffee table, which is flanked by two chairs. Vaughn leads me to the loveseat and we sit down together. A tray of tea has been set out on the coffee table, and Vaughn pours the tea for us.

"Darla, I want to know everything about you, your likes, your dislikes, what makes you tick." He smiles at me tenderly. It gives me a warm feeling inside.

"You are very kind-hearted, Vaughn. I can tell already, just by what I've observed of you." He touches my cheek with his hand and my eyes close as I lean into it.

He pulls me close to him, and leans his forehead against mine. He whispers. "I'm so happy you're here."

We stay like that for a minute, drinking in each other's scents. It feels intoxicating. Then I remember it's because of the marking and try to snap out of it.

I'm here for my sister, then I need to find my way back to Justin. But what if Justin no longer wants me? What if he's no longer alive? The thoughts sober me. *If he's gone, or no longer wants me, maybe fate has dealt me another chance at life with a caring, attentive mate?*

Waves of guilt wash over me for having such thoughts. My mind feels confused, and I'm sure the marking is messing with my mind. It's difficult to keep my thoughts straight when I'm this close to Vaughn.

I interrupt the moment by reaching for my teacup and take a sip. I'm surprised by what I taste. "Oh, Vaughn, this tea is so flavorful. It's really nice."

He smiles as he reaches for his own cup. "It's my favorite. We have it sent from Europe by way of the Trans-Siberian Railway."

"By the way, thank you for being so welcoming and so generous. It's not every day someone holds a ball in honor of my sister and me." I smile demurely as I set my teacup back on the coffee table.

"You and your sister deserve every honor we can bestow on you. You will both be a blessing to our realm. And you are already a blessing to me, personally." He turns slightly toward me and puts his arm around me. I can't help but rest my head on his shoulder.

We sit there in comfortable silence, and I feel myself drifting off. I'm too cozy to move. Some time later I feel myself become weightless, and hear a door open. I feel myself lying on something incredibly soft. My hair is smoothed from my face and I lean into the hand stroking my cheek.

I feel a kiss on my forehead. "Sleep well, my queen."

In the morning, I wake up in my bed, and catch one of the house staff quietly setting out my clothes for the morning. "Good morning."

"Oh, good morning!" I hear a slight accent in her response as she smiles and curtseys. "Breakfast will be in half an hour. I will make sure someone comes up and gets you at that time."

"Thank you." I smile back at her, then pull myself out of bed.

"I hope you don't mind, but I removed your evening clothes last night so you'd have a more comfortable sleep."

I look down and realize I'm in my slip. "Oh, that's fine. Thank you for doing that. I must have fallen asleep in the sitting room."

"It's right next door. In between both of your bed chambers." She smiles and winks as she collects the linens.

"You mean mine and Vaughn's?"

"Mmhmm." She has a cute, quirky smile on her face. "I'll be off now." She curtseys again before leaving my bedroom.

I get ready for the morning, and one of the staff guides me to the dining room, where I run into Nat. Both Natalie and myself are in floral dresses; mine is yellow and hers is soft pink. Vaughn welcomes us, and pulls out each of our chairs to seat us.

Waylan arrives a minute late. He smiles and comments, "You girls look like a dream." Nat and I both smile at the compliment.

We settle down for a nice breakfast, and chat about the upcoming ball. Vaughn decides to regale us with amusing stories of past balls, and has us all laughing. Natalie seems to be hanging on his every word.

At one point, Waylan asks her something. I think he does it more so to get her attention. Although he seems to be enjoying himself, and has loosened up more than I've ever seen him, I see a flash of resentment as he looks at his brother.

Maybe it's because his brother naturally holds the attention of a room. Vaughn does exude a regal and charismatic aura. It must be difficult to live in his shadow, especially for someone with Waylan's temperament.

"So before things start to get busy, I was thinking the two of you ladies may want to spend some time together in the conservatory this morning." I smile at Vaughn, thankful for his sensitivity and his caring nature.

We say goodbye to the men, and make our way out of the dining room. Since Natalie already knows the way, the two of us walk down the corridor together. As we get closer, we're greeted with the sound of trickling water.

The conservatory is surrounded by a concave array of windows, embellished with jade metal. The metal is bent in such a way that it reminds me of the shape of the stained glass windows of a quaint little

church in the town where we grew up. The glass ceiling is domed, focused around a central point from which a floral chandelier has been hung.

Champagne roses and ivy adorn the windows, giving the room an atmosphere similar to a garden. A stone fountain in the middle of the room contributes to the tranquil atmosphere, its steady stream of water adding naturally to the serene ambiance. Combined, the flowery spring inside and the snowy winter landscape outside impart a sense of peacefulness.

Natalie and I sit on one of the comfortable cream colored couches, facing each other. It seems that neither of us knows where to begin. I encourage Natalie to go first. She isn't as forthcoming at the start, but as she tells her story, she becomes more open.

"I know it's a ridiculous sounding story, and I understand if you don't believe me, Darla." I can sense Natalie withdrawing into herself.

"Not at all, Nat. I'm sure my experience was somewhat similar to yours. That's how I ended up here, remember?" I neglect to tell her about Justin, trying to keep the focus on her as she shares her experiences. It wouldn't do to have her worry about my own predicament.

When she's finished sharing, I feel compelled to ask her the question that's been on my mind since I first saw her with Waylan in the rotunda. "Natalie, I have to ask you something. Are you happy here?" I look over at Nat, and her hands are busy smoothing her dress absentmindedly. She seems to be avoiding eye contact with me. "It's okay. Just be honest with me."

"What if I told you that I'm happy here, but I'm unhappy..." she mouths the next two words without using her voice, "...with Waylan?" It's an answer I didn't expect to hear.

She directs her eyes up and at the floral chandelier. "Isn't the chandelier gorgeous, though?" I'm startled by the sudden change in topic,

but I look up at the chandelier. I squint my eyes and then I clue in to what she's directing me to look at. Above us I can see a security camera, discreetly placed in the chandelier.

I realize then, that we don't really have room to speak freely. We are in effect, living inside a gilded cage. I would hope, based on my pleasant experience so far at the palace, that we are in a safe environment.

Then I realize attitudes could change very quickly if it was suspected that we were thinking of leaving our mates. I really don't know how Waylan and Vaughn or even others would react. From that time on in our conversation, we mouth certain words, while speaking others.

"Do you want to leave?"

"No. Yes. I mean I don't know. I really love it here, but I don't like the idea of being mated to Waylan." This makes things more complicated than I thought. Her desire to stay seems to outweigh any desire to leave, but it's not because of her future mate.

"What can I do to help you?"

Natalie seems reluctant to talk about it. It's as if she feels she needs to walk on eggshells around me. That's odd, since she's never been afraid to share her true feelings with me before, just shy about boy talk. I wonder if she's afraid of being honest in general or just about this one subject regarding leaving. I get the sense she's holding something back.

"Right now, there's nothing you can do to help me, Darla." It's at that point I realize I'll be here for a while. There's no way I can leave my sister alone with her troubles. *She's going through inner conflict, related to her surroundings. When she's ready to talk, I need to be here for her.* I feel like I'm in limbo again.

CHAPTER TWENTY-ONE

The afternoon goes by in a flurry, and before I know it, I'm dressed in my beautiful gown, ready to go. The first layer of my dress is a soft, satiny cream material covered with a pattern of coral roses. The top layer is a thin creamy lace overlay, also with roses. The two materials of different textures together give the roses a soft glow and almost a three dimensional appearance.

The bodice has the lace sewn into it, is defined and has been fitted, thanks to the work of the seamstress. Both layers hang freely, flowing outward from my waist. The small train adds to the formality of the dress. My hair is in a half updo, with fresh coral roses adorning the back, right above where my dark hair falls into ringlets.

Natalie's dress is aqua satin, with a fitted bodice extending into a drop A-line waist, decorated with zirconias. Her updo is laced with tiny gems that shimmer like diamonds whenever she moves. She looks absolutely stunning. It's amazing how well our dresses fit our moods today. Mine is more free-flowing and fairy-like, whereas Natalie's is more formal but with a sparkle.

When it's time, we're walked to the head of the grand staircase. As we stand at the top, I look down and see Vaughn and Waylan in their royal uniforms. Vaughn is looking at me with an openly rapt expression, with real joy in his eyes. Waylan glances back and forth between Natalie and I.

I focus on Vaughn as we are announced and are cued to descend the staircase. I feel myself beaming from the inside as I walk toward him. He takes my hand when I reach the bottom, and with a slight bow, he brings it to his lips, brushing the back of my hand. I feel entranced.

Vaughn stays by my side all evening, making necessary introductions, but otherwise he is attentive to my every need. We dance the night away, as though we are the only two people in the room. When I can, I check on my sister, glancing her way. One time, I notice she has an almost bitter expression on her face as she looks at us, not realizing I can see her. *Is that because she is sensing something is missing between her and Waylan?*

But I'm so wrapped up in the enjoyment, spending time with Vaughn on this fairytale evening, that I savor every moment we have together. It's difficult, reminding myself the marking is responsible for the escalating feelings between Vaughn and I. However, I find I need to do so.

Guilt tugs at me as I think about both Justin and Vaughn. Feeling drawn to Vaughn makes me feel guilty, even though the marking is what's driving our attraction. On the other hand, leaving would hurt him and he may chase after me. Who knows what the political aftermath would be— *could it start a war between our prides?*

Plus, Natalie being unhappy yet unwilling to leave, seals my fate. I need to stay in order to protect her. As her big sister, I need to look out for her.

But do I need to sacrifice my own happiness to keep her safe?

And that's when I realize I could have just as happy a life with Vaughn as I could with Justin. They are both so similar—stable, reliable, and level-headed men. Both of them are kind, noble, and exhibit solid leadership. It's as if they had the same upbringing and training.

But Justin has lost so much in his life. He lost his first mate, although I don't know the whole story there. If he lost me, too, it might drive him back into depression and isolation.

No, I have to figure out a way to deal with my dilemma. I wish someone else held the answers for me. The more time I spend with

Vaughn, the more difficult it will be to break things off with him because of the effects of the marking.

Justin would understand my dilemma, because he was part of the original plan and knew the risks involved. He would assume that by now I'd be marked by someone else at my final destination. That's if he is alive and well. *But does he still want me?*

The last thing I remember is Justin falling to the ground, after being injected with something. I pray it wasn't a permanently incapacitating drug and that he is safe. For all I know, he could be locked up in a cell somewhere, or even worse.

The motive behind it may not even be related to the mate issue. It could be due to inter-pack relations or because of a business rival. But I have an inkling that he was attacked because of the mate transfer. Maybe someone made a deal behind his back.

Again, it all comes down to money, power, and I guess I'd have to add in mates as well. *Money, power, and women. One or more of those things might have motivated the attack on Justin. I'm just not sure how it all fits together.*

"What are you thinking of, Dearest?" Vaughn looks down at me with concern in his eyes. "You seemed to be far away just now."

"I was thinking about those I care about, hoping they are safe, and wishing the best for them in the future."

"Do you want to talk about it?" He holds me as we dance, his chin over my head.

"I think the most pressing concern is with my sister. I'm worried about her." I'm not about to mention anything about my plans to have her leave with me if she's unhappy.

"I would discuss it with Waylan, but he's becoming more and more difficult to reach. If only our cousin was here, he could talk some sense

into him. Waylan looks up to him and respects him. However, Waylan's resentment toward me keeps on building. I'm afraid he wouldn't listen to me. If the opportunity arises though, I'll try my best."

"Thank you for your concern for my sister." I can feel my eyes are glassy with emotion and gratitude.

"Anything that concerns you, concerns me, Darla." He kisses my cheek softly.

I wish I could share with Vaughn the predicament I'm in. He's so easy to talk to, and the one person I feel I could trust for good, solid advice. But I can't, because what am I going to say? *"I already have a mate, I'm here to see if my sister is okay, and to steal her away if she isn't."*

No, sharing this with Vaughn is not an option.

It's difficult to keep it from him, though, because he's so caring. I know he can still sense I feel troubled, and just wants to comfort me. I'm afraid if the truth came out he would react in anger, both because of loss and feeling "played". I sigh.

"I know you have a lot on your mind, but let's try to just enjoy these precious moments together." Vaughn takes me aside as the music transitions from one song to another. I lean into his side as we walk to the terrace, where we see the stars in the clear, black sky.

"It is beautiful out here."

"It is, especially when I have such a beauty with me." He looks down at me and smiles affectionately. He gives my cheek the lightest, tender pinch, as if he's just stroking me. I can tell by his gesture he's trying to draw my lips up into a smile.

He's successful and I smile up at him. He takes me in his arms and we dance, swaying gently on the balcony, under the beautiful night sky. I relax into his body and we both let our cares just float away.

Eventually, we move back inside, and I spy my sister alone. I gesture to Vaughn, and we both walk over to where she's standing.

"Would you ladies like a glass of champagne?" Vaughn is the perfect gentleman, paying us equal attention. I see Natalie's eyes light up.

"Yes, please." Nat assents and I nod. Vaughn moves off into the crowd to get us drinks.

"Wow, the way your face just lit up, you must be desperately craving a drink!" I tease her. Nat blushes and looks at me guiltily, but doesn't quite meet my eyes.

"He left you alone here, didn't he? Waylan." I sense Natalie is just happy to have a bit of company.

"He's been gone for quite a while, spending time with that woman in the corner."

I look in the direction her eyes are facing, and see a woman with auburn hair, quietly talking with Waylan in the shadows. I sense a strange aura surrounding her, and I wonder if she's a shifter, or maybe something else? I question if it's just me or if others can sense it. The two of them seem secretive, from their furtive glances around the room.

"It's odd how he wouldn't introduce me to her. I've been feeling a little stressed, while standing here alone."

"Hmm. Because of the ball? Or other stuff?"

"Both." I'm glad she's opening up a bit more, but don't want to push too far.

"So, what's Waylan like tonight?" I notice Natalie tenses with my question. "If you're comfortable talking about it."

Waylan finally notices us glancing over at him, dismisses the woman, and confidently makes his way toward us with a smile.

Nat whispers to me. "We'll talk later." I nod at Natalie, looking over at her, squeezing her hand.

"I'm here for you, okay?"

I see the tension leave her body. "Thanks, Darla. That means a lot to me." She gives me a genuine smile and we hug.

"Ah, our two lovely honored ladies." Waylan steps before me and kisses my hand with a light bow, then moves in between Natalie and myself. He places his arm around Natalie, and attempts to do the same with me. I quickly sidestep away from him and turn. It just looks like I'm repositioning myself for conversation with him.

"Thank you, Waylan." I smile at him. "So, tell me about yourself. We haven't had a lot of opportunity to just get to know each other." Natalie seems relieved I'm making conversation with him.

Waylan smiles appreciatively. "What would you like to know?"

"Oh, hobbies, things you enjoy, embarrassing stories. That kind of thing."

Waylan's smile becomes one of amusement. "Embarrassing stories, huh? Let me think." He pauses, looking upward. "Oh, here's one about Vaughn."

Natalie looks eager to hear what he has to say. "Well, when Vaughn was a cub, he accidentally shifted inside a barrel when we were playing hide-and-seek. Not only did the barrel lid fly off so he was discovered, but he got stuck, and had a barrel stuck over his bottom half. He pulled himself around with his front legs until someone was able to tap one of the staves out of the barrel rings."

Both Nat and I laugh at the idea of a small, regal Vaughn pulling himself around in a barrel.

"What's all the amusement about? I thought I heard my name." Vaughn gently hands us our drinks as he returns.

"Oh, Waylan was just sharing an embarrassing story about you." I smile.

Vaughn laughs in an easygoing way. "About when we were cubs? We had a lot of fun, didn't we, Waylan?"

Waylan looks down for a minute, smiling. "Yeah, we did." When he glances up again I see a look of regret flash over his face.

"He was telling us the story about when you got stuck in a barrel."

Vaughn chuckles. "Yeah, I wanted to put wheels on the thing and have some fun. But someone grabbed a hammer and tapped it apart before we had the chance to figure out how to do it."

Natalie and I laugh at the image. "It must have been so much fun, growing up like that."

"Yeah, we'd play with our cousins for hours, getting into all kinds of mischief. Of course, we were all boys, since girls are rare with shifter parents."

"Well, Darla and I grew up doing more 'girly' things, but Darla had her moments." Natalie giggled.

It was good to see both her and Waylan come out of their shells. "Well, it's true I got into more trouble, but Nat had her time in the spotlight, too. Like when she decided to decorate the walls using crayon."

Nat taps me on the arm playfully. "Well, you should have seen Darla when she fingerpainted all over the table."

"We were just natural artists!" We all laugh.

"That's the thing about being brothers and sisters. We have such a shared past. So many fun memories together." Vaughn is pointedly looking at Waylan, but Waylan is focused more so on his drink.

"Here's to fond memories with siblings." Vaughn leads us in a toast.

It's good to see Natalie laid back and enjoying the ball. Waylan, too. Maybe the two of them just need some help breaking the ice. However, I can't help but notice Natalie's glances over at Vaughn, with a longing in

them. Maybe no one else sees, but being her sister, and having concern for her, makes me hyper-aware of any nuances or undercurrents.

The four of us continue to enjoy our evening together, as we say goodbye to our guests and they leave, one by one. It seems everyone had an enjoyable evening, and appreciated being invited to meet us. Many of them wish us well, with our upcoming mating ceremonies, and hope to see us on that special day.

I smile as I say my goodbyes to each one of them, but start to feel the weight of expectations placed on me. I feel guilt whenever I glance over at Vaughn. He seems so happy with me on his arm. And I'm not going to deny we work very well as a couple, exercising our duties with the public.

Waylan is a bit standoffish as he says his goodbyes, but he does seem more open than he did at the commencement of the ball. Natalie plays out her role perfectly. She may not be as outgoing as me, but she has a genuine, caring attitude that is attractive to others.

When everyone has taken their leave, the four of us have a late night tea in the lounge. Vaughn and I were so busy greeting people, then off in our own world dancing, that we hadn't tried the delicacies served at the ball. Several fresh trays of food are brought into the lounge for us to enjoy.

I think this has been a great night for all of us to bond together. If Natalie stays, I will need to foster a relationship with Waylan, and also with Vaughn, as he is Waylan's brother. I don't want to dwell on all the consequences my leaving might have, so I engage in light conversation until exhaustion takes over.

I look over at Nat and see she's struggling to keep her eyes open. I nudge Vaughn and he notices, giving oblivious Natalie an affectionate smile.

"Well, we should all retire for the night." Vaughn and I stand.

Waylan, not realizing Natalie is using him for balance, stands at the same time. I giggle as Natalie nearly falls sideways on the couch. Her eyes abruptly fly open, and Waylan helps her stand, although she is somewhat wobbly.

"Have a good night." I smirk as Waylan scoops up Natalie and holds her to his chest. Her head lolls into him.

"Good night." Waylan nods to us.

"Waylan. Natalia." Vaughn smiles as he sees Natalie way off in dreamland. He offers me his arm, and I watch as Waylan carries her up to their rooms.

Vaughn and I walk up to our rooms and enter the sitting room.

"I had a wonderful evening with you, Darla." His voice is tender and his eyes are soft as he takes my hands in his.

"I did, too, Vaughn. Thank you for making our welcome such a special event."

"Anything for you, Dearest." He places a tendril of hair behind my ear, then strokes my cheek and I lean into his hand, my eyes closing. He places his hand behind me and brings me in for a gentle hug.

I can feel his body quivering next to mine, like the vibration of a harp string. I'm shaking slightly. He tilts my head up and looks into my eyes, searching. I see a bit of confusion on his face, but then he reaches down and gives me a chaste kiss on my lips.

"Goodnight, Darla." His arm is around my waist as he leads me to my bedroom door. He holds it open for me, and I walk into the dimly lit room.

"Goodnight, Vaughn." I smile up at him and he reciprocates, then he gently closes the door.

CHAPTER TWENTY-TWO

As the days tick on by, and the date for our mating ceremony looms before us, I find my stress level increasing.

How am I going to get out of this without disrupting the shifter society or sparking a war? Then I pause for a minute and reflect. *Do I really want to get out of it?*

These are questions I am facing as the mate pull grows stronger each day between Vaughn and myself. I am in danger of falling for him, and it is becoming so difficult to fight. At the same time, Waylan and Natalie don't seem to be making a lot of progress in their relationship. I wonder why that is.

My days are packed full of activity, preparing for events. Both Natalie and I are being instructed on the history and current intricacies that make the Primorye Kingdom function. I really am finding it to be fascinating, as it's such a unique society.

About a week after the welcoming ball, Nat and I finally have a heart-to-heart. Vaughn could sense we needed some time together away from everyone and everything, so he arranged a surprise for Natalie and I. His gift to us is a day together, away from palace life.

His eyes sparkle as he helps us into the plane. "I hope you two have a wonderful day and some much needed 'girl time'." Natalie's eyes glow as she looks at Vaughn with gratitude.

Although he and Waylan stay back, a security team is sent with us. We strap in, ready to take off. A couple of hours later, we arrive at our destination. Vaughn has arranged for us to stay at a nature resort down south at Lake Khanka. I'm surprised and touched by his generosity toward us.

It is an idyllic setting, and during the late morning we sit on the patio at the lodge, watching the mandarin ducks swimming. They are beautiful creatures, with the most gorgeous colors. Pink bills, deep green and blue crests, purple breasts, gold and orange feathers, and a rust-colored frill around their throats. It's amazing that nature has produced that myriad of colors in one animal.

At Noon, Nat and I sit in a solid wooden gazebo, constructed in an oriental architectural fashion. We are surrounded by colorful wildflowers and wildlife. The weather is cool, but not chilly, and both of us are wearing cream wool coats and the most adorable matching hats, gifts from Vaughn and Waylan.

Lunch has been brought out from the lodge, and the security team sets up far enough away to give us privacy. In addition, the wind whips up now and again, and is generally at a low howl, so we won't be heard as we chat. The south wall is solid, shielding us from the wind.

The setting and atmosphere remind me of a painting I saw when I was young. I always wondered what the story was behind it. It feels a bit like déjà vu, surreal, like I'm now living in that painting.

But at the same time, in that fae-like atmosphere, I am faced with practicalities. They force me to stay grounded. For finally, Nat and I have some freedom to get into the real issues without being concerned about "listening ears".

"So fill me in on everything, Natalie. What's really troubling you, and why so secretive?"

"It's Waylan. I couldn't say anything about this at the palace as there are 'ears' everywhere, and cat-shifters have enhanced hearing. Waylan's very controlling, and I'm worried he monitors what I say and where I go."

"What's up with that? I wonder why he'd act that way."

"He has an envious streak that keeps growing day by day. He can talk of nothing but how his brother is so undeserving of his position and what he has, and even of you."

I feel bewildered. "Me? How do I fit into all of this? He has you!"

"I know. And that doesn't help my self esteem. Before you arrived, he flaunted me like a toy in front of his brother. Vaughn didn't take the bait and become jealous, but instead was practical about it. He worked with Waylan's contacts to obtain his own mate, someone similar to me." I watch as Natalie blushes.

"So it's more that he felt he had something Vaughn didn't, and now Vaughn has the same?"

"Something like that. But I'm worried. He talks about this stuff so much, even saying he should be king, not his brother. I'm worried he might do something to Vaughn."

I can see the tears building up in her eyes. And that's when I realize it.

She's in love with Vaughn.

I go back to my lunch, wondering how I should bring the subject up. It needs to be talked about. I decide to be direct with her. I glance over at her, and wait until she finishes her sandwich.

"You love him, don't you?"

Nat looks distressed. "Love who?"

"Vaughn."

Natalie gasps, looking at me. Then her voice becomes urgent. "Please don't say anything. Waylan is angry enough all the time. He would become explosive if he found out." Her eyes grow larger. "And you! What about your feelings? I am so sorry." She covers her mouth with her hand and I see her eyes fill with tears.

"There's nothing to be sorry for, Nat."

"But he's your mate!"

I sigh. "First of all, you can't control your feelings, especially if they are so strong they're defying your own marking. That's significant, Nat. And even more importantly, although you have all those feelings, you haven't done anything to signify to Vaughn the way you truly feel, or to sabotage my relationship with him. That shows how much you love both of us, that you want us to be happy regardless of your own feelings."

Natalie nods, but looks miserable.

"Secondly." I scratch the back of my neck. "I'm not sure how to say this. But I consider myself attached to someone else."

Natalie looks as if she's in shock. "What do you mean? You and Vaughn seem perfect together!"

"While looking for you, well it's a long story, but I met someone. We are together and were planning on being mated. However, he was helping me find you to see if you were okay. Wires got crossed and my marking was passed to Vaughn in the end." I didn't want to burden her with my worries, so didn't mention any of my misgivings about the way Justin and I parted.

"It's true the marking has pulled Vaughn and I together, but I believe my affection for him is familial. I could care deeply about him as a brother. I've only been staying for you. To make sure you're okay. If you weren't okay, I was planning to take you and leave."

She speaks in a small voice, looking down at the table. "I can't leave Vaughn."

"But if you don't leave you'll be mated to Waylan."

Her face looks distraught. "I don't know what to do. I'm so torn. I can't be with Waylan. Yes, he's incredibly attractive physically, and he does have some positive qualities, but envy has a grip on his soul. And I

know that 'trying to change someone' never works. They have to be motivated intrinsically to change, or it isn't genuine and won't last."

I nod and look at her with compassion in my eyes. "I understand this must be so difficult for you—being in the position you are in. We do have a bit of time, but we can't leave it too long."

"Do you have a plan for leaving?"

"Not yet, but I'm trying to come up with something. I've noticed we've been given no access to phones or computers since I've been here, or I'd contact Justin."

Natalie looks a bit sheepish. "I'm afraid that's my fault. I didn't understand any of this and was scared to death, and tried to get away. I even contacted the police, but when they came, everything was discussed in Russian, and it was 'resolved' right in front of me. Since that time, I've had no access to a phone or the internet, thanks to Waylan."

I sigh. "Well, that would be our number one priority. Finding a way to communicate with Justin. I'll keep trying to think of other options—things we can do from our side to help ourselves. We're in this together, so let's brainstorm over the next while, ways we can deal with our mixed-up situation."

"Yeah, it really is a confusing situation to be in. If I hadn't been taken in the first place, none of this would have happened." Nat has a guilty look on her face.

"But then I wouldn't have met Justin."

"True."

"So let's just deal with the situation at hand. No carrying excess guilt around with you, okay?" We lean in to give each other a hug, and we hold each other for a minute. I close my eyes, trying to send my love and care to her. I know it might sound odd, but after learning more about shifter

bonds, my hunch is that she can feel my emotions when I project them her way.

We'll somehow figure this out. I know we will.

We spend the afternoon walking alongside the lake on the sand, and exploring the nearby meadows filled with different species of wildflowers. Spring is definitely here, at least down south it is. Soon we'll be returning to the north where winter is trying to hold on. But I decide to focus on the 'now' and just enjoy the time with my sister.

Security is always close by, so Nat and I are careful about what we discuss. We talk about some of the fun memories we have of our childhood, and a bit about our parents. I hope they're doing well. They've always been a quiet couple, and because they had us later in life weren't as in tune with some of the things we were into as we grew up.

The generational gap was a bit too wide, I guess. They grew up during a time when TV's weren't a regular staple in the home, and the internet wasn't even a dream on the horizon. Nat and I were of a different species of human—"techno humans", I guess you could call us, since we grew up attached to our phones and the internet. It's amazing we've survived this long without them, living in our current situation.

However, because of our current circumstances, I now have more appreciation for my parents. Without phones and internet, we've been kept completely busy, spending time with others, studying about the region, and doing important tasks. I've never been this long without a phone, not since I got my first one at age twelve. But now I can see there is a life beyond my very own closed-in technological universe.

As dinner time comes, it's a bit chillier outside, so Natalie and I elect to eat inside the lodge. We've had a good dose of much-needed fresh air, evident from our rosy cheeks. We wash up for dinner and make our way to the dining room.

The Chinese lanterns placed at short intervals among the rafters above us are beautiful. Each lantern's orange glow flickers independently of the others. The light bounces off the glossy, black ceiling, creating a mirrored effect. It looks as though a dark night sky is filled with them. Such a cozy feeling.

I notice that apart from our security, we're the only ones in the dining room. In fact, apart from the staff at the lodge, we haven't seen anyone new to us all day. I laugh to myself.

"What is it?" Natalie looks up from her menu.

"I just realized Vaughn must have booked the entire resort just for us today."

Natalie smiles. "You're right. I haven't seen anyone other than staff here and our own security all day."

"It makes sense though, for security reasons. I bet that's one of the stipulations he made in order to allow us to spend the day here alone."

"He's so thoughtful isn't he?" Natalie looks a bit dreamy.

I laugh. "You're so cute."

"Whaaat." She smiles at me and goes back to her menu.

Dinner is a real treat, with all kinds of delicacies fresh from the lake. We both love seafood, so enjoy every bite. Between the ambience, the food, and just being with my sister, this day has truly been special.

And I can thank Vaughn for that. I smile to myself.

We're back on the plane and covered in cozy blankets, ready to doze off during the flight home. *Home.* It's interesting I would think of it that way, since I've been living there for such a short time.

Home is where the heart is.

My thoughts slip away as I drift off to sleep.

Justin.

CHAPTER TWENTY-THREE

The final days before our twin mating ceremony are spent in a flurry of excitement. Well, the excitement of those around me, anyway. The palace staff run by with expressions of both glee and consternation, as they prepare for the significant historical event.

As time passes by, my heart sinks lower and lower due to the weight of guilt I feel toward both Justin and Vaughn. The weight is pulling me underwater, and I'm drowning because of it. With Justin, I feel guilt over my growing feelings for Vaughn. They've been brought on by both the marking and spending time with a man who truly knows how to cherish others. With Vaughn, I feel guilt for not stopping preparations for a ceremony I'm uncommitted to. Oh, and add in the fact I'm in love with another man, who I'm still hoping will somehow become my future mate.

And I now realize what must be done. I must talk to Vaughn about my relationship with Justin, and my lack of commitment to our upcoming union. It will be difficult to explain, especially since our bond keeps growing. Our bond is now something that cannot easily be explained away or disposed of. It's like a complex, living, breathing organism.

So after two days of hoping to run into Vaughn unsuccessfully, I hunt him down. By now, things are completely out of hand. In addition to the decorations and flower hooks all over the palace being made ready for the florists, some special dishes are being prepared ahead of time. Supplies are constantly being flown in, guest rooms set up, and the ballroom and grand dining room are being fully decorated for the ceremony and reception.

I never realized how much time and preparation would be involved for such an event, and it's only compounded by the fact it will be a "once-

in-a-generation" occurrence. Family and friends are flying in from all over the world, some have already arrived, and everything will be widely televised for all their subjects to view. With each growing revelation, it's like I'm standing by watching additional cars pile onto an ever-growing train wreck.

Finding out all of these details makes everything so much harder, but I have to talk to Vaughn about it, so I seek him out relentlessly. After being redirected a dozen times after "just missing" him, I finally find him in one of the guest corridors. He smiles widely at me, looking at me with nothing but adoration and happiness, and I fall into his arms. And it's in his arms that all my concerns fly out of my head and I sink into contentment.

No, no, no! I try to break his spell over me, but the draw is so strong. So that's how I find myself, the evening before the mating ceremony, trying to force a conversation with Vaughn as I attempt to eject us out of the tornado of preparations going on around us.

"Vaughn, we need to talk. It's urgent." He looks into my eyes and nods.

"Walk with me. There's still so much that needs to be done, especially with all our guests flying in."

"I need to tell you some background about the markings and how I got here."

He looks at me. "It's okay, Darla, you may have been marked a few times by others, but I know it's part of the process. Waylan explained a bit to me about how they do a few marked exchanges to get you here, and I understand."

He must see the trepidation in my eyes, and stops walking. He faces me, cupping my cheek with his hand, eyes going wide. "They didn't hurt you, did they?" His mouth sets in a grim line.

"No, nothing like that." He looks relieved, and I appreciate him all the more for his concern for me.

I decide to just come out and say it. "Vaughn, I was hunting for my sister. She got caught up in all this, was basically taken from her life, and disappeared. Then while I was looking for her I was won in an arena fight and marked. The winner helped me to narrow down where she most likely was taken, and he was to pose as my mate..."

We are suddenly swarmed by guests who have found us, entering the guest wing from the stairs, and Vaughn and I are separated. Vaughn is being congratulated, while I'm being welcomed to the family with hugs and adorable kisses from baby-cheeked children. They have all been longing to meet the new princess, soon to become queen.

I find myself with a one-year-old baby in my arms, bouncing him gently, while talking with his four-year-old, inquisitive sister. I can hear not-so-subtle onlookers already commenting on future royal children. Vaughn is looking over with affection and amusement as I try to manage the youngsters.

I smile and chat as though I hadn't a care in the world, while inwardly, I'm screaming in frustration, the need to talk to Vaughn growing.

Aaaahh!

I keep my face smooth, smiling. After several minutes, Vaughn ties up the conversation, thanking each of them for attending. He says we're looking forward to spending time with them during the reception dinner and days following.

I see a couple of eyes twinkling, as one of Vaughn's old friends comments. "It's a good thing we have an extended stay, because we know how *busy* the two of you will be...with palace duties of course!"

I can feel my face become warm, and I'm sure I'm turning bright pink with embarrassment. Vaughn actually chuckles when he sees my face.

"But we mustn't keep you two. Lots of preparations to be done. Francie and I know that from our own experience, and your ceremony is much bigger than ours!"

We say our goodbyes for now.

"Vaughn, is there anywhere we can talk without being interrupted? It's of vital importance that we speak, and now. It can't wait."

We hear more guests coming up the stairs, but Vaughn has seen the seriousness in my eyes. He immediately takes me to an angelic painting and opens a panel, steadies me as I walk through, then follows me. He guides me down a corridor lit with modern light stripping on the floor, down a stairway, and through a maze of dim hallways.

"Is this why I haven't seen you for the last couple days?"

"Uh, yeah, I've been tending to keep to the passageways to avoid being detained." He sounds a bit sheepish. "But if I'd known you were looking for me, I would have sought you out immediately, Dearest."

Vaughn opens a panel to a dimly lit office and turns on the overhead lights. The dark wood furniture and paneling are beautiful, and contrast nicely with the crimson and cream walls. He takes my hand gently, and walks me to a plush crimson loveseat with dark wooden legs.

Vaughn looks at me earnestly. "What's troubling you, Darla?"

I suddenly feel afraid to tell him the truth after all the preparations that have been set in motion. I feel choked up. "Vaughn, I'm afraid you're going to be terribly angry with me."

He takes both my hands in his. "Whatever it is, Darla, I'll do my best to help if it's in my power to do so. I think the world of you."

I see the sincerity in his eyes. My own eyes start tearing up. "The shifter who won me in the arena marked me and was helping me to track Natalie down so I could ensure she was okay. However, we were forcibly separated. I don't know what happened to him, if he's safe, or even wants me, but he and I had talked about having our own mating ceremony in the future."

Vaughn's breath catches. He cups my cheeks tenderly as he searches my eyes. "And what about now? Do you still choose him as your mate?"

Tears dribble down my face, slowly. My voice comes out in a hoarse whisper. "I don't even know if he's alive. But if he is and still wants me, I do." My tears start to come more rapidly, and Vaughn pulls me close to his chest.

He places his lips on the top of my head and kisses me softly. "Whatever your decision is, Darla, I will respect it. Your happiness is my primary concern."

I sniffle a bit, and after a while I look up at him. "Do you really mean that? But what about all the preparations and your guests?"

"It's nothing to be concerned about when you're making a decision that will affect the rest of your life. While I hope you will change your mind and choose me, what I say stands. Your happiness is the most important thing to me in this world. Because, Darla..." Vaughn hesitates.

His eyes are more intense than I've ever seen them. "I truly love you. I love the person you are, the strength you demonstrate, your heart, everything about you. I love *you*." He tenderly kisses my forehead.

"If you are absolutely sure, we can call the mating ceremony off, but if you are unsure, we can postpone the ceremony until you make a final decision."

Vaughn is so understanding it's difficult to believe. I thought for sure there would be some degree of anger from him. But instead, he is

compassionate and sensitive to my needs, regardless of what I've said or done.

"Thank you, Vaughn. You are such an understanding, caring individual, one that I already cherish in my heart." He smiles at me with sadness mingling with hope, and I can sense his longing for me. We both feel the longing, the pull that wants to draw us closer together, and do our best to resist it.

"Another thing. I don't think Natalie wants to mate with Waylan. In fact, I think she's strongly opposed to the idea."

Vaughn sighs. "I'll talk to Waylan about that issue as well."

Vaughn offers me his arm, takes me through the wall panels again, and walks me to our rooms.

"You should get a good rest tonight, Darla. Sleep on it, and we'll talk to Waylan about it tomorrow." I nod, and Vaughn opens my bedroom door for me. "If you need me later tonight, you're welcome to meet with me in our joint sitting room. I'll work from there for the rest of the evening in case you need me for anything.

"Thank you, Vaughn." My voice is hushed. I reach up and plant a tiny kiss on his cheek."

"Goodnight, Darla."

"Goodnight, Vaughn." He holds the door while I enter my room, then quietly closes it behind me.

I wish I could text Natalie, but of course neither of us have phones. I will have to catch her tomorrow. I get into my nightie, and crawl into bed. Tomorrow will be a big day. I can feel it in my bones.

CHAPTER TWENTY-FOUR

The following day comes soon enough and I'm up, navigating my way to breakfast, hoping to talk with Natalie and Waylan. Neither of them are in the dining room. Natalie may have just slept in, if she was able to sleep at all, but I'm sure Waylan has his hands full with guests and preparations.

I know Vaughn needs to dive back into his work, but before he does, he looks at me with a quizzical look and squeezes my hand. "What is it you need, Darla?"

"I need to try to contact him. Is there any way I could use a phone or the internet to try to reach him? I haven't been able to contact him since I arrived."

Vaughn looks confused. "Sure. You mean you haven't been able to *reach* him since you've been here, right? But you've been trying to and that's why you're worried?"

Now it's my turn to be confused. "No, I haven't been able to *contact* him because Waylan removed all access to phones and the internet. Natalie also has mentioned he sometimes monitors her conversations with people, too."

This is the first time I've ever seen Vaughn look exasperated. He groans and shakes his head. "Waylan. I'm sorry for his controlling actions. I'll give you access right away. Here, use my phone."

Vaughn hands me his phone and I start to punch in Justin's number. The phone auto fills in the number with the name "Justin" beside it. "Whaaat? I don't get it." I'm holding the phone as if it's a foreign object.

"What's wrong?"

"I just punched in part of his number and his name and full number popped up."

Vaughn's eyebrows raise and he tilts his head quizzically. "That's odd. What's his name?"

"His name is Justin."

Vaughn freezes. "Your beloved is Justin?" His eyes open wide and he pales. "I need to find Waylan right away. I'll talk to you later, okay?"

"What's going on, Vaughn?"

"Nothing to worry about. I'm going to need my phone to text Waylan if I can't find him. I'll try to reach Justin for you."

"Okay." Now I'm curious. *How does Vaughn know Justin?*

I find my way back to my room, greeting guests and staff on the way, needing some time to process things. I lay down, and thankfully am able to get in a quick nap. I feel ten times better when I wake up, but realize it's time for lunch. I hope to catch Natalie to update her and see how she's feeling.

I feel bad about springing everything on Vaughn last minute, but as he says, I can't give up my own happiness if this is not what I want. The fact that he's not angry but thinking about my well-being reveals just what kind of man he is, what type of king he is. I'm glad I told him, instead of going forward as is. I know he'll look after things from here on in with Waylan.

I arrive in the dining room and it seems I'm the only one there. I wait patiently, but the staff serve me without the others. So I eat, in order to keep up my strength. Close to the end of lunch, Vaughn comes in to grab a bite to eat.

"I haven't been able to reach Waylan or Justin. Neither are answering their phones. Justin's is going straight to voice mail. I'm going to look for Waylan again."

"Okay. I'm coming with you, though."

"My pleasure, Darla." He offers me his arm.

We scour the palace searching for Waylan, engaging in conversation every few steps with staff, either asking about Waylan's whereabouts or answering questions related to preparations. Add to that all the greetings to the guests we run into on the way. It's slow-going and exhausting, and I feel we're getting nowhere.

A while later, Vaughn's phone beeps. He checks his texts. "Waylan." We change direction and walk into a large mud room that contains coats and boots, and we both put on a set before stepping outside. We walk to one of the buildings behind the palace library.

"This building houses our university." Vaughn gestures ahead of us. "Waylan is fascinated with the science lab, which is near the back end. He says he has something important to show us.

"They've been working on several cures in the lab, including one using shifter stem cells to stimulate human cell regeneration." I nod excitedly and we continue on our way.

Since it's such an important ceremonial day, Waylan's news must be groundbreaking, if it's drawn him out to the lab. My excitement increases, wondering what type of medical advance has been made. We walk down the hallways, past offices and classrooms, until we get to the medical science wing. Waylan meets us there.

"Waylan."

"Vaughn."

They nod to each other.

Vaughn addresses the issues without beating around in the bush. "I need to talk to you about the mating ceremony. Neither of the girls are ready for this. Darla and I are canceling ours, and I think you should postpone yours. Darla has mentioned that Natalia is still sorting out her feelings."

Waylan's face hardens, so I address him. "Please be sensitive toward my sister and consider her happiness. She's uncomfortable talking with you about how she feels, but I know she isn't ready for the ceremony." I try to be diplomatic, and just ask for a postponement.

"And what about losing face, Brother? All these people have come for the ceremony!"

"It doesn't matter, Waylan, in the scheme of things. It's better that issues get sorted out before anything is made official. We'll still have a joyous celebration, but it just won't be a mating ceremony."

We stand in the hallway, as a group of security staff gather.

"Actually, I have a better idea." Waylan puts his arm around Vaughn. "But let me show you what's been discovered first." We step through the doorway into the medical sciences lab.

"I'm sure it's exciting news, knowing what the team has been working on. Looking forward to it." Vaughn smiles and looks a bit relieved. Perhaps he expected Waylan would react differently to his request to postpone the ceremony. It seems like he's willing to talk about it, so it's a good start.

Then suddenly everything is turned upside down. The next few moments happen in a blur. Waylan's hand, which was around Vaughn's shoulder, has stuck some type of syringe with green liquid into his neck, while a group of men hold him in place so Waylan can press the plunger all the way in.

I see Vaughn drop to the floor in agony, in a forced shift, bones cracking and material ripping as he changes into his large tiger form. Then he lays on the floor, unmoving.

"No! Vaughn!" I instinctively rush to him and find myself on the floor, trying to find out if he's okay. "What have you done to him?" I panic.

I'm being immobilized, and feel a prick in my shoulder. "Just a sedative. Should calm you down." A man in a lab coat looks at me, somewhat regretfully. Everything goes hazy.

When I can finally maintain a grounded thought, I see I'm in a tiny room, with three white walls and one transparent wall. I gasp as I realize I'm in a cell in the compound's lab. My anxiety shoots through the roof.

Just great. I'm a guinea pig? My thoughts clear a bit more. *Where's Vaughn?*

Then I see flashes of orange and black, behind the ever-moving group of people in white who are walking and standing, and sometimes crouching, in front of me. No one comes to talk to me, and I try to figure out what they are doing. After a few minutes, I gasp. Vaughn is laying on the floor in his tiger form, asleep or unconscious, and things are being done to him.

Is he hurt? Are they trying to help him?

Although my view keeps on being disrupted by the men and women in lab coats walking back and forth in the room, there are moments when everyone in the room stands still to observe the medical procedures. I can see each time fluids are injected into Vaughn's tiger, and how minutes later they would withdraw his blood.

What the hell are they doing to him?

I watch as they mix his blood with other chemicals, until they make a thick substance. A vaguely familiar woman with auburn hair stands behind Vaughn. She passes her hand over the substance and it flames neon green, then it becomes a charred black powder.

Waylan's tiger lies opposite Vaughn on the floor, but awake and alert, as the woman sprinkles the powder in round patterned lines from one tiger to another. At the junctions she lays down runes. She waves her fingers from Vaughn's side toward Waylan's side and I gasp at the result.

The orange in Vaughn's fur glows like fire and starts bleeding into the black lines on the floor that adjoin the tigers. The black lines spreading from one tiger to the other look like small streams of lava.

Finally, all the orange disappears from Vaughn's fur, and the lava-like liquid seeps into Waylan's fur, causing it to glow like fire. Vaughn lays there, still motionless, now black stripes on white fur, all color gone. I strain, but am unable to tell if he's still breathing, or if they've killed him.

My mark feels like it's burning, and through my reflection in the window I see it glowing like fire. I gasp as I recognize that Vaughn no longer holds my mark. However, I realize with dread that I can still feel the active marking binding me.

Waylan stands as his black stripes sharply contrast with his orange fur, like fire and coal beside each other. His tiger turns to look at me, and I can see his catlike smirk. He knows he holds my mark now.

Waylan walks out of the lab and deeper into the building. He roars, and the volume is so extreme that glass shatters, and some of the lab scientists are thrown to the ground, along with the lady who manipulated the runes. My window shakes, and thankfully the shatterproof material crumbles, opening up access to the rest of the lab.

A fire breaks out as a result of spilled chemicals interacting with each other. I realize now is my best chance to escape, since Waylan is no longer in sight and the others are distracted. Even better, the sprinkler system goes off in the lab. While they are attending to the fire and dealing with the chaos, I quickly walk out of the room. A few doors down I slide through an open doorway, into a staff room.

I'm in luck! I grab a lab coat hanging from a hook and quickly put it, a mask, and a pair of goggles on. I hope this makes me less conspicuous as I move through the facility. Now the only one I have to worry about is Waylan, since he knows my scent.

Disguised, I hang back for a while, try to stay calm, and brainstorm for a plan to get Natalie and myself away from this place. I don't know the full extent of power that Waylan has, but if his roar is any indication, then his power must be immense. While I'm thinking about my next steps, I see a key on a hook, labelled "Master Key". I swipe it, knowing it will be helpful, and possibly our ticket out of here.

The best solution I can think of right now is taking Natalie, stealing a vehicle, and getting to the nearest airport. *Or the nearest embassy? Or maybe the Trans-Siberian Railway?* Neither of us has a passport or travel documents readily available to cross any borders, so we're stuck in Russia for now. We're either taking a domestic flight south to get to the consulate, or travelling west by plane or railway.

I use the master key on a lock to a room labelled "Computer Lab". I log onto one of the staff computers in guest mode, and look up Google Maps. I answer "yes" to the popup asking if I wish to allow Google to know my location. I see that I'm far north of Vladivostok, in Eastern Russia, as I had surmised. I look up the Consulate General, and find the location.

We definitely need a vehicle. One of the security rooms should have sets of keys for the vehicles, I'd think. Or the actual garage. The keys will definitely be close to the garage. Let's just hope there isn't a keypad with a security code.

I make a mental note of the things I'll need to get out of this place— security code, car keys, Nat's location.

I need to find and grab Nat first, then check the garage to see if we need a security code.

I feel terrible about leaving Vaughn behind in the lab, but I have no chance of being successful against Waylan and his loyalists by myself. It will be a lucky break if Natalie and I can get out unharmed.

Besides, I don't know if Vaughn is even alive.

The thought sobers me. He was a good man, and a fair and just leader. I can't imagine what will become of his people now, without his leadership. His brother intends on ruling with an iron fist. I can tell, based on his comments made to Natalie and his controlling personality.

I wonder if the role of prime ikati *was automatically transferred to Waylan in the same way my marking was.*

But it's not my first concern. Natalie is. I must find Nat, and quickly.

I make my way toward the end of the university compound. I cross to the back entrance of the palace, and walk down a corridor from which the house staff comes and goes. I open a door and walk along the first floor until I find a closet of uniforms.

I take out a maid's uniform and enter the staff dressing room beside it. I ditch my lab outfit and put on a black dress, pinafore, and white frilly maid's hat over hastily braided hair. I go back to the closet and rummage in the bottom, and find a pair of black oxfords.

I find a broom closet and pull out a caddy with cleaning supplies. I'm hoping to become invisible, just a staff member, no one to take notice of. I take the back stairs, intending to find my sister's rooms. Thankfully, the light stripping helps me with my footing.

At the top of the stairs, I stop on the landing, and peer through a glass disc which lets in a stream of light. This area is unfamiliar, so I continue to the right corridor that branches off from the landing. I travel in the approximate direction of Natalie's rooms.

After checking a few more times through peepholes, I finally see some familiarity, and press the illuminated button at the side of the wall panel. The panel slides horizontally, and I step into the well-lit corridor leading to Nat's rooms. I walk down the hallway, passing unnoticed by several guests, staff, and security, and knock on her door lightly.

I hear Natalie's voice, and a surge of relief washes over me. I hadn't realized I'd been holding my breath until that moment. "Come in."

I turn the door handle and walk in. She doesn't seem to notice me, and continues pinning up her hair in front of the vanity. I clear my voice.

"Oh, you can place the linens in the bathroom if that's what you're here—"

"Nat."

She spins around, nearly falling off the padded stool. "Darla?" Her eyes open wide as she takes in my costume. "What are you doing dressed up like that?"

"We need to get out of here. Now."

"What do you mean?"

"Waylan has taken over, and we need to go."

She looks panicked. "What about Vaughn? Where is he?"

I shake my head, and she looks frantic. She rushes over to me, placing her hands on my arms, searching my eyes. "He's okay, isn't he?"

"I don't know. Waylan attacked him. The last I saw of him he was lying on the floor..."

"What about your bite mark? You can still feel he's alive, right?"

"There was some sort of ritual. Waylan now somehow holds my marking."

She focuses her mind then gasps. "He holds mine, too. Nothing's changed with my marking."

I nod. "Then we've got to go." Natalie doesn't wish to be mated by Waylan, so we've got to leave right away.

Nat crosses her arms stubbornly. "I'm not leaving without him. I won't leave Vaughn behind."

"We'll have to come back for him later, Nat! It's too dangerous to try to take him right now. Besides, there's no way we could lift an

unconscious tiger-shifter between the two of us. He's got to weigh at least a thousand pounds."

"Wait! He's still in his tiger form? Then that means he's not dead." I can see relief flooding her face. Her eyes look watery.

"Waylan left him in the lab, so for now he doesn't seem to be a threat to Vaughn. I wish I could tell who is loyal to Vaughn and who is to Waylan. I would have told someone to take a team to the lab if I knew who to ask."

"What do you have planned?"

"We grab coats and boots, find car keys, and drive to the airport or railway."

Natalie looks torn. She doesn't want to mate with Waylan anymore than I do, but I can tell she's not going to leave Vaughn unless she knows he's safe. And I can't leave Nat until I know she's safe.

I sigh. I just don't know what to do. I stand there perturbed, wracking my brain. *I'm between a rock and a hard place—damned if I do and damned if I don't.*

Suddenly, I feel throbbing through the *ailouros* bond. I gasp, since I haven't felt a soul since I was delivered to The Circle. I can feel my link with the *ikati.* My body starts shaking.

It's Justin! He's here!

Relief floods me and I tear up. *He's alive!* I can feel his candle, and it's burning larger and brighter by the second. Somehow he's found me, and he's on his way! I feel guilty for ever doubting his love for me.

"Let's go!" I squeal. I grab my sister's hand, and start pulling her toward the bedroom door.

"What are you doing? I told you I'm not leaving."

"I know. But Justin is coming. I can feel our pride bond. He'll help us out of this predicament. We just have to stall things as long as we can."

Natalie is insistent. "Let's get back to Vaughn. I need to check on him." I see that stubborn streak we share. Plus she makes a good argument. "If he's awake, he'll know best how to handle things and know who's loyal to him. If not, we can look for something in the lab to mask our scents until we find a vehicle. If we can't access a vehicle then we can hide undetected."

Natalie walks behind me down the hallway, hoping not to be recognized. We enter the corridor of staff tunnels behind the wall panel. We sneak downstairs, into the mud room for coats and boots, and out the door between the library and university. We walk briskly on the path outside—and right into Waylan.

I know I need to delay things as long as I possibly can, to give Justin more time. So I do something that under other circumstances may seem like a futile attempt to prevent the inevitable.

I run.

CHAPTER TWENTY-FIVE

Empowered by my display of defiance, Natalie runs in the opposite direction, toward the compound. I hear Waylan's laughter behind me. "Run, run like the wind, little rabbits. I'll even give you a head start."

I know for apex predators such as Waylan, the fun is in the chase. He might enjoy this, but my only goal is to buy time. I run into the beech forest, thinking the trees may slow him down, or force him to follow me in human form. However, I know he will easily track my scent wherever I flee to.

I don't know how much of a head start he will give us, but if my sister can somehow evade him as well, that will buy us a bit more time. Every minute counts, since I know it will take time for Justin to arrive. I can feel the rest of his team as well. *Good. He'll have backup.*

It's questionable how many pride members are loyal to Waylan, but I would hope very few. People genuinely like Vaughn and he has good rapport with them. But greed for wealth and power corrupts, and who knows what Waylan has promised his followers.

I run deeper into the forest, choking on the cold air. I'm glad we were able to snag a couple of coats and boots, but it doesn't stop the searing pain of the cold in my lungs. I know I can't continue indefinitely like this, and I'll eventually lose my cover because I'll end up having a raging coughing fit.

Waylan must have gone after my sister first, since I have yet to hear him chasing me or sense him stalking me. I run by a copse of trees and trip over one of the roots, face-planting in the snow. I wipe the snow off my face and out of my mouth, and have a hacking fit. I rest there for a few minutes, since the trees grow so tightly together, and will at least block

Waylan's tiger from pursuing me. His human form is another story, but he is a big guy like his brother.

I'm still coughing uncontrollably, but it's more of a rumbling in my chest as I keep my mouth closed. Finally, it slows down until I'm just choking on a cough here and there. I wonder if I should move on, or take a stand here. If he's stuck to his human form, he'll be more vulnerable. I search around the copse for possible weapons. I find a sharp, jagged piece of breccia rock that looks like it may be useful, and a large, thick stick. I tuck the sharp rock in my pocket and slide the stick into my coat. I don't know if they'll be of much help, but anything is better than nothing.

I put a thin layer of snow over the root I tripped over, thinking Waylan might trip as I did. He has a much longer stride though, so chances are lower that he will. Otherwise I can't see much else I can do but conserve my energy and calm myself.

Wait a sec! I can climb a tree!

My adrenaline starts pumping again. I find it fairly easy to climb one of the beech trees, and hope I'm out of reach at 25 feet. I rest in the crook of a branch and wait.

I don't have to wait long before I hear him calling out in a sing-song voice, taunting me. "Darla! Darla!" I can hear his amusement as he draws closer.

His eyes connect with mine over the distance, and he sprints over to the tree, bare-chested, stopping several feet away. He starts laughing. I feel irked that he would find humor in the situation.

"You do know tigers can climb trees don't you?"

I'm betting on his tiger being too heavy, especially since cat-shifters are larger than typical tigers. I don't answer him.

He sighs. "You're really going to make me come up and get you aren't you?"

I stay silent, focusing on holding onto the tree and observing his next move. I watch as Waylan does a partial transformation. My breath catches and I groan. I'd forgotten about the partial shift. It means he has the strength and claws to make it easier to climb, but lacks the weight which would be an obstacle for him.

I watch as he rapidly scales the tree. I stretch out my body and reach out to the closest tree in the copse. I manage to grab onto a branch while stepping on another, pull myself close to the trunk, then hold on.

"Hey, stop that! You'll hurt yourself, little rabbit."

Waylan leaps and clings to a spot above me. I can see his muscles ripple on his feline-like body. He speaks firmly. "Climb down or I'll carry you down. Now."

Waylan has me cornered, and there's not much I can do. So I shimmy down the smooth trunk as Waylan watches, and scurry into the thicket. I pull out the branch and breccia rock. Waylan descends, then leaps from his perch, landing in the snow. He transforms back into his human form, and approaches me.

"Come now, sweet little rabbit, you didn't think you could outrun me, did you?" His voice sounds almost affectionate, and he smiles at me.

I watch as the tattoos on his skin glow like fire. With their intricacy, they are beautiful. He comes a little closer, noticing my defensive stance, and tries to coax me out of the thicket, as though talking to a skittish fawn.

"Come on, Darla. It's okay. I'm not going to hurt you. Both you and your sister are invaluable to me. Let's go." His lips quirk up in amusement. "Put the stick down, now."

In response, I throw the stick at him, which by reflex he dodges. It gives me an extra second to slide between the trees behind me where everything grows even more densely. He sidles up to the trees to try to force his way through, and as he becomes stuck, I pull out the breccia

rock, slitting his skin in a finger-width stripe down his side. Red stains the snow as blood dribbles from his side.

"Yaaaa!" His voice comes out in a strangled roar and the trees around him sway. I suddenly regret poking the proverbial bear. I turn around and run like hell.

I have about a minute before I'm tackled to the ground. Thank goodness for the thick layer of snow cushioning my fall. I feel his hard body pressed against me as he lays on my back, pinning me down, and he whispers in my ear.

"I'm not mad, you know. In fact, I love the chase, the exhilaration. The feeling of catching my prey and enjoying it at the end of the race." Then he sweeps his lips over my cheek, and kisses it softly. I shiver. "But I'm not a brute. I can be as gentle and reasonable as my brother." His hand strokes my hair, softly, as though trying to calm me. I take in a shaky breath.

"Unfortunately, we have to get back now." He sounds reluctant. He gets up, places me on my feet, and brushes off the snow remaining in my hair.

He crouches to my height and takes my hand. "But before we go back, I want you to be aware that if you throw any kind of wrench into my plans this evening, I won't go easy on your sister." I can feel my face blanching as his eyes pierce my own. "Do we have an understanding?" His vague threat nearly petrifies me, but I'm able to nod my head.

Before I know it, he's picked me up and has me slung over his shoulder. "We're behind schedule." He sets off in a run, back toward the palace. As my body is jerked around, I see from my upside-down position that his side has already healed.

But then I notice something that may be significant. Below the residual blood on his skin in the exact place where I wounded him, the flaming tattoo no longer glows.

"It's never been done before, *prime ikati.*" I overhear one of Waylan's advisors responding to his command in the hallway. I listen carefully to try to understand Waylan's plans, or to find a dynamic between him and his men that could be exploited.

"I don't care. Are you disobeying my order?" Waylan growls.

"Not at all. I'm just saying there's no guarantee it will work, and if it does, we don't know the ramifications of such actions. There could be a variety of side effects we don't anticipate."

I look at Natalie, wondering if she's figured out the subject of discussion, but she gives me a nearly imperceptible shake of her head.

"I'm willing to risk it. The benefits outweigh the risks. Go get them ready."

"As you wish, Your Highness."

Waylan's advisor enters the room where I was placed upon our return. "Guards, Ladies, come with me." We follow the advisor deeper into the palace where he instructs the guards. Half the guards take Natalie farther into the palace, I assume to her rooms.

My guards take me to my room and open the door for me. I step through the doorway reluctantly, not that I have a choice, and into the group of women scurrying around. The group looks relieved to see me, and words tumble out of their mouths. "We need to hurry. There's not much time since they've moved the ceremony earlier. We have to get you ready for the mating ceremony."

I'm clearly confused. "What ceremony? I'm sure it's been cancelled."

They all insist, speaking at the same time in a jumble of words I can barely discern. "No no no. It's tonight. The double mating ceremony. We must get you ready."

I'm still confused, then realize Waylan must still be planning on having the ceremony with Natalie. *I guess I'm going as her Maid of Honor or whatever they call it at a shifter ceremony. We should have run when we had the chance. Stubborn Natalie. How can I get her out of this? I'm sure she doesn't want to do the ceremony with Waylan, regardless of what he may think. But then his warning...I can't afford to do anything risky.*

I let the women get me ready for my sister's ceremony. They dress me in a sparkling rose-gold gown that reflects different facets of light. Another woman brushes my lips with matching lipstick and applies a light coat of mascara over my dark lashes. When they're finished, they're all smiles, and one even claps her hands together in delight.

Although I'm full of anxiety over my sister's plight, I still manage to be polite. "Thank you, Ladies." I smile at them.

"Our pleasure!"

The guards deliver me to the grand ballroom where I danced, what seems like a lifetime ago, with Vaughn. Instead of going through the main doors, they open a set of side doors that are obscured by a dividing wall. It is similar to the waiting area for the *ailouros* ceremony. Except this time I'm afraid my every action is being watched by the man who has the power to harm my sister.

Inside the alcove sits two chairs. One is empty, and the other is filled by my sister, looking gorgeous in an opal, iridescent gown. I sit in the empty chair and her hand reaches out then clings to mine. She looks as anxious as I feel. My concern is for her safety, but apart from my earlier stunt, playing "tag" with Waylan, I haven't done anything to incur his

wrath. Nat should be safe. If being mated to Waylan could be considered "safe".

I lower my voice to a whisper, putting my mouth right up to her ear. I don't know how exceptional the shifters' sense of hearing is, just that it's exceedingly more pronounced than ours. "You don't have to do this, you know? I can figure something out."

Maybe if I make a scene Nat could get away. I evaluate the idea. *The risk is too high. I'll have to figure something else out.*

She looks at me, paling, and nods her head insistently. She whispers back to me and completely surprises me with her answer. "I want to do this."

Through a joint in the wood, I can see her mate-to-be sitting in his royal uniform in the front row. He is looking ahead, and I see him glance our way and smirk. *If he wasn't such a prick, he'd be a very attractive man.*

"Are you sure? What about Vaughn?"

Her lip trembles. "I've changed my mind. I'm going to become Waylan's mate." And I know I won't be able to budge her from her stubborn position. Just like I couldn't persuade her to leave earlier, once she dug her heels in.

I wonder how Waylan has a hold on her. *He must have threatened her with something.* I look toward the door, and the guards are stationed there. No easy escape.

"Hey, I support you, whatever your decision is, okay?" I don't understand her about-face, but I'm sure she'll explain herself later. As I hold her, I feel her trembling. She pulls back from me and offers me a small smile. I squeeze her hand tightly and she squeezes mine back.

One of the members of the royal court gets up and addresses the crowd in what I assume is Russian. I can see through the wood joint that

Waylan is making his way to the front of the room. He stands there, while the oration goes on.

Then the crowd stands, and the orator looks toward the alcove and gestures for us to come forward. As we walk from the alcove toward Waylan, I hear a gasp from the crowd. Then Waylan turns to face us, and I see his jaw drop, a sense of awe on his face. All of a sudden, he looks incredibly nervous, but for the first time, I see his eyes light up as he breaks out in a genuine smile.

The orator continues to speak in Russian, and Waylan answers back when required. Then the orator asks a question of Natalie. Waylan whispers to her. "Say 'da'." Natalie does so. The orator asks both of us questions, and Waylan guides us through the ceremony with the correct words in Russian.

Waylan is given a ceremonial knife, and pierces his hand. He holds Natalie's hand and pricks it gently, and they press their hands together. Everyone in the crowd applauds, and conversation starts up.

Waylan gestures to me to hold out my hand. "In support of your sister." He smiles at me.

At that moment, I'm distracted by the main doors being flung open. Waylan pricks my hand and presses it to his own hand, as Justin rushes in.

I feel tears build up in my eyes, as I smile with relief and wave at Justin with my other hand.

He's here!

I am about to rush over to him through the noisy crowd, when suddenly both my knees and Natalie's buckle underneath us and we fall to the floor. I'm in agony.

CHAPTER TWENTY-SIX

Justin stops for a moment, turning deathly white, looking at Waylan and trying to read the situation. Then he rushes up to us, as Waylan greets him with a big smile. "Justin, my cousin! You made it! You're a bit late because we started early, but there is plenty of food and drink to go around." Waylan laughs and claps him on the back.

But Justin pays no attention to him and crouches down next to me, concerned. "What happened?"

"We just did the part of the ceremony where I demonstrate support for Natalie, and I fell to the floor. Justin, I feel so strange." I rub my forehead, feeling a bit sickly. He draws his lips together in a thin line and helps me up, supporting me, while Waylan helps Natalie to her feet. I hear a low growl from Waylan.

"Waylan, what's going on?" Justin looks fierce. "What is she talking about?"

"Ah, it's a long story..." He scratches his head.

"Where's Vaughn?" Nat and I look at each other. Justin notices our glance. He rubs his hand through his hair. "Ah, Waylan, what did you do?"

Waylan speaks formally. "My brother is—indisposed right now." He looks between Justin and me as though trying to puzzle something out. He seems confused. "Darla, you know my cousin, Justin?" I nod.

"She is my betrothed." Waylan's eyes go wide at Justin's revelation.

Waylan insists otherwise. "No...no, she was Vaughn's betrothed." He steps backward in shock. He actually looks a bit afraid.

The majority of the guests have filed out of the ballroom by now. Justin's team and Waylan's guards have moved to where we are.

"There's something I'm not getting here, Waylan. Darla's sister is mated with you?" Waylan nods. "Then why did Darla's *ailouros* link just change color?"

"She's your *ailouros?*" Waylan takes another step back with Natalie in tow. He groans, pinching the bridge of his nose with his thumb and finger. "Oh hell, Justin."

"Please don't say you somehow did the impossible and completed the mating ceremony with Darla, too." Justin studies Waylan's face. Waylan is silent and won't make eye contact with him. "Damnit, Waylan! I told you not to mess with that stuff!"

I can hear Justin's wheels turning. After a minute, he sighs. "Okay, if you manipulated it, there's got to be a way to undo it."

"No." Waylan looks determined and takes a step toward Justin.

"No, what? No, it can't be undone or no, you won't undo it?"

"I'm keeping them both, and you can't stop me."

"Stop being a stubborn little prick, Waylan. I don't want to hurt you."

Waylan smirks and draws up to his full height, still shorter than Justin, but to me they're both giants. "She's my mate now. You hurt me, you hurt her. In fact, you'll hurt both of them." Justin looks uneasy.

Dick speaks up. "There are ways around that, Waylan. Besides, any man who uses that as an excuse to get out of a fight isn't really a man, is he?"

Waylan rolls his eyes. "Who invited you, Richard?"

"That's Dick to you."

"Yeah, well I don't have time to dick around, *Dick*." Waylan starts unbuttoning his royal coat, one button at a time. "Well, let's get to it then, Justin."

"Waylan, please reconsider. You know you can't even come close to beating me."

Waylan speaks under his breath. "That's where you're wrong, Dear Justin." He lays his coat over the back of his chair, untucks his white dress shirt, then starts unbuttoning it.

"Justin, something happened to him in the lab. He transferred something from Vaughn in a ritual. I think it was some sort of power. His roar did equivalent damage to that of an earthquake." Justin gives me a worried look.

Waylan removes his shirt, and everyone except me gasps as they see his fiery tattoos. Justin seems to be calculating.

"One more chance, Waylan. Please reconsider."

Waylan laughs. "Hahaha! What a bluff. For once I'm stronger than you, Justin. I'm not some kid to be pushed around."

Justin's tone is somber. "You know I never saw you that way, Waylan. You were always like a little brother to me." Justin removes his suit jacket, his tie, and starts working on his dress shirt.

Waylan pauses what he's doing, then makes a concession. "Look, I'll give *Dick* enough time to look after the girls before we start this."

"Thank you, Waylan." Justin hesitates as he looks at me. I can see the longing in his eyes, but holding me would only enrage Waylan because of the mate bond.

I move over to him and whisper. "When I cut Waylan earlier, his tattoos underneath stopped glowing. Not sure if it means anything." Justin nods.

He turns to his men. "Dick, Parker, take the girls to the medical lab and find what you need. Keep them safe." Justin and Waylan continue to strip in the ballroom.

Dick leads us to the back of the palace then in the direction of the lab. When we get to the science wing in the university, we see rooms with missing glass. A clean up crew has already been through the area. We

quickly rush to the lab as I fill them in on what happened earlier during the day.

"I want to warn you that I'm not sure what kind of condition Vaughn is in, and I hope to God he's still alive. He was lying there on the floor in his feline form when I snuck out earlier during all the chaos."

We dash across the last corridor and into the main testing lab. I hear Natalie gasp with relief. "He's alive. He hasn't transformed back into human form. But what happened to his coloring?"

She is apparently shocked by Vaughn's monochromatic coloring. She rushes to his side and strokes his fur. It looks damp, a result of the fire sprinkler from earlier.

"It was a result of the ritual. All the color moved from Vaughn to Waylan in a fiery glow, making Waylan's fur look like lava and coal. You saw how his tattoos look in human form."

"What does that mean?"

"The power radiating off him was immense. His roar alone created all the destruction down the corridor. He shattered the windows, there was debris everywhere.

"See the empty wall of that cell?" I point to the cell I had escaped from earlier during the day. "He broke apart that shatterproof material with his roar and wasn't even in the room at the time."

Dick and Parker are down on the floor checking Vaughn. "He's got a strong pulse and he's breathing steadily. Was he subdued and later knocked out by the ritual or was he medicated to get him into this state?" Dick looks up at me.

"He was medicated."

"You mean Waylan didn't even challenge Vaughn for kingship?" Dick grumbles. "That's low."

"The kingship seemed to have been transferred to him automatically along with my marking. I heard some referring to him as *prime ikati* and 'Your Highness' even though there was no type of ceremony."

Dick is texting. "Derby says the guys have headed outside. I need to take care of you girls and mute the mate bond."

Dick starts going through the fridge and cupboards for supplies. He starts making two piles of sterilized items. He prepares two syringes of some type of medication. He goes next door to get a gurney, followed by Parker.

Natalie is still stroking Vaughn's fur. "Natalie? I know you didn't want Waylan as your mate. Did he threaten you?"

"He threatened me with your safety if I didn't willingly participate, Darla."

What a coward.

"He did the same to me—threatened your well-being if I interfered with anything. I would have done something if I was guaranteed we'd get away safely."

Dick and Parker help us onto the gurneys. As I sit there I wonder out loud, "What will this do to us?" Dick is using an alcohol swab beside my rolled up sleeve.

"It will block any pain. Because of the mate bond, you may feel sensations as your mate goes through a painful physical experience. Since your mate is about to go into battle, this will alleviate Justin's worry of having to hold back for the sake of the two of you. He'll actually be able to fight."

"Will we be knocked out?"

"You shouldn't be, but you may not be able to move much. For some it immobilizes them, for others it just makes them feel very weak." I nod

my head, and Dick pierces my shoulder with the syringe. He keeps an eye on me while preparing a second syringe for Nat.

"I don't feel so good." I'm feeling a bit woozy and dizzy. Parker helps lower my back until I'm lying down. He winds the winch near my feet and it elevates my back slightly.

Dick helps Natalie into a supine position after her shot and elevates her back a bit.

"Should I worry about Justin? He's never been defeated, right?"

"He's never been defeated, and is much stronger than Vaughn, even though Vaughn is the strongest shifter in Eastern Russia. Waylan has always been far below Vaughn's strength, so no threat to Justin in the past. But something obviously happened during the ritual you witnessed, and Waylan has unassessed strength, to the point where he's confident he can beat Justin."

I try to nod my head, but have difficulty moving my muscles. If I didn't have the drug starting to move through my system, I'm sure I would feel the anxiety and rush of adrenaline that comes with untold worry for a loved one.

A loved one. It's true. I love Justin.

Even though I'm having difficulty feeling emotions, I know in my head and my heart that I love him with every ounce of my being.

"What has Waylan and Justin's relationship been like over the years?"

"Waylan always looked up to Justin as a big brother. He was envious of his actual brother because Justin and Vaughn were close. But they let Waylan join them. Over the years, Waylan's envy over Vaughn increased, but he always held Justin in high esteem. He wanted to be like Justin.

"But at the same time, his envy has caused him to seek power. He got into some pretty nasty business when he was younger and power-

hungry, but eventually returned to the pride. However, from what you described earlier about the ritual, he's apparently maintained some of his less savory contacts.

"The fact that he refuses to try to find a way to release you from the mating bond when he knows you're Justin's, shows there's been a change in him. His desire for power has grown."

"So his lust for power has overridden the bonds he had with Justin."

Dick nods. "I wouldn't rely on those bonds to dish out mercy. He finally has what he has always wanted, control of the kingdom, his newly found physical power, and has taken what he thought was his brother's mate, but happens to be the mate of one of the most powerful shifters in the world."

"He's out to prove something."

"Yes, that he's worthy of Justin's attention, and even more so, he's trying to prove to himself that he's a worthwhile person."

Parker gives some insight. "However, even with his lust for power, he decided not to use you girls as bargaining chips in the end to ensure a win against Justin. So that shows there's still some decency within him. Plus, he didn't murder his brother, just left him incapacitated."

"Is there any way we can see them? I need to know Justin is okay."

"It's too dangerous to go anywhere near them if they decide to fight this out. They know you're in this part of the compound so they'll avoid this section of the university. But maybe there's another way to view them..." Dick texts on his phone. He turns on a monitor hanging in the corner from the ceiling, used to project lab samples.

"Derby is sending video feed. I'll cast it so we can watch."

Dick sets up the screencasting on his phone, and we see two nearly naked men in the snow, talking. Overhead lights have been turned on, causing the snow across the field to sparkle and glow. Not that they'll need

the lighting. As feline shifters, their night vision would be extraordinary due to the reflective material on their retinas. But at least it will allow us to view the fight clearly.

I can hear Justin speak. "You've changed, Waylan. You've let envy cloud your mind and your judgment."

"No, I'm just ambitious, trying to make myself better, more powerful."

"You were fine the way you were. You don't need to prove anything to anyone."

"I want to be respected."

"To be respected, you need to act respectful first. What you did to Vaughn was not respectful or honorable. He's your brother and loves you."

I can hear the bitterness in Waylan's voice. "You both just saw me as a tag-along."

"That's not true, Waylan. I've always loved you as a brother. There's still time to change your mind. We can somehow straighten this mess out."

"It's too late for that. I'm sorry I didn't know Darla was your mate. But now that I've done the impossible and have two mates, I won't give that up. It means a stronger line of descendents, and a stronger dynasty. Surely you can see my point?"

"Waylan, those things you have now, you've stolen. You didn't fight Vaughn as tradition requires. You 'stole' the kingdom by stabbing him in the back—literally. You manipulated Darla during the ceremony without her realizing. And somehow you've taken power that is not your own.

"Any victory today won't belong to you, as you didn't earn any of those things. You're lying to yourself if you think those things make you a better person."

Waylan shakes his head, and the tattoos on his neck make it look like flames are being painted in the air.

"I'm done talking. Let's just get this over with."

"If you won't give up my mate, then I have no choice, Brother."

"We fight, traditional rules." They both grasp each others' arms, up to their elbows, to seal the deal. They start walking away from each other.

"What's happening? What do they mean by 'traditional rules'?"

"They've agreed to fight in accordance with a set of rules made several centuries ago. They include pacing off initially. An honorable fight, no assistance, no weapons. Waiting for the other to shift if the fight goes that way. And the winner takes all..." Dick sounds reluctant to continue.

"Okay, that doesn't sound too bad."

"Well, the most significant rule is..." Dick pauses. "It's a fight to the death."

CHAPTER TWENTY-SEVEN

I struggle to move, but my body is like jello and it won't obey me.

"What do you mean, 'to the death'?"

"I'm sorry, Darla. I don't want to see either of my cousins hurt." He then mutters to himself. "Even though Waylan is such a prick these days."

Dick crouches down, checking on Vaughn. I can see him pondering.

"I don't understand why it has to be to the death though." My emotions are like liquid, and I sound more zoned out than stressed.

"Apart from it being the traditional way to challenge, the only known way to break the mate bond is through death. And unless Waylan agrees to seek an answer through the stuff he was dabbling in, Justin has no choice but to fight to the death for you."

Dick's voice becomes low and serious as he looks up at me from his crouched position. "He was going crazy without you. Even though there was no longer a marking, it was as if one existed while you were separated. I've never seen him like that before."

I feel terribly guilty, knowing Justin's heart was faithful while mine was being pulled in different directions. "It was different for me, Dick. Although I love Justin, my feelings were so convoluted. I also care a great deal for Vaughn."

"That's understandable, since the marking can elicit strong reactions."

"And Vaughn is also a remarkable man. He and Justin are two of a kind. Men with solid character. I feel so wishy-washy beside them."

"Don't be so hard on yourself, Darla. Being marked by several people in such a short period of time would make anyone's head spin."

I catch sight of Natalie in my periphery. She doesn't seem to be moving. "Dick, can you check on Natalie? She looks so still."

"Sure." He stands up and walks over to Natalie to check on her. After a minute, he speaks. "Her pulse is strong and steady, and she's breathing fine, but I'm afraid she's out cold for now. That doesn't usually happen, but nothing to worry about. I gave her the same dosage as you."

"How is Vaughn?"

"He seems to be breathing okay. It would help to get him back into his human state though. It would be easier to assess his condition, and would make it possible to move him."

"Is there a way to do that?" I ask, surprised.

"Yes. Unfortunately, it involves another chemical injection to force a shift the other way if the patient is unable to shift by themselves."

"Is it dangerous?"

"Well, there is always an element of risk when forcing a change in either direction, but the rate of reaction is very low."

"How low?"

"So low I've never seen negative effects before. But then again, we've only ever forced shifts due to medical reasons or when someone is in distress."

Dick assembles what he needs with Parker's assistance, and gives Vaughn an injection. *Poor guy, he's been poked and prodded with needles. Hopefully, this will be the last one.* A minute later, we hear crackling and snapping as Vaughn transforms from his huge tiger back to his naked human form.

My eyes open wide, and Dick looks stunned. Vaughn's hair is now white.

"Has that ever happened before?" Dick shakes his head in reply to my question. "Do you think it means anything significant?" I'm worried

that what they did to Vaughn's tiger in the ritual will have consequences for his human body.

Dick and Parker carefully transfer Vaughn from the floor to another gurney. Dick looks pensive as he covers Vaughn with a light sheet. "I don't really know. I'm not completely sure how it affects his tiger form either. We're assuming the ritual initiated a transfer of Vaughn's power, your mark, and his position as *prime ikati*. We don't know how much power was transferred, if it's permanent, and what condition Vaughn is in because of the transfer."

"But his vitals are all good, right?"

"If they are, it just means he is able to maintain the most basic functions to sustain his life without support. We need to do a full medical examination before we know what kind of condition he is really in." Dick starts texting again.

Within three minutes a medical team and some of Vaughn's security rush into the lab. *They must have run all the way here.*

The security guys look frantic. "We've been looking everywhere for Vaughn. Security's scattered all through the area outside, scouring the grounds, searching for him. We never thought to look in the lab for him since he never comes here, and his scent was nowhere to be found. So we thought he was a distance away from here. We have a helicopter scouting farther out near the borders. We've just called everyone in and back to their regular posts."

"It's so odd. He has no scent. And why is his hair white?"

The medical team surrounds Vaughn, and equipment is brought in from the adjoining room. Natalie's hospital bed and mine are pushed against opposite walls to make more space. They put a cuff on Vaughn to measure his blood pressure, check his heart rate, then monitor his temperature and respiration rate.

A blood oxygen level sensor is placed on his finger and they set up an IV drip. Another needle. *He's going to feel like a pin cushion when he wakes up.* They continue in a flurry around Vaughn as they assess his condition.

I manage to tilt my head slightly to view the monitor. Justin and Waylan are warily circling one another, sizing each other up. The circle becomes smaller as they close in.

Suddenly, Waylan rushes forward to take a swipe at Justin. Justin ducks, and somehow Waylan overbalances and goes flying over Justin. He recovers quickly in a somersault, spinning around close to the ground, prepared with a block. He tries to take Justin's legs out from underneath him with his own leg. Justin anticipates the move and leaps over Waylan's powerful leg, dealing a kick of his own aimed at Waylan's head. His kick is blocked, and Justin springs back off the barrier Waylan makes with his hands.

Dick comes over and stands by me. "They're testing each other. They haven't sparred in a long time, and Justin's experience is second to none. He's fought some of the most talented shifters in the world. Waylan's got much more power than before, but needs to get used to his newly found strength. His balance was off during that first strike, but he adapted and his equilibrium was much better during his second move."

Justin waits for Waylan to make the next move. He must sense impatience from Waylan, which is not surprising, considering Waylan's temperament. Whenever Waylan moves, even just slightly, his glowing tattoos simulate flame-writing in the black of the night. I wonder if this is distracting or illuminating for Justin. I hope it somehow gives him an advantage.

Waylan closes the gap, and starts sparring with Justin. I watch punches, kicks, and blocks on both sides. Justin is allowing for the new

level of strength Waylan is projecting, but Waylan is still overbalancing and it looks like his equilibrium is off at times.

They move apart from each other, and both make a partial shift. They remind me of the catmen who ripped my car open like it was a can of sardines, except this time the pattern on their fur is stripes instead of rosettes. Their fighting style seems to be similar to their human moves, except their bodies have more height and bulk, can leap a lot farther, and have teeth and claws that can easily tear through flesh.

I swear that as Justin rains blow after blow on Waylan with his sharp claws, that the fiery glow on Waylan becomes less. I'm not sure what it means, but I hope it means Waylan's power is diminishing.

Waylan has difficulty keeping up with Justin, struggling to utilize his power. He uses his momentum as the smaller underdog, showing he is having difficulty adjusting. He breaks free from the onslaught of blows and leaps backward, out of range.

"Is Justin playing with him?"

"No. He's giving him a chance to adapt and get used to the changes in his body. Justin's always been a very sportsmanlike fighter, holding fairness as paramount. However, Waylan is fighting at his usual skill level, just with more powerful blows."

I watch as the two catmen round each other, sizing each other up again. Waylan moves in again, and they start to fight, this time with harder blows and kicks. Although it's difficult to tell, because Waylan is now blending into the night, it looks like he's taking the brunt of the blows.

"What's happening now?"

"Waylan is an emotional fighter. He has always allowed frustration to take over, making him impulsive. Justin has always been patient and level-headed while fighting, allowing him to calculate his moves."

The fighting becomes more vigorous. Waylan lapses into a routine of repetitive moves. Justin is thinking his moves through.

I carefully observe every move. "It looks like Justin is able to preserve more energy. Waylan seems predictable and is tiring."

"That's right, Darla. Justin is anticipating they'll end up doing a full shift. With that shift, power and size have a major increase, but stamina drops severely. Justin is preserving his energy for the next phase of the fight."

The two of them back away from each other, giving each other plenty of space, then run in opposite directions, into the birch forest that lines the field.

"And now they'll shift for the final stage of their fight."

I hear a groan from behind the medical team. *Vaughn!* I wish I could sit up, but all I can do is move my arms a bit. Dick walks toward them, observing from a distance. After a few minutes he returns.

"They must have injected a stimulant into his IV to wake him. He's awake, eyes open, and taking sips of water." Dick sits on the edge of my hospital bed and puts his head in his hands. He rubs his face and looks toward the middle of the room.

I feel the moisture in my eyes as they glisten with tears. Although my feelings are muted, I still react, which shows the depth of my emotion. My care for Vaughn runs deep. We sit in silence for several minutes.

I turn my attention back to the fight. "What are they doing now?" I stare at the screencast.

Dick walks closer to the screen to get an idea of what Justin and Waylan are up to. "They're hunting each other".

"What? How does that work?"

"Well, tiger-shifters rely on stealth as one of their primary tools when going up against an enemy."

I whisper to myself. "I wish Waylan would see he's never been regarded as an enemy."

Dick continues. "After stalking the target, the tiger-shifter initiates an intense surprise attack, to get the upper hand. They're good at short, focused attacks. Usually it's enough to immobilize their prey. Their overall stamina is limited, and they need to recover from their attacks before launching each new one."

"It looks like Justin has an advantage with the stalking part." I can see the glow of Waylan's coat contrasting with black. He looks like a glowing silhouette from some angles, and like a black panther touched by embers in other positions. I can't make out Justin's tiger anywhere.

"If he's downwind, he's got even more of an advantage. Waylan won't be able to pick up the direction of his scent." Waylan continues to slowly creep forward, ears twitching.

Sure enough, Justin launches a surprise attack, claws slicing across where Waylan's mane protects his throat. He draws some blood, while the two of them battle it out. They are standing on hind legs, balanced by their warring paws fiercely banging against each other. I can tell they're protecting their throats and spines by fighting this way. Harsh growls and short guttural roars come from both of them.

It reminds me of when Nat and I were little. We made card "tents" by standing two playing cards so they leaned on each other. If one wasn't balanced properly against the other, then both cards would fall down. The tigers are balancing off each other in this way, and Waylan's tiger's "stolen" strength is compensating for Justin's enormous size. I've read that regular Siberian tigers can stand up to eleven feet when fighting on their hind legs like this, but shifter limits must be much higher. The times I've seen Justin fight, he's superseded those limits.

Then the two of them break away, and prowl parallel to each other for a couple of minutes before attacking again. Justin's paws take swipes with their razor-sharp retractable claws at every opportunity they can, and I see he's figured out that deactivating the glow can be done by scraping Waylan's flesh and causing it to bleed. I can't tell from watching on the monitor, but Justin must feel it's somehow weakening Waylan physically since he keeps repeating those actions.

Another flurried attack, followed by a prowl. The next time the attack ends with Justin grasping the underside of Waylan's neck with his teeth, and holding on as he is tucked upside down. They lay still for a couple minutes like this except for paws swatting when they can, then start up their flurried fighting again.

I observe what Dick mentioned about stamina. Between each ferocious interval of fighting, is a break, the parallel walking or the grasping and holding until the next interval. I gather only a game of gradual stamina reduction or a decisive blow is going to end this fight.

The two tigers continue to fight this way. I notice Waylan weakening as the glow noticeably vanishes from his fur. He blends into the night more fully now. I see him stumbling more often, while Justin holds his ground.

Justin's teeth sink into one of Waylan's front legs, and there is a snapping sound. Waylan's front leg becomes useless in the fight, and he now has more difficulty protecting his throat.

During the next flurry of fighting, Waylan's front leg is pinned, while the other one hangs uselessly. Justin finally gets a better grip on Waylan. Instead of ripping out his throat, I can see Justin trying to force him to submit. But instead of staying close to the ground in submission, Waylan pushes his back paws into Justin, giving him leverage to flip the two of

them over. Justin's hold on Waylan's throat is relentless, and his canines won't release Waylan unless he submits.

"Justin is giving Waylan the option to yield. He doesn't want this to go to the death."

I nod as I watch the two of them grapple in the eerie glow created by the snow's reflection. With all his strength, Waylan pushes his hind paws against the ground, digging in, forcing the two of them into a standing position on their back legs again. Waylan is trying to use Justin's height against him, forcing him to bend his neck in order to keep his grip on his throat. Because of the awkward position, Waylan is able to get his paw free and take a swipe at Justin's face, hoping to get him to release his throat.

However, Justin's incredible size overbalances the two of them, and Justin crashes down beside Waylan, his canines still buried in Waylan's throat. Justin tries to release Waylan, but it's too late, and the result is not pretty. Waylan's throat has been ripped open, and blood is pouring from the deep gash. Several seconds later, Waylan shifts back into his human form.

As Justin shifts, I hear him yell. "No!" He stops shifting halfway and picks up Waylan, running toward the university.

CHAPTER TWENTY-EIGHT

"He'll be coming here, to the medical-science wing."

"The girl is awake."

"Natalie?" I call across the room. I'm unable to see her because of the medical team in the middle of the room. I hear a tiny murmur from her.

I watch as the medical team prepares the room for their incoming critical patient.

"Blood type for transfusion?"

"Checking records."

Vaughn is moved beside Natalie to make more space.

I feel the mate bond break. I still can't feel much emotionally, due to the injection Dick had given me earlier, but I feel the break.

"He's dead." Natalie's quiet voice is emotionless.

I can briefly see Vaughn and Natalie as the medical team moves around.

Vaughn struggles to get up. "No!" His voice is hoarse and he sounds choked up. I can see a tear make its way down his face.

Natalie reaches out her hand to hold his as he falls back onto the mattress and faces her. They lie there beside each other, and I can see Vaughn's back shaking as he deals with his grief. I know Vaughn is trying to draw strength from her.

Justin bursts into the room, half-shifted, with Waylan in his arms. He sees the med team and places Waylan on the hospital bed. They get to work on him immediately.

Justin shifts back fully into his human form and starts pacing. He goes to the sink and immerses his head under the tap, and I see red liquid run

off him into the sink. After a minute, he pulls his head out from under the stream of water. Then he scrubs and scrubs, trying to eliminate all traces of liquid death.

He starts pacing again, looking over at Waylan, running his hands through his hair. Dick taps his shoulder and hands him a hospital gown, bringing him out of his trance. He ties it over his naked body, then sees me. He walks over, pulling me up into a wet hug.

"Justin."

"Darla." Justin's lip is trembling. He carefully lowers my head back down.

We listen closely as they work on Waylan, trying to decipher what the team is saying to each other. "Pulse check."

Two members are off to the side murmuring to each other quietly. "...started healing already until the moment he died. The throat wound is now not as bad as it was originally. If they can just revive him..."

"Continue compressions." Justin holds my hand as we listen and wait.

Both Natalie and I gasp. "The mate bond is back." We hear beeping on the cardiac monitor. Then Waylan flatlines again.

"Justin, quickly, mark me." He looks at me. "While the mate bond is broken. Please."

He nods and bends over me quickly, piercing my skin with his canines. Then everything goes black.

I wake up and turn over. I see Justin sleeping in the chair beside my bed. His sleepy eyes open.

"Good morning, Princess." He gives me a sleepy smile, but I can still see the worry lines on his brow.

"Good morning, Justin." I smile at him.

He kneels beside the bed, stroking my hair. "So how do you feel?"

"I feel tired." I yawn.

"Waylan made it. The doctors worked on him all night." He pauses, searching my face. "What about the bond and the marking. Did it work?" He grasps my hand, looking at me with hope tainted with fear in his eyes.

I jerk up into a sitting position, suddenly remembering the details of the night before. I force myself to feel.

"I can feel..."—Justin looks as though he's holding his breath as I speak—"...your marking."

I squeal and throw my arms around his neck. We're both laughing and shedding tears at the same time. We hold each other for several minutes, and I melt into his arms. I feel so relieved, so comforted, so...at home. Home is where the heart is, and I know who my heart belongs to.

Then Justin looks at me directly. "Darla, be honest with me. Is this what you want?"

I respond without hesitation. "Yes, Justin, I just want you." He pulls me onto his lap and hugs me from behind.

"Are you sure?" He pauses. "What are your feelings for Vaughn?"

I speak truthfully. "I did feel drawn to him, very much so. But I feel it's more like a brother-sister bond. He is someone who I highly respect."

"So, there's nothing romantic you'd like to explore there?" I can feel him holding his breath again.

"No, nothing at all. Dick told me that a lot of the draw to Vaughn was due to the marking. I had ample opportunity to explore things romantically with him, but instead we built a friendship. I just want you, Justin. You and only you."

He sits me on the bed and looks me straight in the eyes, searching. "Then I have no other option than to do this." He slides to the edge of the bed.

"Do what?"

Justin slides off the bed and onto the floor, pulling me to the edge so my legs hang over the edge. *What's going on?* I feel confused.

He positions himself on one knee, then reaches into his pocket and pulls out a little velvet box. He opens it and inside is the most beautiful ring, a diamond set in rose gold, with intricate tiny roses and vines. My eyes open wide.

He looks up with sincerity as he searches my eyes. "Will you, Darla, make me the happiest man alive, marry me, and become my mate?"

"Yes!"

I reach for him and he picks me up off the bed, twirling me around as we laugh together, then settles his lips on mine. His kisses are tender, filled with gentleness. I cradle his head in my hands. I touch my nose to his.

"Yes." Our foreheads touch and we hold the moment. "Yes, I will marry you and become your mate."

As he holds me in his embrace, I feel enveloped in his love. He gently presses his lips to mine, and I want time to stand still. To cherish every second with this man who has stolen my heart and made it his. Our kiss is tender, pure heaven. Something I will never take for granted, having gone without it for what feels like forever.

I'm in his arms. I'm safe. I'm loved. All I can hope for now is that Natalie finds the same happiness. *Natalie...* I gently pull away from the kiss, and Justin can tell what's on my mind, just by looking at my face.

"There's a lot to tell you about last night. After the marking seemed to work on you, I immediately told Natalie. She was desperate for

someone to mark her, to break the mate bond, even if they just held her mark for now. Vaughn volunteered without hesitation."

My smile is so bright I'm beaming. "Natalie is in love with Vaughn. Her feelings were so strong toward him, even after Waylan's marking, although she never acted on those feelings out of love and respect for us."

"I know for a fact it's mutual. Vaughn is in love with her."

"You do? Really?" I recall bits and pieces. "Well, Vaughn was so taken with her initially that he wanted a similar mate for himself. And I know he's felt a great deal of affection for her even without the draw of the marking."

"I know Vaughn. He never would have admitted he had feelings for her before because she was Waylan's marked mate. He's always kept clear boundaries, and never tried to take from others. But I can tell he loves her. I know my cousin better than he knows himself.

"Last night in the infirmary the two of us stayed up late, talking while you girls slept. When I asked him about transferring her mark to someone else—well, that's when he snapped out of denial. He realized he never wants to let her go.

"He's known her as long as you and I've known each other, but he suppressed any romantic feelings for her because of the circumstances. He no longer has to suppress those feelings, and he's going to be honest with her about how he feels."

I feel so happy for her, knowing their feelings are mutual. I'm excited to talk with Natalie about this turn of events, ripe with possibilities. I hope I can catch her soon, once she and Vaughn have had their discussion.

"What's Vaughn's condition?"

"We're really not sure yet. Only time will tell. He may still be the strongest shifter in the area, even if he's been weakened."

"What will happen to his throne?"

"Well, with my win, I also won back the throne from Waylan. I'm bequeathing it to Vaughn."

"You have no desire to be king?"

"Just king of my own home and life, with my own lovely queen by my side." He smiles at me, softly. "It's not the first time I've passed the throne to Vaughn."

I'm completely taken by surprise. "Really?"

Justin scratches the back of his neck and looks a bit shy. "I'm by far the strongest shifter from Eastern Russia. Vaughn has always been second strongest. But life in the palace is more Vaughn's thing, even though I grew up here with him. So when we came of age, I abdicated and Vaughn became the next king."

"I'll have to get some embarrassing moment stories about your childhood from Vaughn and Waylan."

Justin's expression changes and his tone becomes serious. "Actually, you may not be talking with Waylan for a long time."

"Why's that?"

"Waylan will be tried for treason because of how he backstabbed Vaughn and stole from him instead of challenging him. However, Vaughn and I are going to push for imprisonment and rehabilitation with the *prime konseho* instead of the death penalty. I think Waylan can change his ways and become a contributing part of society without being a risk to others. He's still young, and several family members, including Vaughn and myself, are willing to take him under our wings. If he's willing to change, that is."

I nod my head in agreement.

"But about other things, Darla. How would you feel about a wedding and mating ceremony in a palace?"

I gasp and put my hand to my chest. Then I pause and reflect. "Well, on one condition."

"Whatever it is, I'll do my best to make sure it's taken care of. What is your condition?" He smiles at me and takes my hand in his.

"That it's *you* I'm marrying."

As he sits down on the bed, he pulls me to himself and places me sideways on his lap. He leans in and nuzzles my neck where my mark is, breathing in the scent of my hair.

Justin places his forehead against mine and smiles. "I think that could be arranged." We touch noses, then his lips find mine and gently brush against them. His lips gently settle on mine, and he kisses me with tenderness. He touches my lower lip with his tongue, and my lips part slightly. His tongue caresses my own briefly, leaving me longing for more.

Justin's hands cradle my head, and his kiss continues, becoming more insistent. I find myself falling into the passion of the moment, allowing my thoughts to leave me, and to just focus on loving this wonderful man here with me. I feel all sense of where I am disappearing, and as if I'm floating, falling.

No wonder they call it "falling" in love.

Justin unlaces the front of my lavender nightdress the staff had dressed me in. The upper part of my chest is revealed, showing a bit of cleavage, and Justin gently lays me down on the bed. He drags his lips down from my mouth to my neck, then along my upper chest. The sensation is intoxicating.

I reach my hands underneath Justin's shirt and he pulls it off. He lifts me back up from a lying position and holds me close. The sensation of his skin on mine feels amazing.

Justin whispers in my ear. "You mean the world to me, Darla. You are my everything." I press closer to him and squeeze him in a hug.

"I love you, Justin."

"I love you, too, Darla."

We hold each other for some time, our hands stroking each other's hair, just basking in each other's love. I feel perfectly happy at this moment.

"Justin?"

"Yes, Darling?"

"Could we get married sooner rather than later? After the last scare, I'd rather be safe than sorry."

"How soon are we talking?"

"As soon as possible."

"I think that could be arranged. Let me send out some texts, and see what Vaughn and I can work out."

We wander down to the dining room a bit later in the afternoon, in search of food. Staff from the kitchen pull out leftovers from lunch and prepare us both a plate. I feel like I'm starving. Then I remember I've missed a few meals. We sit next to each other at the dining room table.

Justin can't keep his eyes off me. "I didn't know if I'd find you again. We used every contact we had, followed every possible lead, searched high and low, with no luck."

"How did you know I was in Eastern Russia?"

"I didn't! I was at the end of my rope, and thought to enlist Vaughn's help, since he and Waylan had invited me to their double mating ceremony. I didn't know you were here until I felt you through the *ailouros* bond." Justin takes my hand and leans forward.

"I put two and two together and tried to contact Vaughn, with no luck. No cell service since the drive is so remote. We rushed as fast as we could." I sense Justin's urgency as he speaks. "I figured you were about to be joined together with one of my cousins. I was hoping we had enough time to prevent it."

I shake my head. "Waylan moved the ceremony up, due to his impatience."

Justin nods. "That sounds just like him. I must have walked in right after he completed the bond with you."

"He told me I was supporting Natalie so I thought it was a bridesmaid thing. The ceremony was in Russian, he'd threatened to hurt Natalie, and I was distracted by you coming through the door—my head was spinning. But I had no clue I would end up as his mate."

Justin spoke softly, brushing a tendril of hair behind my ear. "I'm so sorry I wasn't here to protect you. I was relieved when the bond showed me you were here, since I thought you'd be safe with my cousins. At the same time I was stressed at the thought of you bonding with one of them. But I had no idea Waylan had taken things this far."

"It's not your fault, Justin. If it wasn't for that guy, Snake..."

"You mean Slice?" His mouth quirks in amusement.

"Yeah, that guy. We wouldn't have been separated. By the way, what was all that about? What happened to you?"

Justin sighs. "He told me the terms had changed and you were going to The Circle to be re-marked. He felt we were too close, and wanted to make sure nothing disrupted the transaction with the buyer. That's why he loaded extra men on the plane in the first place as 'excess cargo'..."

I crack a quirky smile. "'Excess cargo'? Edible snails?" Justin snorts at my terrible pun.

He continues. "He dropped me back off in North America at a different location than where we'd left from. It took some time for us to reassemble the team and get started, since I was still knocked out for a few hours."

"But still—I now dub thee 'Just-in-time'."

Justin groans. "That was even worse."

I laugh. "Go on. Sorry for interrupting. I'm just in such a giddy mood."

Justin wears a smile of amusement. "I can tell." He chuckles at my silliness.

"I gave the money Slice paid me to Vaughn—Vaughn thought he'd paid a finders' fee. He thought the women were willing participants who had consented from the beginning. He had no idea about how the system had been manipulated over the years." Justin shakes his head.

"It's like going back a few hundred years, to when women were auctioned off to wealthy shifters. Mandatory marking now provides protection, but I still don't like the idea of these marked exchanges."

"Well, something has to change with the way shifters obtain mates. It's still barbaric going through the arena situation as a woman, being given no fair options." It's high on my list of priorities as *ailouros*.

"I agree. However, we need to come up with solutions that will bring about the same results without endangering the shifter population as a whole. Do you have any ideas yet?"

"Not yet, but once we're settled back home, it's a project I'll be working on as *ailouros*. The first question I have is about the scientific reason why most births are male. There's got to be a reason for it. I think it may be a good place to seek answers."

"Oh! I never even thought of that, Darla. It should definitely be researched if it hasn't been already. Good call." Justin smiles at me and squeezes my hand.

"From a different perspective, if the women had options and *chose* the arena competition, then I'm okay with it. To me, it's the lack of choices for the women involved that is barbaric. Yes, both my story and Natalie's have wonderful endings, but it may not be that way for all women. It's something to be researched as we consider presenting any changes."

"Well, there's one thing you're wrong about."

"Hmm?"

"Your stories don't have wonderful endings."

"What do you mean?"

"Your stories have wonderful *beginnings*. This is the start of something new and precious for all of us, Darla."

I can't help but smile at Justin.

CHAPTER TWENTY-NINE

Vaughn and Natalie walk into the dining room, hand in hand. I smile at this development. Justin and I stand.

"Natalie, you and Justin never had the opportunity to formally meet." The two of them exchange greetings, then Natalie and I hug while Justin and Vaughn embrace.

"So you and Darla wish to hold both a wedding and mating ceremony as soon as possible! How about four days from now? All the guests will still be here and the major preparations have already been done. It also gives a few days to bring over Darla and Natalia's parents and any other close friends the girls may have."

"Girls? As in plural?"

Vaughn seems a bit shy, which is unusual for him. "Well, Natalia and I had a deep discussion about it, and I've asked her to be my one and only. After observing what Darla has been through and the risks involved, we decided not to wait. Less anxiety for both of us. Otherwise, I don't think we'll be sleeping due to worry.

"So Justin, you up for a double wedding and mating ceremony?"

"Absolutely, Vaughn, if Darla and Natalie are in agreement."

Natalie and I are excited about the idea. It will be an incredibly memorable day, and bring all four of us closer together. So we get down to the nitty-gritty details and make some decisions. Then we make an appointment with the lady who planned the original double mating ceremony, and tell her what our wishes are.

"Four days?" Her eyes were like saucers. "Well, if you're sure. Here are some options that need to be considered..."

She begins to lay out a schedule for dress fittings and all of the details for the bridal party. The men will arrange flights and palace accommodations for remaining relatives. She delegates her assistant to deal with the catering from the kitchen, florist, cake creator, and more.

Thankfully, the palace has already been decorated and most guests have been situated. However, there is still a lot to be done. The excitement in the hallways is evident from the guests and staff. Although there was some upset due to Waylan's actions, the palace will still host a once-in-a-generation event.

I don't think the responsibilities of becoming queen have completely hit Natalie yet, but she is a keen learner and will have plenty of time to adjust to her new role. She and Vaughn have been growing closer, due to their previous affection for one another, the marking, and strong natural attraction. I think they are perfect for each other.

They have compatible personalities, ideals, and values, and both have solid character. They make a good couple, and I can't wait to see how their relationship grows over the years. I smile wistfully.

As for my own *ailouros* responsibilities, I haven't forgotten the poverty issue, the problem of how mates are obtained, or that the shifters are teetering on war with the humans. Once we get back home from this unexpected and amazing journey, we have our work cut out for us.

Vaughn and Justin arrange for our parents and closest friends to be flown in. My parents are definitely surprised, to say the least. They had recently returned home from their vacation overseas, and were starting to become alarmed at not being able to reach either of us.

Although they haven't been involved much in our lives during recent years, they still have concerns over our upcoming marriages. They feel it is all so sudden, since it is all new to them. Not introducing them to our future spouses previously has contributed to that.

"Darla, you're both serious about this?" My father's brows are knit together in concern.

"We know the two of you are so independent, but neither of you have ever talked about these men playing a part in your lives." Mom seems troubled.

"Yes, I want to spend the rest of my life with Justin, and Natalie wants the same with Vaughn."

"As long as you're sure. We just want the two of you to be happy with your spouses."

"How are the two of you doing? We haven't had a chat in ages."

"We're doing okay. Dealing with normal life issues, now we're done travelling for the present. We've missed you girls since you moved away." It's the first time my dad has admitted this to us since we settled across the country.

Mom speaks in earnest. "We really do, Sweetheart. We've missed the two of you."

We've never been really close with our parents—they've always been a bit distant—but maybe things are about to open up for us. I've heard some parents relate better to their adult children and have a more open relationship with them. Maybe we'll be able to connect better with our parents now we're older.

The idea of being closer to family, both Justin's and mine, gives me a feeling of warmth and support. I smile, happy that things may change with our parents. Although we're unable to share about shifter society, there are plenty of other things we can share. I'll make sure to spend time with them before the wedding.

My best friend, Susan, is a bit miffed at me. I can tell, even though she tries to hide it behind her bubbly personality. She talks a mile a minute. "Wow, it seems like everything is happening so fast! I'm so

surprised—Natalie's always been so cautious. I can't believe the two of you are getting married! And to royalty! I'm so happy for you. Really. I wish I'd been kept more in the loop though.

"Just remember I'm always here for you to talk, vent, or whatever you need, whenever, okay?" She hugs me and gives me a special squeeze. "Love you, Darla." I can see tears glistening in her eyes.

My parents' reservations begin to fade away, while sharing afternoon tea in the conservatory gardens with Natalie, Justin, Vaughn, and myself. The men easily charm my mother's socks off. She thinks it's wonderful that Natalie and I have met such "fine young men", as she puts it. I overhear snatches of my dad's conversation with Justin, as I sit with my mom. Natalie and Vaughn are close by on a stone bench, no doubt having a moment of conversation about the upcoming nuptials.

"So tell me, Justin, what kind of business are you in?" My father sits forward in his chair to engage with him.

I smile at my mom and put my arm around her. Together we enjoy the garden atmosphere and colorful blooms. They look so odd against the snowy background on the other side of the conservatory windows.

My mom sighs, enjoying the atmosphere. "It's the best of both worlds inside here. The beautiful white landscape without the cold, plus the scent of the gorgeous indoor flowers. So far the conservatory is my favorite room in the palace."

"Wait until you see the ballroom, Mom. It's absolutely amazing. Everything is so ornate. Add in the decorations and it's like a dream. We couldn't have hoped for a more beautiful place to have our weddings and receptions."

"Well, I'm very happy for both of you girls." She pats me on the hand. My mom and dad have never been very expressive or social, so to

see them engaging with others and discussing feelings is something very positive and important to me.

"I'm so glad you're here with us, Mom." I squeeze her shoulders in a half-hug.

"I am, too, Darla." She takes my hand and squeezes me back.

Natalie and Vaughn move closer to us, and Justin and my dad join us. The six of us spend the rest of the afternoon together, now that my parents have both been reassured. I am relieved they are so accepting of Justin and Vaughn.

During mealtime, the large dining hall is full, with all the guests lodged in the palace. Some of those from our pride back home are in attendance. It's nice to see the familiar faces.

Waylan's room has been cleared out, and Justin stays there. Natalie and I have swapped rooms. Justin and I also have a sitting room separating our rooms, and when we need a bit of time to ourselves, we have our "oasis". The night before our ceremony, we sit there together, just holding each other.

"I'm so glad I have you, Darla."

"And I'm so glad I have you, Justin."

There's a tender moment when we explore each other's eyes, then Justin gently kisses my lips. I reciprocate, and his lips brush my cheek, the corner of my mouth, and my lips again. He sweeps his tongue lightly across my bottom lip, and my lips part for him. His tongue touches mine, and I feel electricity coursing downward through my body.

Justin's tongue is probing while his hands cradle my head, and the passion begins to swell inside me. As if he can feel it, Justin kisses me more intently. I feel like I'm soaring, without wings. I'm suspended in mid-air, flying, and can't get enough of Justin's love. I feel truly happy and content, while at the same time desire builds inside me.

Justin's hand goes through my hair, gripping it firmly, while his other arm scoops my body flush with his. He starts kissing me down my chin to the underside, then down my neck to the bottom of my gown's sweetheart neckline. He kisses me across my collarbone as my head leans backward. Want and need stir inside me.

Justin supports my head as he brings it to his own, so our foreheads are touching. We are both panting, out of breath, as though just finishing a sprint. We brush our lips together a few times before sitting back and examining each other's eyes again. It would be so easy to get lost in one another.

Justin whispers. "We have a long day ahead of us tomorrow. We should both get some rest." I nod my head, reluctantly agreeing.

Justin offers me his hand. He walks me to the door at the side of the room that leads to my chambers.

"Sleep well, Princess. I'll see you in the morning."

Although it took some time for me to get to sleep, I am up early, excited and nervous about what the day will bring. Justin and I have an early breakfast in our attached sitting room together. We don't have a lot of time, but we enjoy our few minutes together, chatting while drinking morning tea and coffee.

When our time is nearly up, Justin and I are in each other's arms. "Think about it. The next time we are together will be when we're ready to complete the ceremonies." He winks at me and strokes my hair.

"It feels surreal, that today is the day, and this time I'll be bound to the *right* man." I giggle. He smiles and kisses me on both cheeks, as he finally puts an end to the incessant knocking on the sitting room door.

"Come!" Staff spills through the door, and we're both swept away in waves toward our rooms.

The ladies are back to ready me for today's ceremonies. There are four hours until the start, so they begin right away. My Maid of Honor, Susan, is with me as she is also being dolled up.

My hair is being curled for a half updo, one of my favorite hairdos for formal occasions. I feel the warm iron as it spirals my hair, then smell the sweet lemony hair spray as it lands on each curl to make it last. After that, the stylists work on shaping my overall look so it's soft and appealing. They showcase beautiful, shiny curls down my back while framing my face at the front with two ringlets. They adorn the top of my head with an intricate braid, laced with ribbon and tiny flowers.

Once they finish my hair, an update is given on the preparations for the events. The guests are now being seated for an early brunch in the dining hall. Afterward, the lounges and parlors will be open so they can chat and relax before the commencement. The grand dining room is already prepared for the reception, and the food is well on its way. The ladies now start on my facial treatment, smoothening my complexion with a luxurious exfoliation, followed up with soft creams.

A stylist faces me toward the mirror. "It's like art. You need a nice canvas on which to begin your painting. We now have a soft, smooth canvas to work on." I have never really considered makeup application to be a form of art, but I now realize the skills used when painting a portrait are the same ones used when applying makeup.

After the primer is blended into my skin, one of the ladies prepares the stylus to start the airbrushing. This is only the second time I've had airbrushed makeup, the first time being for the previous ceremony. From experience, I know the result will be flawless.

Once my makeup has been applied and set, we are ready for our dresses. Natalie and I had decided on coral dresses for our Maids of Honor. For the bouquets and palace decorations, the color scheme is coral, with purple and aqua as the accenting colors, plus plenty of greenery.

The coral dress for Susan has a vertically pleated satin bodice with tiny off-white rosebuds and green leaves. The lower part of the dress has a layer of chiffon over the satin. The dress accentuates her figure, and she looks gorgeous.

Natalie and I chose matching wedding dresses in off-white, in the same style as the dresses for our Maids of Honor, but with tiny coral, aqua, and purple rosebuds on the vertically pleated bodices. To complete our bridal outfits, we both have off-white veils, with tiny matching rosebuds, that flow beyond our shoulders. I can't wait to see how Natalie looks.

Once we're completely dressed, my bouquet of coral roses, accenting flowers, and off-white satin ribbons is placed in my hands. Susan walks up to me.

"Darla, you look unreal. I can't describe how gorgeous you are. You're going to knock Justin's socks off." We giggle together.

"I'd love to know I have that effect on him."

"I'm sure you already do!" She pauses. "Darla, I'm so happy for you and Justin. He is getting the most amazing and caring friend as his beautiful bride. You mean so much to me. And even when things get hectic and busy, I'll be there for you."

"Thank you, Susan. You mean so much to me, too." My eyes start to feel moist and I choke up a bit. "I'm trying not to cry so it doesn't ruin my makeup."

She laughs. "Don't you dare cry!" I join her in a good laugh, as my nerves are flowing over the top and spinning me around emotionally. "Better to laugh than cry."

There is a knock at the door. We both call out in unison, then giggle. "Come in!"

CHAPTER THIRTY

The door opens and I see Natalie standing there, looking like a fairy queen. In addition to the wedding and mating ceremonies today, Natalie will have a coronation ceremony as she becomes queen. She looks the part. She is breathtaking.

Although Natalie and I have matching bridal outfits, her hair has been done differently. It pours over her back in long ringlets with a crown braid on top, with a beautiful rosette crown woven in.

We move out of the crowded room and into the hallway. Natalie and I hug each other carefully so as not to get tangled in bobby pins from our veils, in florist wire from our bouquets, and in ribbons and rosettes. We walk to the main mirror in the upper hallway as the palace photographers take photos. We look so alike, yet seem different with the auras we are projecting.

Natalie seems so wistful and fairy-like in the way she carries herself today, whereas I have a more engaging air. Both of us are incredibly beautiful in our own ways. We smile into the mirror and at each other as the photographers take photos of us posing around the ornate decor, with paintings of cherubs on the walls.

The photographers stop us every few steps to get the photos they are seeking. We eventually find ourselves at the stairs leading to the main floor. There are new flower arrangements in coral, aqua, and purple that evoke the feeling that spring is in full bloom. Throughout the palace, it is. And in my heart it is, also.

After descending the staircase, we arrive at the first set of double doors where Natalie stands. I am led to a second set farther down the hall. Once we are settled, the doors open for our Maids of Honor. I stand

aside so I can't be seen, and am not able to see inside as a result. The doors close as both Maids of Honor walk down two different aisles at the same time.

I'm directed to move in front of the doors. I hear the music change, then the doors open and I see everyone standing. I'm astounded at how many people are in attendance. The room is now a double ballroom with a balcony. A dividing wall must have been opened for the room to be so expansive. I walk forward, one slow step at a time into a wonderland, a florist's dream. The beautiful chandeliers sparkle from the noonday sun, and the flowers give an ambience that is creamy and soft.

I look to the front and see Justin, standing next to Vaughn. The aisles are angled like spokes on a wheel, so Natalie and I will be next to our future husbands and soulmates when we arrive at the center. I see Justin watching me in wonder as I approach him, one step at a time. My filmy veil softens my view of everything. I finally reach him and stop beside him. He and Vaughn are now back-to-back, both facing their brides.

Justin gently lifts my veil and I can hear him gasp, his eyes wide. His smile brightens even more, and his eyes glisten. He looks like he's in heaven. As we go through the ceremony, in both Russian and English, he takes my hand. I can feel him trembling. He looks into my eyes and speaks his vows with sincerity.

"Darla, when we met that first evening, I could feel the sparks between us, and I knew you were the one for me. We've been through extraordinary circumstances, yet found our way back to each other.

"This, I promise you. That I will never take you or your love for granted. That I will cherish you and always put your needs first. That I will nurture and protect you all the days of our lives. Until death do us part." Justin places a ring on my finger.

I speak my own vows and place a ring on Justin's finger. Then we step farther away from those witnessing our union. A legal document is waiting to be signed and witnessed, sealing our marriage. I remove one of my lace gloves.

A thick pin is used to puncture both Justin and my thumbs discreetly, since there are those from the non-shifter community in attendance. We join our hands together, ensuring the blood from our thumbs intermingles at the site of the wounds.

I can then sense that the mating bond is sealed. However, it feels different than the time with Waylan. I don't feel like falling over, and I feel complete. I can sense Justin's feelings through the bond. The joy, the wonder, the rapture. The love he has for me is so immense it could never be measured.

"You may now kiss the brides."

Through my periphery, I see Vaughn reach down to Natalie. Justin cradles my head, tilts my chin up, and bends toward me, caressing my lips with his own. He is so tender, and I feel a rush of love through our bond.

The bond is truly amazing. In my mind, instead of two separate candles, we are now one candle with two wicks, burning brightly, side by side. I feel so cherished.

I am in awe. The whole ceremony has been surreal, like a dream. More beautiful than anything I could imagine. For I am marrying my beloved, the one I want to be with for the rest of my life, both now and when we're old and grey. This is forever.

Once our ceremony is complete, and the onlookers have finished clapping, Justin, the two Maids of Honor, the groomsmen, and myself stand off to the side. Now comes Natalie's coronation. She and Vaughn move to the center of the room where she is firstly joined to the pride,

with another discreet touching of fingers, then Natalie makes her vows to the people of the region.

My head is still swirling, getting used to the mate bond and the overwhelming feelings it initially brings on. Justin gestures to me that it's time to stand behind the new queen, to act as witnesses and sign the royal document. The document is signed by all four of us, and Natalie is now Queen of Primorsky Krai. Another discrete brushing of Vaughn's pricked finger over Natalie's mark with her words of acceptance, and Natalie has completed the *prime ailouros* ceremony.

Joyous celebration rings out. People are overjoyed about the ceremonies and the coronation. After many years without a *prime ailouros*, they now have a beautiful, caring queen to fulfill that role.

The celebration moves into the dining hall where people are seated. Floral garlands adorn the walls, doors, and a lattice archway. The eight of us in the wedding party will sit at a head table for everyone to see. The chairs are dark wood with navy cushions, brocaded with gold, and the tablecloths are off-white, similar to the color of the walls.

Beautiful bouquets of flowers in our wedding colors grace each table. Flowers woven together with greenery join the bouquets together, creating a gorgeous theme of connectedness. Aglow with candlelight amidst the other sparkling decorations, the reception looks stunning. Natalie and I walk in our satin layered heels, with lace-gloved hands holding onto our new husbands' arms, and take our seats.

We are both pleased to see we will be seated beside each other at the table, with our husbands flanking us. After our husbands seat us, I grasp Natalie's hand and squeeze, smiling at her. I can tell she's feeling overjoyed.

Justin is at my right, and pulls me into his side for a hug. He looks down at my face and touches my nose with his. He gives me a tender kiss.

The house staff start serving us, and the food looks and smells delicious. As the meal goes on, we enjoy the laughter and camaraderie around us.

"I feel so at home with everyone, Justin."

"I'm happy you do. I was raised here, and consider everyone to be my family. And now you are my family, the one I hold closest and dearest to my heart."

"And the one you share your chocolate-covered strawberries with?" I eye his plate with an innocent look.

He laughs. "Yes, here, Darling." He feeds me a chocolate-covered strawberry, and I close my eyes as the bright strawberry taste mixes with the intoxicating chocolate.

"Mmmmm."

Justin whispers. "Just seeing your eyes close like that and hearing you make that sound..." He kisses me softly on the cheek while he discretely squeezes my thigh.

After dinner, we have our first dances together as newlyweds and mates. I'm relieved Justin is such a good dancer, and all I need to do is follow his lead. I get caught up after a while with the twirling and movement, and just relax into his chest as we sway.

"My Darla."

"Mmmmm. I love the sound of that."

Natalie and Vaughn are so enraptured with each other. I smile as I watch them dance. They are such good people and deserve to be happy.

Susan is having a blast with the other groomsman. They've hit things off well and are having fun. Justin's groomsman, Nelson, and his mate, Katie, are clearly enjoying themselves. It's been so nice to see them again. Natalie's old roommate, Julia, looks comfortable, swaying in another man's arms.

The day is perfect, everything I could have ever wanted for my dream wedding. As the day extends into the evening, family and friends greet us, as others step out into the conservatory garden. House staff serve drinks to guests in the parlors and lounges. As the sun begins to set, Justin and I step into the conservatory to watch the colors saturate the sky.

Strings of lights on slo-glo mode turn on, creating a magical feel as the world transitions to night. Chandeliers have been dimmed and lamps set to create a romantic evening ambience. Candelabras throughout the main areas on the first floor have been lit, and people enjoy mingling, spending time with family and old friends, and getting to know new ones.

I've become so used to the palace photographers following us around, that I barely notice them now, unless they ask us to pose for formal photos. They are constantly snapping photos of us with our guests, creating a historical record of everything.

In a couple of weeks, Vaughn and Natalie will set out to do a royal tour of the Primorye region, meeting and greeting the people of the realm. Natalie will start in her role as *prime ailouros,* nurturing the people in Eastern Russia. I will surely miss her after Justin and I return home and to our regular lives. Knowing how connected Justin is with Vaughn and those who live in the Primorye region sets me at ease.

I begin to fade after such an intense day, and Justin suggests we retire to our rooms for the night. We say our goodbyes, and Justin scoops me close to his chest to carry me up the main stairway. I'm laughing, as it feels amazing to be so close to Justin, and because it feels like I'm flying. He carries me upstairs, and directly to his room.

Justin uses his foot to open the door and, once we are inside the room, to shut it. He carries me to the bed and carefully lays me down on the soft covers. He takes off his formal jacket and lays it on a chair back.

He walks to the bed and stares at me as if in wonder. "You look like an angel, the way the moonlight is shining on you." I glance down at my dress, and realize the satin and chiffon have an ethereal quality to them.

He sits down on the bed and cages me with his arms. "I don't just mean your dress, my sweet. Your face, eyes, lips. The glow from you. I can tell it comes from inside. From your soul."

I beam up at him, gently touching his arms. "I'm so perfectly happy right now, I can't even express how much. I feel perfectly content here with you."

"I'm so excited about what the future holds for us, my love." Justin nuzzles me on the neck, close to where he marked me. I feel waves of pleasure and warmth consume me.

I can barely contain my happiness and feel like I could burst. "The future holds so much for us, and together we'll get through anything, no matter what comes our way. I'm so thrilled to be walking this journey with you."

"As I am with you." Justin kisses me gently on the lips. He leans his elbows down on the bed, and shifts himself so he's lying beside me, yet above me with his upper body.

My eyes close with his lips' caress. I feel his arms go around me and lift me to a sitting position. I feel him tug on a thin satin ribbon behind me, and know he's undoing the lacing down the back of my dress. He continues to kiss me as he unlaces me. He inhales sharply as his hand comes in contact with my bare back.

His kiss becomes more intense, and I barely notice when he has fully undone the lacing, I'm so caught up in the moment. He places tiny kisses on my cheeks, nose, forehead, then again on my lips. Then my lips willingly part for him as my mind spins into a wild dance of passion.

Our tongues and lips embrace in a universe where time stands still. When we come up for air, I feel him gently removing my lacy gloves. The shoulders of my dress slip down, revealing my white lingerie beneath. His hands gently caress my shoulders, and he sits back to take a better look at me.

He shakes his head. "You're absolutely breathtaking."

He strokes a ringlet of hair from my shoulder, cradles my head, and starts kissing my neck, whispering, "Darla, my beauty."

He lets his lips drift downward and over to my shoulder, then to my collar bone. My head bends slightly backward, and I feel his gentle touch as he grazes my neck. He continues back down to my collarbone and I let out a tiny moan of pleasure.

When he gets to my lacy white bra he asks, "May I?"

I look into his adoring eyes, feeling the strength of his love for me through our bonds. I draw his hands to my sides so they slide across the satin and lace, and around my back. The movement of his hands sliding along the sides of my breasts to my back feels amazing and I let out a small gasp. I feel a tiny tug, and my bra becomes loose around me. Justin gently peels the bra from my body, all the while looking at me. Once my bra falls away from me, I hear him gasp.

"God, you're so beautiful."

He draws his hands from my back along my sides, and gently brushes the tips of his fingers along my breasts. I shiver with pleasure. He continues his gentle caresses on my chest as his mouth softly comes down on mine, his tongue brushing against my lips.

My intake of breath is staggered and I can feel myself quivering, wanting, anticipating more. Justin responds to my desire by taking both breasts in his hands, moulding them and caressing them more directly but gently, with his fingers. My eyes close and I moan softly.

"Justin that feels...oh..." My words stop as I feel his wet tongue slowly roll over my right nipple. Electricity courses through my body. He dampens my other nipple with his tongue, and softly suckles my breast, while making a rotating movement with his finger on my other wet nipple. His tongue taps softly and repeatedly on my nipple, and he switches between tapping and gently licking and sucking, back and forth on either side of me.

My desire is increasing to the point where I feel wanton and willing to do anything. The muscles in my abdomen move slightly forward, then relax downward and backward. My body involuntarily repeats the motion, my hips rolling forward then backward.

He takes turns gently sucking on each breast, while caressing the other, and my nipples harden, to the point where I can handle a bit more pressure. Justin nibbles on one, and gently pinches the other, and I let out a moan. By now I've finished undoing the buttons of his shirt, and can feel his hard chest beneath my hands.

He removes his dress shirt and pulls me to himself, so we are fully skin on skin. I feel his warm body against mine, and the slight friction as he pulls me upward and onto his lap. I'm straddling him beneath the folds of material settled around me in a pool of soft, white waves.

His lips crash down on mine and I feel his tongue sweeping inside my mouth, electrifying me each time it touches my own. He nibbles on my lip while he massages my breasts, then closes the space between our lips again, teasing my tongue with his own. We take a few seconds to breathe, and I'm panting.

I nibble on his ear, blowing gently, and leave a trail of kisses from behind his ear down his neck. I can feel his light chuckle on my cheek as it brushes his neck on the way down. He reaches underneath my breasts,

supporting them in his hands, stroking his thumbs around my damp nipples.

I reach his chest and try to drag my tongue and lips downward, but I'm stopped as his hands are blocking me, cradling my breasts. I sit back for a moment, and see the teasing look on his face. He now knows what my absolute weakness is, and I don't want him to stop playing with my breasts.

I feel his hardness directly beneath me as I'm straddling him. He gathers the ripples of material from around me with one hand, while cradling my head and tilting my body backward with the other. I lean back on my elbows, arching upward, so he can pull my dress down over my legs. He places it over the end rail at the bottom of the bed, then twists back so he's facing me.

He traces his fingers along my white garter belt, and to my silky thong. "Mind if I...?"

My voice comes out in a whisper. "It's okay. Go ahead." Justin tears off my soaking thong, and gazes downward at me with hooded eyes. He shakes his head.

"I can't believe you're mine."

As he pulls me to himself, I whisper in his ear. "I'm all yours, and only yours."

Suddenly, his mouth is on mine again, passionately, longing, searching, and I feel the need and desire building inside me with even more intensity. He pauses for a moment to wet his thumb in his mouth, then brushes it gently between my legs as his lips crush into mine. I feel his tongue dominating mine, while his thumb gently works in circular motions below.

My hands move down his back to his waistband, underneath it, then slide around to the front, where they undo his belt buckle. As I work on

his button, he lowers me backward on the bed, then slides his mouth downward to my breast. He strokes my nipple with his wet tongue, then taps his tongue lightly and rapidly against my nipple before he subtly nips me. My abdominal muscles raise slightly, as he slides his fingers farther down from where his thumb is, to where my wetness is.

He kneels up and slips his pants down, then fully removes them so he's left in his boxer briefs. He lies on top of me, his legs between my white hose which are attached to my garter belt. I feel his bulge press against me, rubbing me between my legs, as his fingers and thumb reach under and massage around my area saturated with wetness. His lips find mine again, and his kiss is vigorous.

"Ohhh, Justin. Please, more." I'm so full of need, of want. Just for our bodies to be as close as they can to one another. I need to feel him. All of him. I need to feel him inside me.

I see the lust in his darkened eyes, as he draws his mouth back down to my breast, and I'm like putty in his hands. One of his hands is on my other breast, and he's moved his other hand up slightly to make circular motions again. I can feel the edge of his hardness pressing into me between my legs with only a thin piece of fabric between us now. The entire experience is so erotic. I feel my heart pounding a mile a minute, and my excitement builds. My hands are behind him, and I'm pulling him into me. I can tell I've soaked through his soft boxer briefs.

"One sec." Justin kneels up, and pulls his black boxer briefs down his toned body. I gasp when I see how excited he is. He chuckles at my reaction. As he pulls his briefs off, I get on my hands and knees in front of him on the bed and surprise him by taking him into my mouth. I hear his not-so-subtle moan.

"Ohhh, Darla."

I swirl my tongue around the tip, tasting his wetness. I suck on him, then envelope more of him in my mouth. As my breasts hang down, he massages them, wetting his fingers between my legs and then rubbing the moisture on my nipples. I hold him around his waist, pulling him farther into me, stroking my tongue along him, sucking on him, while moving my head back and forth.

It feels so intimate. I'm giving my husband, my mate, pleasure in a way no one else can give him. I am his one and only, and it's not something I take for granted. He picks me up and lays me back down on the bed, and lies on top of me, caressing my cheek, stroking one of my ringlets back.

"Darla, do you mind if I taste you?"

I smile, and my voice sounds dreamy. "Just the idea of your mouth on me excites me."

Justin laughs and inhales deeply, taking in my scent. "I can tell."

I feel Justin dividing my legs and see him looking down at me hungrily, as he gently caresses me with his fingers. I feel so vulnerable. Then he slides back, lowering his head between my legs, and I feel the soft stroking of his tongue. I relax, and it feels amazing. He probes his tongue inside me and I love the sensation. I can feel him licking me inside and out, and allow myself to sink into the pleasure of the experience.

He softly caresses me in circles with his tongue as he did with his fingers earlier, and the very light touch, just barely there, is incredibly erotic. He probes himself inside me again. But I want his face to be close to mine. I love the intimacy I feel when his face is up close. I put my hands around his head, and gently guide him back up to me. He dives onto me, kissing me passionately.

I can smell my scent on him. "My scent..."

"It's intoxicating, it's like a drug, Baby."

Things intensify even more and our hands caress each other. Justin's mouth is on my breast again, tapping my nipple softly with his wet tongue now that he realizes how much it stimulates me. Our torsos are moving together, causing friction. Our bodies have heated up to the point where there's a slight sheen of perspiration on our skin.

My legs wrap around his waist, and Justin moans as he's pulled hard into my pelvic region. Between being so tightly woven together and the friction, I can feel my excitement grow even more. My craving for him just increases, to the point where I'm sliding my pelvis up and over, with a driving need to feel the tip of him at my center. I tighten my muscles at my entrance around him, and he gasps.

"Darla, are sure you're ready?" I can tell he's having difficulty controlling himself.

"Yes, Justin." We both embrace each other tightly, and he tenderly kisses me on the lips.

"I love you, Darla."

"I love you, too, Sweetheart."

I place my hand around him to guide him into me. I feel him probe then draw back. He repeats this action until he's most of the way inside me. I can tell he can't hold back any longer, and he slides the rest of the way in. We stay like that for a minute. I wrap my legs around him again, now that he's inside me.

"You okay?" He softly kisses my face and nose.

"Yes. It feels amazing. I can feel your heartbeat inside me. It's pulsing."

His lips cover mine as he draws back and gently pushes back in. I moan softly, and he takes that as encouragement to continue. We start to fall into a rhythm, and I can feel my level of pleasure rising. He leans on

one arm while using his other hand to stimulate my breast, and it feels incredible.

We move as one entity; there is no beginning or end to either of us, and it evokes deep emotions in me. Being joined together with my husband, my soulmate, like this is indescribable. I feel something deep growing inside me, not just desire and pleasure, but a warmth, a light.

As he pushes into me, my feet automatically try to pull him even farther in. He moans. He pulls back and thrusts while I pull him toward me. I want him so badly, desire him so deeply. I'm insatiable, like I've been living in a desert all my life and have just had the first drop of water spill on my tongue. My thirst keeps growing with each additional drop.

Our movements become even more rapid and I can no longer control myself as Justin presses harder and deeper into me. I never dreamed being intimate could be like this, this wildness, threatening to take over me. Suddenly, I feel like I'm being flooded with pleasure, like a water level rising that is about to fill me to bursting.

"Oh, Justin...I'm gonna..." Justin's pace picks up frantically. A wail leaves my lips as pleasure shoots through my body. Wave after wave hits me as I feel Justin thrusting harder and deeper.

"Oh! Justin! Justin!!!"

Finally, I hear a deep groan tear from his lips and it feels like a fluffy cloud of cream is filling me up to the brim. We wait, joined together, as the aftershocks hit us. I'm quivering, almost shaking.

Justin stays inside me, and I can feel him still filling me with his creamy velvet in time with the aftershocks, as I tighten around him with each tremor. His heartbeat pulses deep in the core of my being. It's an incredible feeling. We stay that way, holding onto each other for a few minutes, as Justin caresses my face with tender kisses.

"I love you so much, Darla."

I'm emotionally moved by his heartfelt declaration and I can feel my eyes glisten with moisture. The love I feel for this man overwhelms me.

"I love you too, Justin. I'm so glad I'm yours and you're mine."

He kisses me softly on the nose and forehead. We stay together as long as possible, Justin still inside me, bodies intertwined with each other, until we are naturally separated. Then I lay on his chest while he plays with my hair.

"That was absolutely incredible, Darla."

I lean over and kiss him tenderly on the lips, smiling. "It was, was it?" He can tell I'm in a teasing mood.

"Mmhmm. I loved every moment, every touch. It was amazing." I give him a big hug, holding him tightly, then kiss him gently all over his cheeks. He pulls me to him and I giggle. We kiss on the lips, smiling at each other.

"This has been the most perfect day, the most amazing day of my entire life. And it's all thanks to you." I give him a tiny tap on the nose.

"Well, I think you had something to do with it, too." Justin quietly laughs into my hair.

"I can't believe we're finally together, married, mated, joined together. I can feel a new warmth inside me that wasn't there before."

"That's the mate bond you're feeling, now that we've been intimate."

"Mmmm. I love how it feels."

I see a mischievous glint in Justin's eyes. "And I love how *you* feel. I can't get enough of you, Darla." I can't help but laugh at his dreamy smile.

"You're too cute."

"Cute? Aren't I a strong, ferocious, manly tiger?"

"Hehe, you also have an adorable kitty side."

"Well, I think the only one around here who's adorable is you, Darling Darla." He gives me a little tickle then holds me as he kisses me

tenderly several times on my lips. "Mmmmm. My wife. I love the sound of that."

Now it's my turn to get a bit mischievous. "Well, you know there's a saying that as long as I'm happy you will be, too."

"There is?"

"Yes—'Happy wife, happy life.'" Justin snorts at my silly quote.

"Well, I will do anything in my power to make sure you're happy, Darla. Regardless of whether or not it affects my own happiness. You deserve the best in life, and I'm so privileged to be the one who has the honor of giving you those things."

"I don't want any 'things'. All I want is you." We kiss, tenderly.

We hold each other until late into the night, speaking of our love for each other, dreams for tomorrow, and how the best days are yet to come. I drift off, my head on Justin's chest, content, feeling like the happiest woman in the world.

One thing our journey over the last few months has shown us is that fate drew us together for a purpose. Even with so many twisting turns and obstacles, we were led right back to each other. Fate has shown we were meant to be.

Now it's time for our future to unfold...together.

ABOUT THE AUTHOR

Anjula Evans is a writer living in the Toronto area. This is her third novel. She started writing and illustrating children's books in 2014.

She enjoys time with family, writing books, and composing music.

Manufactured by Amazon.ca
Bolton, ON

20441823R00166